Winterking

Also by Paul Hazel

WINTERKING

Volume III of *The Finnbranch*

Paul Hazel

The Atlantic Monthly Press

BOSTON / NEW YORK

FIRST EDITION

Title-page illustration by M. C. Escher

LIBRARY OF CONGRESS CATALOGING-IN-PUBLICATION DATA
Hazel, Paul.
    Winterking.
    (The Finnbranch; v. 3)
    I. Title.   II. Series: Hazel, Paul.   Finnbranch; v. 3.
PS3558.A889W5   1985   813'.54   85-47786
ISBN 0-87113-026-2

BP

Published simultaneously in Canada

PRINTED IN THE UNITED STATES OF AMERICA

For Natalie Greenberg

Ah, it's a long stage, and no inn in sight,
and night coming and the body cold.
— Herman Melville
 in a letter to Nathaniel Hawthorne

I.

The River

1.

The photographs of that time, printed from glass plate negatives, reveal a landscape at once more barren and roomy, a world puzzlingly larger (not merely less cluttered) than the world bequeathed to us. The pastures to either side of the House-tenuc, the sixty river miles between Devon and New Awanux, had then only lately begun to close again with trees. But the trees are small, all second growth; the men do not as yet seem uncomfortable beside them. Their expressions reflect no amazement at the huge bald earth nor any knowledge of their little place in it. Their reputation for being perceptive, while not entirely undeserved, did not truly encompass the land. To them it was Eden though the fires of workshops and mills made a twilight by midday over the rutted hills. The lie which their fathers had carried across the Atlantic persisted with the sons. But the land had never been Eden, not even when a wilderness of gloomy wood had covered the valley. The last naked men living along the upper reaches where the river was narrow and stands of sycamore still crowded out the sun knew all the while it was Hobbamocko, not Jehovah, who ruled there. The English, however, who had covered their genitals far longer than they had been a nation or gone over the sea, never asked them.

So it happened that Jehovah's white clapboard houses, like a species of mechanical mushroom, sprang up inexhaustibly. There were four on the Stratford flats. In New Awanux itself there were twenty. Old Okanuck, son of Ansantawae, the wind of memory blowing across his mind, sat laughing merrily in the corner of the longhouse and struck his hams. Alone, he had burned seven of Jehovah's houses, had walked up to them boldly across the green commons, bearing a torch in each hand. The ghosts of those burnings still flamed in his eyes. The warriors saw it and were cheered.

"The land did not want them," old Okanuck said. "If it had, those houses would have grown back, like the madarch, drawing their substance from the bones of the buried wood. So our longhouses grew then, year after year in the same place, nested in the damp, in the oak-shade, taking their strength from the ground."

A smile sank in his toothless mouth. Like the earth he had darkness inside of him. And foxcubs and black birds, he maintained, shaking with laughter. And a thousand oak trees, windstorms and the seeds of spiders. "Only see that I am planted deep," he howled gleefully, "and I will grow a world again. A better world." Old Okanuck winked. "No Awanux."

They gave him his pipe.

When the silence had lasted for many heartbeats, a boy with thunderous brows reached across to touch the old one's shoulder. The faces of the men turned on him disapprovingly. But Okanuck, setting the pipe aside, gave him an encouraging nod.

"The Awanux are many," the boy said angrily.

Okanuck did not take the boy any less seriously but grinned. "We are more," he said kindly. With a sweep of his outsized hands he motioned the boy to sit nearer and to share the pipe. Okanuck watched as the boy parted his lips and sucked in great quantities of maggoty smoke. But, though the smoke filled the boy's chest, inside there was emptiness. The smoke was drawn in and lost.

"Once," the boy said, uncomforted. "Perhaps it was different then. But now it is they who increase."

Okanuck leaned forward. "They are only a frost," he said slyly, "a frost on Cupheag, on Metichanwon, a chilly smear on Ohomowauke. . . ." His brows were lifted. Despite his age his hair was black as oak-shade. "Who, knowing the frost," he asked, "fears it?"

Outside the longhouse the valley was sealed by cloud. Okanuck felt no resentment. He laughed.

"The earth is under it," Okanuck said. "Deep down. Undying." Gingerly, with the clawed edge of his toes, he dug for lice, scratching in the mat of dense feathers on the underside of his black and cobalt wings.

"Crows?"

"Surely not," was the immediate answer. "Dark, nameless birds. The type doesn't matter. But water birds of some sort, I should think — though, of course, the shapes are drawn from the earth, not the river." He smiled. ". . . Pulled aloft from the fields and then transformed, one pattern to the next, until they soar." Turning in his desk chair, the speaker pointed. "The white birds, on the other hand, emerge directly from the sky."

He paused, appearing to search for a phrase which, in fact, he knew quite precisely. "As though," he began again, "some quality in the white horizon . . . in the whiteness itself . . . exactly matches the whiteness of the birds." He let that sink in. "See, near the top — to the left of the center line — how the birds begin all at once, sky and birds in one tessellation — simultaneously. You do see it?"

The younger man nodded but continued to examine the woodcut of white and black birds silently.

Pleased with his explanation, the speaker went on smiling. He was perhaps a decade older than the younger man, just a shade past thirty and already balding. The woodcut hung on the south wall of the study. It had taken him the better part of six months to save for the print. Now as his gaze traveled appreciatively over the repeated images of birds, his sense of uneasiness in the younger man grew a bit sharper. Yet for another moment he chose to ignore it. He tipped a little farther back in his chair.

His name was George Harwood. He was an assistant professor of Awanux. He had a blonde wife and a five-year-old daughter, neither of whom he could quite afford. He lived with both in three cramped rooms in the basement of West Bridge Hall, where individual scholars before him had lived since the time of its founding. His duties, for which he was paid only slightly more than the wage of an instructor, included tutoring a dozen or so of the more promising young men. And this young man, with his long, odd, unboyish face, was accounted to be the most promising.

Indeed, Harwood had long since been aware of a twinge of jealousy whenever he considered Will Wykeham. Harwood himself had once been thought of as something of a prodigy, a man to be watched. This was not boasting. When he was barely nineteen he had produced a thousand-page study of the myths of the Flying Dutchman, a study of such scope and interest that, he had been assured, with a very little tightening it might well have found a berth at the college press. But there had been interruptions. He had been burdened with other matters and the work had dragged on without completion.

Wykeham, of course, had yet to accomplish anything of equal breadth or learning, a paper on Chaucer, a few brief articles on Milton, jewel-like, it was said, nearly perfect but on a small scale. The younger man had a talent for appearing to inhabit the author's world, an instinct for the nuances of language now fallen out of use, an instinct which permitted him to suggest a number of rather clever interpretations, wonderfully clear once he mentioned them but previously escaping the attention of more seasoned scholars. The senior faculty noticed him. On

one occasion hearing Wykeham deliver a paper on *Paradise Lost*
the Dean himself had whispered discreetly to Harwood, "One
might well suppose the boy had lived in the Garden and had
spoken personally with the Snake." Harwood's mouth had
twitched up at the corners. The Dean, who was a kindly man
and inclined to like undergraduates indiscriminately, promptly
forgot the remark. It was envy that caused Harwood to remember it nearly half a year until at Greenchurch, on the edge
of panic, the words came back to him.

Beyond the window the river was blurred with cloud.

Having turned away from the woodcut, Harwood found the
younger man looking at him intently. For an instant Harwood
had the curious feeling he was staring directly into the blank
March weather. The eyes, while not large, conveyed an almost
overwhelming bleakness, as though through their slight open-
ings Harwood glimpsed the cold mist and the hills beyond them,
fading north in the rain. But it was the long square face that
had most shaken him. The strong features, gathered close to
the center, left an expanse of unexpected whiteness. It was a
face with room in it. Whatever trouble had momentarily set its
mark there, the face itself, with a surprising sense of quiet,
remained essentially free of concern. Harwood found himself
suddenly ill at ease.

"You said they reminded you of crows," he said unevenly.

"I'm sorry. Not really." Wykeham's voice came from miles
off. "I was just thinking of crows." For a time the younger man
looked past him, staring through the window at a clump of elms
set off at the edge of the broad college lawn. "I saw one this
morning. A great scruffy-looking fellow. Too big for a shore
crow. It was waiting for me by the post office gate when I went
for the mail."

"Waiting?"

Wykeham's frown vanished. "I think so," he said. His eyes
turned abruptly toward Harwood. "You might say a prophet
of doom." Wykeham reached across his chest and into the inner

pocket of his jacket and drew forth an envelope. He dropped it
on the desk in front of Harwood.

"You may read it," Wykeham said. "But the short of it is,
I shall be leaving New Awanux by Saturday."

With one pink hand Harwood reached halfway to the letter.
Both men shared a love of light holiday literature. Harwood
lifted an eyebrow. "Oughtn't you have said," he bantered, " 'I
must be gone before morning'?"

Wykeham managed to smile and sigh all at once. "Really,
George, this is serious. You might at least have a look."

The envelope was addressed: William Wykeham, Esq., College Station, New Awanux-on-Housetenuc. The address, set
down in yellowish-brown ink, was large and florid, with much
embellishment and too many capitals. Harwood glanced at it
dubiously before pulling out four sheets of white paper. He laid
the letter on the desk in front of him and began to read.

"My Dear Mr. Wykeham, Undoubtedly the lawyers have
informed you of the untimely demise of Michael Morag. Clearly
your guardian was a just man and died peacefully (as his service
deserved), leaving your affairs in good order and myself, as I
believe those same lawyers must dutifully have written you, to
manage and discharge them in his place. I regret I had not the
pleasure of meeting him. Indeed he must have been a most
pleasant man as is well evidenced by the comforts of the parsonage wherein for so many years he resided, where I (by terms
and covenants of the Will and by my appointment lately to this
parish) consider myself now fortunate to have established my
own household.

"I am told that yourself you never met the Reverend Mr.
Morag, although it cannot be more, at least not greatly more
(if it is not too discourteous to remind you), than sixty miles
from New Awanux to your properties here in Devon. AND THE
TRAINS RUN WITH SOME FREQUENCY! But then, of course, you
have been traveling and had only come to these shores, as it

were, and at that for the first time, when you matriculated and
have since been much involved with your studies.

"So, as it happened, we both missed knowing the good Morag.
More's the pity. Such a thoughtful man! Did you know that
even on his deathbed, seeing his end and seeing as well, I might
say, that another would soon come after him, he had four hundred
bottles of the finest porter laid freshly aside in the pantry. . . ."

Harwood began to fidget in his chair.

"Yes, I know," said Wykeham, shaking his head. "It would
appear he is something of an ass."

Harwood looked incredulous. "He says he's now your guardian."

Wykeham nodded. "Yes of course," he put in quickly, making
as little as possible of the other's surprise. "My father and
mother died when I was quite young. A shipping accident I am
told, although it hasn't prevented the lawyers from. . . . Not
that I minded." He paused. "You might skip the second page.
It's the third that matters."

Harwood shuffled the papers. His forehead wrinkled. Damned
if he could think of Wykeham at the mercy of lawyers and
guardians. Frankly, now that he put his mind to it, he could
not think of anyone less likely to be intimidated by men of any
stripe. But guardians. That was new. He hadn't suspected
Wykeham was an orphan. Without really thinking what he was
saying, he blurted out: "This Morag fellow left some property,
is it?"

"No."

"It says — let me find it — a will. . . ."

Harwood became aware of Wykeham's eyes again.

"Morag was the executor," Wykeham said quietly. "It's my
grandfather's will. The property has been in my family for years.
The executor, who is always a minister of some sort, gets the
use of the parsonage. Now that Morag is dead there is a new
man."

"Y-yes. Quite," said Harwood, annoyed at getting it wrong and almost stammering. It's those damn eyes, he thought. He was still holding the letter. "But what is this business about leaving school?"

"It begins on the third page," said Wykeham.

Harwood glanced hurriedly at the second sheet but realizing Wykeham was watching, he put it aside for the next.

The first paragraph consisted mainly of accounts: so much for tailors, for booksellers, for a wine-merchant. Harwood added them mentally and was shocked by the sum. The man's robbing him, Harwood thought, but then he noticed that the bills were in every case Wykeham's. Paid, all paid, Harwood thought gloomily. He moved in his chair and settled down again to read. There was mention of builders and gardeners and a particularly old man, a gamekeeper, who for no reason was being especially difficult and then:

"So I would be obliged, Mr. Wykeham, if you might spare a day to come and talk with him."

Harwood went back to read it once more.

". . . 'South Wood' is cleared. Morag, to do him credit, saw to that last autumn before his decline. He was wonderfully thorough and found twenty new men for the work, each under fifty. Nonetheless, you may be certain, I rechecked the Register myself. Not a man born before '96 and most thirtyish or younger. I mean them to start fencing 'Black Wood' as soon as the ground warms. So there is progress! All the same there is rather a hitch up at 'Black Wood,' in the Keeper's Cottage, to put it exactly.

"John Chance he calls himself. The man's nearly eighty and hunched over like a tree in a gale. Still he fairly howled when we tried to evict him. He says we 'daren't' move him, says he has a paper that gives him rights there, though of course he wouldn't show it. But the police won't touch him. They were boys on the place when Chance was younger. He taught them to snare rabbits or some such!!? In any event, they're no help nor want to be. So Chance stays where he is. And I am powerless.

"It's you he wants. He told me himself, twice. 'Send me the Heir,' he shouted (shouted, mind you). 'He'll speak with me.' Naturally, I said it was quite out of the question. But I really don't know what else to do — what with the ground almost ready. And the delay will cost! So I would be obliged . . ."

Harwood skimmed the rest, down to the name, Timothy Longford, and a postscript, scribbled precariously close to the bottom, inquiring whether Wykeham would be kind enough to secure two volumes, already purchased by Longford and only waiting delivery, at a bookseller on Abbey Street.

Harwood turned the last page over.

"Is that it?" he asked rather defensively, afraid he had missed something else. "You're leaving school in order to fire a gamekeeper?"

Wykeham seemed to concentrate very hard. "In a way I suppose I am," he said carefully. "Except, of course, I very much doubt I shall end up firing him." He stood. "I just wanted to say good-bye." Wykeham held out his hand.

"You are serious."

As he squeezed Harwood's fingers Wykeham smiled.

"It would seem that I must be."

2.

Harwood met with two more students after lunch but was not, he realized, very helpful. When the latter had gone, he spent another half an hour looking through his notes for a Saturday morning class on Blake, trying to decipher, without quite remembering how it went, the line of an argument he had made at least a dozen times. At last, seeing no improvement in his wits, he closed the book resentfully, rose and, taking his coat from his chair, hurried out onto the common without thinking to fasten the door. The afternoon was still bitter with the hard breath of sleet in the wind. The cold went straight through him and he pulled the coat tighter.

The coat was nearly twelve years old and had a frayed collar; little strips of torn lining trailed beneath the hem. He could well imagine how he looked in it. For the price of the woodcut he might have purchased a better than adequate replacement. But the chill wouldn't last, he was certain, for it was nearly April and with the good weather he could get by in his shirt-sleeves. Damn, he thought, remembering the door.

In the middle of the common he turned. There were puddles all around him; his shoes squelched as he zigzagged over the huge brown lawn until he was brought up short under the clump of elms. In the shade of vanished summers troops of young men had worn away the grass, leaving a patch of bare earth. In the drizzle the patch had become a shallow pond. Harwood looked about dismally. He was just turning his neck when something stirred in the branches: a black smear. But when he faced it squarely, he saw it was a crow. Its raffish head crooked sideways, absurdly, like a thief caught in the act.

It's the money, Harwood thought with a start. He remembered the extraordinary sums he had seen in the letter and knew, in a moment of utterly useless honesty, he would have chucked school himself, would have chucked it, in fact, a damn sight faster than Wykeham.

His Grace the Duke of West Redding pulled out his watch and, scanning the face, made a mental note to remind Maintenance to adjust the wall clock by a minute. He was sharply aware of the quiet. As he waited he listened. He heard the faint patter of rain on the windows, the distant clank of his private elevator as it climbed the two hundred eleven feet from the public corridor in the bank's main lobby. The ledger which had been in his personal care for thirty-eight of his sixty years lay closed on the desk in front of him. Precious little leisure he had had in those years; although, truthfully, he had not sought it. He had been eager and clever, capable of prodigious work and infinite care. The young men of his own generation, who by station and training might have seemed more worthy of the chance, had professed to be horrified by his diligence, his eighteen-hour days, his independent and consuming studies of asset depreciation, exclusions and trusts. To be perfectly honest, if by some miracle he could have been given a second crack at it, he doubted he could have managed it again himself. A miracle indeed! The Duke touched the closed ledger with his manicured fingers. He did not choose to open it for one last look.

This morning, as he dressed, he had found himself whistling. He had stood at the window of his town house overlooking the Park. Gazing across at the shadowy towers of the College, he had seen a quizzical smile reflected back at him in the glass. Certainly he had no immediate plans, but it was agreeable and stimulating to think of what he still might do. On his doorstep he had waved aside his driver and, unmindful of the rain, had instead set off walking. He had taken a roundabout route, following the High Street down to the river and only then turning, nearly reversing his tracks, before heading north again along Chapel Street. Even so, the public doors had not yet been opened when he marched into the office of the senior clerk.

"Send me Houseman," the Duke had said.

Caught between duty and surprise, the senior clerk had sputtered.

"He's quite bright, I believe," the Duke had said reassuringly.

The clerk had small black eyes and a dry mouth like a lizard's. He had shaken his head slightly. "Your Grace," he had said unhappily, "he's no more than a boy."

"He's twenty-two," the Duke had said, half to himself, ". . . as I was."

From behind his desk the Duke rose, large and unbent despite his age, and came out into the center of the room just as the young man slid the brass cage to his left and stepped from the elevator. Houseman himself was tall, only casually erect, with thick, long arms and huge square hands which at first glance seemed ill suited for quiet tasks with ink and paper. Now, although he had been watching for months, the Duke found himself studying the young man with renewed curiosity.

He saw clearly what had made the senior clerk nervous. Although they met you straight on, Houseman's alert dark eyes, having made their judgment, were inclined to look about on their own. For a moment the young man's face had turned, gazing down over the city through the rain. The dull sound of thunder rolled on the air. It was not a face, the Duke decided, made content by waiting.

"Thank you for coming," the Duke greeted him.

Houseman nodded.

"You would do me an added favor," the Duke said, "if you would sit in my chair." His voice was quiet, his own face still.

Houseman's gaze lingered there a moment, then unhesitatingly he walked behind the desk. But he stood, his back to the room, as though transfixed. On the window, one drop edged toward another. When the wind joined them, they fell.

"They were all betting you would pick Roger Henshaw," the younger man said.

"He's not gone without notice. Remember that. You will have need of him."

"I know," Houseman answered, without irony. "I would have picked him if it had been my choice."

The Duke smiled.

"Then you will remember." The Duke pulled a second chair up to the desk so that at last Houseman sat in the first, the great chair, his hands to either side of the ledger.

Houseman felt at once that the chair suited him as it would not a smaller man.

"What is expected?" he asked.

"In a very few minutes," the Duke said, "a young man will come here. A summary record of the affairs of his family is before you. He does not manage them and will not, even in part, for several years more. For the moment you will deal almost exclusively with a man named Longford. There are letters concerning him in the vault. From what I have seen he is a fool, as the two others I have known in his position have been. That does not matter. For thirty-eight years it was one of my responsibilities to make certain that the trustees and guardians were of no significance. Now it is yours. It is entirely legal. Longford holds but a limited copy of the will. He cannot begin to imagine its true scope or complexity. The full will is here. Its authority, duly granted and affirmed, rests — as long as you have the confidence of the heir — with you. In time the young man will doubtlessly wish to share some little part of it himself but only by way of amusement. You will find he really has no interest in day-to-day business. It's the long view you must take with him. If you do, he will be generous."

The Duke flicked his watch open.

"He will want to speak with you at some length," he said, "to see what you are like. You must be entirely candid. He will make a point of that and yet I shouldn't worry. It will not be a test. If he hadn't faith in my judgment, I should not have been here to greet you."

"Shall I see him often?" Houseman asked.

There was such a long silence that Houseman, who under other circumstances would have been immune, became embarrassed.

"Only once," the Duke said finally. He took a deep breath. "That is the reason for this talk. Generally you will confer by letter."

One side of the older man's face twitched ever so slightly. It would have been kinder, Houseman knew, to ignore it. But at the very last moment, when he might have let pity rule him, it struck him that there was something important here and he would not let it pass.

"Yet, Your Grace, you know him. And rather well, by your description."

The Duke did not look up. "I knew the grandfather. Met him here in this room." His head straightened. "Just once."

Both men heard the clank of the elevator.

The Duke was already standing. By the time the brass cage slid back he had slipped from the room. Nevertheless the door to the outer office remained slightly ajar. There was another long silence.

When the dark young man stepped onto the carpet, Houseman found himself listening to the rain rather than staring. For a moment the room seemed dwarfed by the sound of rain. The

young man came no closer and Houseman realized that he too
was listening. Then the wind changed, taking the rain away
from the glass. The young man went on listening. Small creases
turned up at the corner of his mouth.

"You have my thanks, Your Grace," Wykeham said fondly.

With a deep satisfied click the door pulled shut.

A bell on a hook jingled when he entered the shop. The wind
had reversed his umbrella, cracking two of its ribs. Wykeham
abandoned it by the door. A pool of water collected under his
feet. Trying to get his coat unbuttoned with numb fingers, at
first he did not notice the woman sitting by the warming stove
and peering up at him angrily. He dug about in his inside pocket
for a handkerchief.

"Is it books you're wanting?" the woman said impatiently.

Her voice was foreign. The sound of distant streets rang at
the back of it, the old faded music of crowded twilight streets
where as a girl she had walked boldly under the eyes of sailors.
She had not known then that those same streets stretched over
the sea nor had she known the dream of the man with his black
whiskers, a parcel of books in his duffel, when he smiled from
the doorway.

"Bodø?" Wykeham asked. The woman's face, which once
may have been as haughty and brave as the pictures of heroines
in her husband's books, was no longer pretty, but when she
laughed with surprise he was nearly certain it had been so.

"Do you know it?"

"I have stopped there," he said, coming across the floor to
stand by her, warming his hands at the stove. Her eyes shone
like gold in the dusk of the shop. "My ship lay over in the
harbor," he said, "buying herring. Too soon we were gone."

Wanting to keep him she said, "It is so far away. You could
not have been more than a boy."

Someone was shuffling along the dark aisle lined with books

or rather the shadows of books, brown and sour as leaf-mold, piled high to the ceiling. "Nora," a man's voice called out sharply.

A gray head ending with a grizzled beard thrust itself into view. It belonged to a short, wiry man of about fifty. He had on an old sailor's cap worn to the same indefinite color as his hair. He glanced about suspiciously. Grown apprehensive under his gaze, the woman turned from him.

"I will make tea," she said. "You would like that."

"Yes," Wykeham said softly. "That would be kind."

Wykeham sat in an armchair watching the empty street fill with rain. In silence they drank the tea from delicate china cups whose touch made the shopkeeper moody and uncomfortable. He finished while the tea was still too hot and put the cup down.

"Well and good," the man said. He made a point of not looking at his wife. "This is, after all, a business."

Wykeham put aside his cup.

"Is there much of a market for antique books?" he inquired mildly.

"Ah!" the shopkeeper cried. "Not just old books. I have everything!" He pointed down at the floor. "Underneath," he said, "I have two great rooms. And above." He raised his arm, lifting it dramatically. "Six floors, groaning under the burden." He smiled inwardly, his impatience forgotten. "One must try to have everything."

"Will you have a cake?" asked the woman.

"Yes, thank you," said Wykeham.

The shopkeeper did not blink.

"There is not a book so awful," he said, "that it will not have its adherents. Or a book, however marvelous, that doesn't for a time fall out of fashion. Sooner or later, then, I have them: old books, yes. But new ones as well, picked up for a song and waiting discovery."

"You have, I believe," Wykeham said, "two volumes on order for the Reverend Mr. Longford."

The woman stopped. She knew she had no more to offer him.

"You are not . . . ," she said.

"Hardly." Wykeham smiled. "I am merely doing a favor."

"Perhaps there is something." She looked around desperately. "Carl, where is that nice picture book on Norway?"

It was not what she meant to say. She had not wanted to involve her husband, but she was frightened and the words fell from her mouth.

Wykeham looked across at her. "I regret," he began.

The shopkeeper had risen. He walked to the front of the shop, where he rummaged under the counter. He kept his back to them but she knew he was listening.

When he stood again before them, two small books under his arm, she still had not spoken. Yet she reached out impulsively. Digging between her husband's shirt and the dry leather bindings, she took the books into her own fragile hands. The shopkeeper grunted with surprise.

Ignoring him, she turned back the front cover of the largest volume, finding a bill resting on a lithograph of a huge, naked Indian. The bill was marked in her husband's clear black letters. Timothy Longford, Greenchurch Parsonage, it read, £8, Paid. She was quite certain Wykeham had seen it.

"That will be ten pounds," she whispered, looking straight up at him in terror.

Wykeham paid without protest. When he had gone, she went upstairs immediately and got into bed, where she lay on her pillow, listening to the storm. But it was the sound of the crowded streets she heard and the knock of the herring boats, rocking in the great distant harbor. Later, when her husband came into the room, his eyes were watchful. Nevertheless, thinking of his wife's cleverness, how with a cup of tea and a half-eaten cake she had earned him more than double the price, he gave her a grin.

A strand of her light brown hair lay wet on her cheek. The years in a different country had made her timid and she would not look at him. It had been another woman altogether, a girl of seventeen who in another place and without encouragement dared talk with strangers. She had not meant to remember her. She had put her away. It was for her awakening, into a world that had no place for her, that something was owed; for that she had demanded payment.

Wykeham sat at his desk past midnight, under the yellow light of the one lamp that had not been packed away. But for a few clothes and a suitcase the room was nearly as bare as on the day he had first seen it. The furniture had gone to storage, the odds and ends put into boxes to be carted off. He loved the feel of the small empty room, blank as the cell of an Irish hermit, loved it more because he so seldom chose to live plainly. Wykeham had always been fascinated and excited by things. As a result the rooms where he had lived had often had the thick and complicated air of thirdhand shops where everything is treasured and nothing is thrown away: bicycle parts had rested in the bath, books in the foyer. Pots, pictures, and embroideries, the enameled tooth of an extinct elephant (preserved in the jaw), a chimney brush without bristles, a shepherd's crook, several fish scalers, a pair of surgical scissors and a Chinese lacquer screen, among many more such notable items, he had only lately picked from the clutter, labeled and set out for the movers.

Deep in the evening, before he had finally sunk back into the desk chair, turning at last to the letters, he had swept the floor. Under the single electric light the plain, tea-colored boards, now dull and grim, had reminded him of the thin brown layers of hardened silt he had sometimes seen in the exposed rock in the hills above Ohonowauke. There were millions of years in the stone but almost none of it barren. In the dry beds of ancient streams he had found the remnants of the changing but never

ending abundance of life, bred generation upon generation, out-
dated and puzzling but seemingly imperishable. Only now and
then there had been a brief gritty band, a patch empty of bone
and shell, as though for a season even the gods, wearied of their
hosts and retainers and with a momentary sigh of relief, had
ordered them gone.

The open window looked out onto the common. The storm
had gone and with it the last smoke-like rags of clouds, blowing
eastward over the sea. The air that crept under the sash, stirring
the sheets of white paper, was no longer bitter.

He finished printing the address on a thick package tied with
cord, then set it aside. On a fresh sheet he wrote the name of
a girl. He had been careful. There had been nothing promised
between them but he felt he owed her an explanation. They
had said good-bye rather formally at the entrance of the library
where she worked behind the order desk on the main floor. She
had stood quietly watching him descend the stairs. When he
had turned, she had waved.

"It doesn't make sense," she had told him.

"I know that." But he knew that it did.

She spoke Latin and German, had studied Greek, but had
never been out of the city. They met in the evenings, after her
work, in a room in the King's Hotel. He had talked to her of
ships and of all the places they had taken him.

"How have you gone so far?" she had asked.

"I started early."

But she had never been content with that. "I will make a
covenant between you and me," she had laughed, baiting him.
"You will tell me everything about all the great, sweet places
that ever were and I will show you the mysteries sailors dream
of when they are far from land."

She was nearly thirty, ten years older than she guessed he
was. Some mornings there were puffy circles under her brown
eyes. Often, as though troubled, she said his name with her lips
only. Now she had turned on her side, her slender legs curled

up and rubbing his. He had told her of Antioch and Alexandria, the Canaries and the westward bulge of Africa, of camels and the Greenland ice, the Shoulders of Jupiter, the docks at Spithead and Madeira and the channel towers at Dover burning lime. But he had never promised.

He sealed the letter and took another sheet. Across the way a few cold lights glittered. After a long time even these winked out. Two more letters lay carefully folded at his left hand. It was very late but he did not move from the chair. He felt no weariness. Once again the world stood before him. He looked out over the common, its darkness made blacker by the fissured shadow of a grove of elms.

The crow alighted on the window ledge. Its sly head twisted around on its neck.

"Why are you not asleep?" Wykeham asked it.

"Like you," the crow answered, "I am waiting for dawn."

3.

In those years the mails, delivered throughout the city by postman on foot, moved more rapidly than is now the custom. On Saturdays the first delivery was completed by eight-thirty. In the outer districts, where the houses were spread apart, and on a few of the larger plots, where there were barns though there was no livestock, the second occasionally dragged on toward evening. But along the congested streets of the center city the second post arrived no later than noon. At twelve-thirty Harwood's blonde wife brought the package in from the porch and left it on the kitchen table. When she came in once more from the back for the wash and found the package still there, she called out to her husband.

Harwood emerged from his study where despite the howls of his daughter he had been trying to rearrange his notes on the Dutchman. His skin was white and dull and he was wearing suspenders over yesterday's shirt.

"No one sends me things," she said in that tone that told him she was making no special claim, only speaking the truth.

A streak of sunlight fell across her faded skirt. Her knuckles were red and her forearms were wet to the elbows.

He sat down at the table and began fumbling with the taut cord fastened with sailors' knots. She stood at his back, looking over his shoulder in silence. Inside the heavy paper there was a coat of new, thick bog-smelling tweed. He made a vague gesture, as though apologizing because his good fortune excluded her.

"You had better go thank him," she said.

At one o'clock a dozen letters lay unopened on the counter of the empty shop on Abbey Street. Out of idleness Nora took them up. Her husband, mumbling to himself, was unpacking cartons. His voice rumbled loudly but without meaning. Her thoughts took no notice. With skillful indifference she sorted the letters, bills into one pile, orders into the next, a third for the private correspondence that went back and forth between dealers with rumors of acquisitions, estate sales not listed in the papers, quiet inquiries and lies. She spread the unopened letters in front of her like a gypsy woman, alone in a booth, reading the cards out of habit.

During the night she had dreamt she had fallen asleep in a tower. When she awoke, still knowing it was a dream, that she had only dreamt of waking, she had found that an immense hedge of thorns had grown up around her. She had gone to the window and opened it. The cold, raw morning air streamed in. But the din she had expected, the sounds from her father's stables, the clatter of carriages in the yard below her, had gone. In the hallway outside her door she discovered her little maid, her smock, and her flesh as well, turned to a fibrous dust. The tiny gold ring that had been her own gift to the girl was hanging loose on the narrow bone of her finger.

Toward morning Nora had awakened in her bed, next to her husband. The delicate pink color of the sky had told her that the rain was over. Something was within my reach, she thought, but I have not touched it. She placed the last letter down on the counter. In a small, spidery old-fashioned script she read her name. Within the envelope there were several folded pages and a steamer ticket on the *Konge Harald* for Bodø.

* * *

The Duke, who had known Wykeham rather better than the others, anticipated the letter and had directed his butler to bring the post in to him as soon as it came. There was a single, deferential knock on the door of the solarium. The man entered briskly, bearing a square silver tray on which the creamy white envelope rested. When he had set it down, the man stepped aside and waited discreetly.

"There will be no answer," the Duke said. The man prepared to go but the Duke leaned back his head. It was a smooth, dark, aristocratic head, not the sort of a head of a man of business. Nonetheless His Grace had had his start in business and had given his life to it. The title had come late and had seemed to him both unnecessary and humorous. Yet he had never protested. He suspected, though nothing had been said directly, that Wykeham was somehow behind it. Fortunately, the title was not hereditary. He had never married and had no children to be disappointed. Nevertheless, the prospect of its eventual mortality pleased him. While, over these last months particularly, he had felt his days shortening, he had never cast a covetous eye on more of life than God, in whose affective agency in human affairs he maintained a guarded disbelief, had allotted him. Unlike most men, unlike Wykeham himself, he was certain, the Duke wished no more of the world when he died than it bury him.

"Your Grace," the man said.

"If you will, John," said the Duke, "have my driver ready at six."

When the man departed the Duke unsealed the letter and found exactly the blunt, authoritative expression of gratitude he had expected. He had been single-minded in his devotion to Wykeham. That their relationship consisted almost exclusively of the contents of the letters between them, his own, of which he still preserved copies, all bearing the same postmark, Wykeham's sporting stamps of almost infinite color and variety, stamps of green mangoes and Spanish kings, cathedrals and gardens in Burma, coming to him from every longitude and meridian on the face of the globe, that his devotion was the product not of smiles and handshakes but of written words did not matter to him. Letters, if one took the time, could be made clear and definite and might, with appropriate care, escape the imprecision which so characterized the shifting, haphazard life he saw about him. Of course the relationship would have gained no footing at all had Wykeham not responded in kind. The Duke remembered his pleasant shock of surprise when he had read Wykeham's first letter, now thirteen years ago, when Wykeham ought to have been a boy of seven.

The letter had come by steamer from Egypt. The Duke had expected some childish babble about pyramids or perhaps, because children so rarely notice what adults take for granted, nothing about pyramids and in its place a great deal more than he cared to hear about the ship's monkey. Instead Wykeham had written about women — and not the women of the bazaar, leaning over their boxes of figs and shouting to buyers, but rather the wave of young English women who had come out with their engineer husbands, women in heavy skirts despite the climate who spoke tirelessly of their Queen's setting a formidable example and sent home for dogs.

He writes as if he were a Roman emperor, the Duke remembered he had thought, as though the boredom of the long voyage had sharpened the boy's perceptions and given him a double set of ears and eyes, the second detached and sardonic, gazing with amused interest over the dark plowed earth of the delta, over the sky's illimitable whiteness, watching, listening to the hobnob of women as though he were watching and listening to the strutting and hooting of birds.

What he had not expected was the invitation, dated six months in advance — for October — to a dinner at Wykeham's Devon estate. Puzzled, the Duke laid the letter aside on the table. The butler had long since gone beyond hearing.

"What do you make of that?" His Grace asked no one in particular.

It was not chance that brought them. Yet it must have seemed like chance to the two young women arriving separately but within a few moments of one another at the information desk in the waiting room at Water Street Station. The Duke lifted his eyes from the timetable to look across at the dark-haired woman asking the track number of the evening train to Devon and at the woman behind her, listening closely to the clerk's answer. The answer given, he watched them turn quickly away, in both faces the same apprehension and seriousness. He recognized at once that in some fashion they were Wykeham's and that each had come alone, unaware of the other. His eyes followed their long legs and slender hips into the crowd. In his imagination younger women were always slender, and he congratulated himself on sharing Wykeham's admiration for the clear bold grace of slender women. He wondered whether Wykeham had managed to sleep with both of them.

The waiting room was dim. The air, pulled in from the platform, was full of the smell of steam. When he looked around again, he had lost them. He stood off to the side, watching quietly, for he knew there was plenty of time. A man pushed hurriedly past him, inquiring anxiously at the desk. He was tall and balding. He had on a new gray overcoat of such elegance that for a moment the Duke was certain he must have met him. Then suddenly he got a glimpse of the man's wet shoes. He has walked here through puddles, the Duke reflected, disappointed. The discovery remained on the Duke's face, mingled with bewilderment, until he overheard the clerk answer: "Devon? Certainly, sir. Track nine." His Grace smiled. Wykeham, he thought, still enchanted but wiser.

Harwood turned his eyes doubtfully and began to hunt for the gate.

"I beg your pardon," the Duke said, moving nearer. "Nine is out by the river. If you will permit me . . ."

"I'd be obliged," Harwood said. He fell in beside the older man gratefully.

Neither was carrying luggage.

"I'm not actually catching the train," Harwood said.

"Like yourself," said the Duke mildly, "I have been planning to miss it."

It was Harwood's dinnertime and except for the coat he would not have come. But the obligation nagged at him. Late in the afternoon he had gone to Wykeham's room in the college, thinking he still might find him. When he had knocked, no one had answered. He had tried the next door and met a sullen-looking boy who barely knew Wykeham and was of no help. He had intended then to return to his rooms but walking across the courtyard, he had encountered a groundsman counting a few crisp bills with his blackened fingers.

"Paid me right well," the man had answered him breezily. "Not many like him. Though I'll admit I had a bit of trouble with all them boxes." He folded the bills twice and thrust them into his pocket. The man grinned. "Engaged me for three hours and paid me for six, it's being Saturday and all and my own time. Though I'd have settled for four. But me and Jake got him off."

"Where?"

"Down to Water Street."

"I-I'm sorry I don't —" Harwood stammered.

"To the trains."

Watching Harwood turn and rush into the street, the groundsman shook his head. But then it had been his experience that education, if it did anything, made it harder for those who had it to find their way around.

* * *

An hour before closing Carolyn simply walked away from her desk. The woman who worked with her had to admit she hadn't been of much use anyway. She had arrived late and kept going to the bathroom. When, looking owlish and tired, she managed to stay at the desk she uncrinkled a piece of paper, read it again then crushed it only to repeat the process a few minutes later. The circles under her eyes seemed to darken like bruises. "Why don't you just go home," the woman had whispered to her kindly. But as a matter of pride, she stayed. Gradually the students marshaled behind her desk drifted to other lines. Carolyn no longer looked up. The clock behind her started the little whirring sound it made before it announced the hour. She closed her eyes tightly. Then she collected the paper, slipped the strap of her bag over her narrow shoulder and went toward the stairs. He had never made a secret of how and when he was going. He had simply taken for granted, she thought, hating for a moment his arrogance, that because he had not specifically requested it she would not come to watch him go.

Before she expected it, Nora was through the doors of the station and out on the platform. The woman walked stiffly in front of her. Because it was already dark and she did not know the way, Nora hurried after, climbing when the woman climbed a steep metal bridge which crossed the track bed nearest the station. A heavy puffing engine passed sluggishly under her. The steam came up from below.

He will have forgotten me, Nora said to herself, though she clutched in her hand the ticket that only he, although his letter had been unsigned, could have sent her.

Half believing it was a college prank, she had left the shop and gone out into the streets she seldom walked and barely knew even after a dozen years in this land of strangers. On her way she had stopped and looked into store windows, gazing at female mannequins of frozen elegance, wearing clothes she had never dreamed of. In the end, standing before a slovenly red-faced agent in the office of the steamship line, she waited as he searched through the records. Yes, of course, the ticket was valid. She saw his sly, conspiratorial smile. He leaned forward over the desk on his fat arms. He remembered now, he said, the man who had made the purchase. He had no doubt, he told her, that the young man had ample reason to be grateful.

Her head throbbing, she retreated into the darkening street just at the moment when Wykeham stepped out of his cab. A second cab had drawn up behind. Two men began unloading trunks and boxes onto the sidewalk. The streetlamps were coming on and lit her pale tense face. She hadn't meant to stay out so late. She couldn't think of what after their brief, odd encounter in the shop she might actually say to him.

Feeling foolish and yet determined, she drifted into the street. When she had crossed over, the young man, who had kept his back toward her, had already disappeared into the monstrous old station. A breath of night air swirled around her legs. She stood among the trunks and boxes holding herself so still it almost seemed to the men easing boxes down beside her that she was waiting to be lifted onto the loading cart.

"Your pardon, miss," one of the men said to her. "Is there something?"

Nora hadn't noticed the man and so did not hear what he was saying. The boxes were growing around her like the wild black hedge that had surrounded her in her dream. Indeed she felt like the girl in the dream: beset on all sides by great dangers and yet somehow made larger to meet them. She was frightened. But because she was frightened she also felt she carried inside her a braver destiny.

The man jabbed at her with his finger. "Miss," he repeated.

She saw him then. At the same time she saw the tag on the box he had set at her feet. She gave a startled laugh. It is fate, she thought recklessly, not certain it was so. In the tiny old-fashioned letters that had been on the envelope she had read his destination.

Selecting a door at random, she walked past the man and into the immense dimness of the waiting room.

The train loomed in the blackness, hissing to itself.

"There," the Duke said.

Harwood walked ahead but the Duke lingered. Hearing the other's footsteps stop, Harwood turned and looked over his shoulder.

"Are you coming?" he asked.

The Duke shook his head. He smiled. "I can see from here."

Harwood nodded and went on.

His Grace held back in the shadows. Perhaps no great harm would be done if Wykeham should see him. After all, he had been invited to Greenchurch and so presumably Wykeham, ignoring the prohibition or perhaps rewriting it, intended that at last he should meet him face-to-face. But for thirty-eight years he had been the Will's most faithful servant and the Will was clear on that point, as it was on so many others. His Grace would be granted one audience with but one member of the family. Thereafter, while he was free to maintain an active correspondence with its male heirs whether in residence at Greenchurch or scattered over the globe, he must never seek another meeting. And he had met (and therefore should have been satisfied) the grandfather, Joseph Wykeham, a grave young man when he stepped into the Duke's office, tall and well spoken and, according to the records, slightly younger than himself. But of course that had been long ago. Joseph had died or at least had been declared missing, then dead. Then, from time to time, His Grace had written the improbably named Sebastian, the father, who had been born abroad, married early and who with all hands had gone to the bottom in the Gulf of Iskanderun without once writing back. It was young William, for reasons which even now remained largely obscure to His Grace, who had been set alone on the Turkish coast and, thereby surviving the disaster, began seven years later to send letters addressed starkly to West Redding, Leeds Bank, New Awanux, the Americas.

It was for William only that the Duke maintained a lasting affection. And yet when the boy, finally a young man, had come in from his wanderings to begin his studies, His Grace had kept his distance as the Will required. The letters still flew back and forth, crossing a few narrow streets where once they had crossed the oceans. But the Duke had come no nearer. Faithful to his trust, even when the latest Wykeham (for there never seemed more than one at a time) announced that the Duke's term would be ended or later when it was learned that Wykeham (the first Wykeham to enter the bank in more than a generation) had come himself to meet the new man, even then, faithfully, His Grace had left the room as Wykeham had come in.

The younger men were left to each other's company. That was as it should have been. The Duke had been the servant of the Will for thirty-eight years but for thirty-eight years he had been its master as well. His hand went into his pocket, touching the letter. Well, the whole bloody tangle is Houseman's now, he thought. How then was he still bound?

The Duke lifted his head.

The realization came to him, almost as a physical shock, that he was looking directly across the platform at Wykeham.

4.

It was simply that there was no time (both too little and none at all). It seemed to happen all at once. In an instant there were men and women of no consequence, milling about the platform, preparing to mount the steps as soon as the conductors had opened the doors. While Carolyn was herself preparing, although for what she was not yet certain, Wykeham was suddenly walking ahead of her. She had no idea from where he had come. His dark head was turned, staring upward into the cars as he passed them. Carolyn opened her mouth. Then she saw the woman beside her, a woman she had not before seen, suddenly rush ahead. In the same instant the conductor swung open the door.

Wykeham stopped, waiting for the thin metal door to be hooked back. From beneath the engine there still came a clattering and the laughing curse of steam. And yet, as if by stopping, he brought her to a stop as well. She waited, feeling, just for the moment, as though the world itself had stopped. She did not move. The woman went by her. Carolyn saw only her profile, sick with longing, and knew beyond dispute or reason that this woman too had followed him.

It happened all too quickly. The conductor came down the steps. Wykeham climbed up. He turned left into the car and was gone. Other people moved into the car, finding their seats, lifting bags and huge bundles onto the racks. He was surely one of them. The woman's lips moved but, as though trapped by the glass, they made no sound.

It was George Harwood who first noticed her. She was not especially pretty although he guessed that once she might have been. Such things are hard to judge but he suspected that she was several years his senior. He had not meant to look at her. He had caught a glimpse of Wykeham just as he stepped onto the train. He had run forward to meet him but a crowd of passengers blocked his way. Harwood turned, walking slowly back in the direction he had come, looking up into the windows. It was, he thought later, simply because she looked so surprised and in his experience people on trains, their destinations and perhaps even their lives clearly in mind, never did.

The edge of her cider-colored hair fell across her shoulders. Her eyes were wide open, grown round. She looked, he decided, like a woman in a tale for children. Caught by a gust of adventure, he wondered not who she was but where she was going. For a moment, with the extravagance of one who has read too many books, he fancied that her journey might take her in and out of sorrow to the ends of the earth. Harwood shrugged, aware suddenly that he was being foolish. In the cars the passengers had settled. He still had not seen Wykeham.

The conductors reboarded the train, leaned out and looked down the tracks. The engine uttered a scream.

The last porters scattered. The Duke listened to the pad of their feet as the the platform emptied. Only he had seen them all, the dark-haired woman wandering aimlessly under the windows, the man a few paces behind, his hands thrust clumsily into the pockets of a coat that was too grand for him. He had not thought about them, nor about the other woman although he had watched her as well. Even Houseman, though he should not have been there, had gone from his mind.

The wind came in off the river, catching the edge of a sign

above his head. The sign creaked and groaned. The Duke listened without hearing. But all the while he had watched. He had seen Wykeham's assured steady gait as he walked between seats, striding with the same unhurried ease with which he had once stepped from the elevator into the room with its great windows. It had seemed a long time ago and yet the Duke hadn't needed to explore his memory. It had been the same long face. The Duke had watched him stop at the front of the car, reach up with his hand to place a small package, the one thing he had carried, onto the rack. And His Grace had kept on watching although, from the first, he had been certain.

Wykeham dropped his hand. Showing no consternation, though the other had no right to be where he was, he slid into the seat beside Houseman.

The Duke shook his head. He would see Houseman fired. He could do that much. It's a different world, the Duke thought sadly. Nothing will make it the same. But all at once he felt that he had got it wrong.

He cocked his head with a slightly puzzled air.

The pale light fell on Joseph's dark face.

It hadn't even occured to the Duke to confuse the matter with family resemblance. He had looked and he knew. In that he had not been mistaken. His Grace was nearly invisible in the darkness but he stepped deeper into the shadow. I must be getting old, he thought. And yet, he was almost smiling as he saw the two young men in the window, William with Joseph's face, Houseman with a face that once might have been his own.

How then is the world different, the Duke wondered, if the years are nothing and there is no time?

5.

At first the train moved slowly, crawling past docks and shipyards. Twenty minutes from Water Street Station Wykeham could still see the outer reaches of New Awanux, the slums gone, but the buildings no less slovenly. For a time the tracks left the river, and the train, now rocking gently, clattered past derelict houses. It depressed him to think of the men who must live there, men he imagined who rose early, starting out along the edges of the roads in darkness to walk to the mills at the city's heart. The great trains sped by them but there was never enough for the fare.

His thoughts made him restless and he was pleased when at last the river swung back into view. Far out in the channel he saw by the lamps hung from their cabins the small black shapes of trawlermen returning late from the bay. He found as always a sort of reassurance in the fact that there were yet some men who steered their own lives. They would ride down into the bay again in the morning, just as fishermen had done for thousands of years and would do for thousands more.

The thought comforted him. Perhaps they were not entirely free, for the sea bound them, but they were as free as men needed to be. He understood such men for he had spent the greatest part of his life in crossing the oceans.

Helped by the memory, he stared once more into the dark. Because he was thinking, he did not hear at first the words of the man sitting next to him.

"Barnum," Houseman repeated, "Phineas T. Barnum, to set it out whole."

Wykeham looked perplexed.

Houseman allowed himself the satisfaction of a grin. Even by his own harsh standards he had to admit, given the little time there had been to manage things, he had performed a miracle. But now that he had secured Wykeham's notice, Houseman waited. There was a great deal to be discovered about Wykeham and it was best to be careful.

Wykeham recognized that look. The first months with a new man were always dangerous. At the start, as good a man as His Grace had made foolish errors. His strength was that he learned from them. Toward the end, in some few matters Wykeham had even begun to trust his judgment, although it was backed by less experience, as much as his own.

But in this the Duke had failed. Already the prohibition had been violated.

He will be disappointed, Wykeham thought, that his last decision did not do him credit. Still, Wykeham hoped for the best. He even smiled, lightly, because Houseman, who had smiled once, was now trying very hard not to.

"Barnum?" he asked.

"Surely you've heard of him — the man with the circuses," Houseman answered. "I rented the stable car from his agent in Bridgeport. Where else was I to find one large enough?" Then despite the best of his intentions he broke into a grin. "They use it, he told me, for shipping elephants."

Wykeham turned. "Painted red I would gather."

Houseman nodded. "With large yellow letters." Hearing himself, his smile vanished. " 'The Greatest Show on Earth,' " he said softly. He could imagine what Wykeham was thinking. "But —" he began.

"But?"

"It's dark," Houseman filled in quietly. "We loaded in the dark as well. It was after midnight, yesterday. Or this morning really. Too dark to see the hand in front of your face. The car went right into the barn. The tracks were there just as you said they would be. Apparently had been for years although you could see they served no purpose. Hadn't any, until that is —"

Wykeham watched the sudden change in his expression. At least he isn't stupid, Wykeham thought, not very much relieved.

Houseman was no longer quite looking at him. "Well, whatever it is went in by itself and no one's the wiser. I closed the doors myself." He managed to turn toward Wykeham. "I was there," he said without apology. "Someone responsible had to be. And I saw to it." He waited. "But even I couldn't tell you what was in there." He waited again. "In any event," he said, "now it's done. And it will be with you in Devon."

"It's a horse," Wykeham said although the question had not been asked directly. "A rather peculiar and rather unusually large horse," he said in answer to the unasked question that followed.

Houseman kept his hands in his lap and nodded.

"You realize," Wykeham said without a trace of awkwardness, "that you should not have come."

"His Grace said," Houseman started but he saw that led nowhere. "There are things that will need doing at the other end. Arrangements . . ."

"Which I shall see to. Or others will. I am not without resources. Letters were written. I already have at Greenchurch, I believe, several dozen men in my employ. New men, I will grant you. Like yourself, untested —"

Houseman looked pale.

"Of course, I recognize you acted out of the best of intentions," Wykeham added. "And I have always appreciated a certain zeal. I expect that His Grace saw that in you. Perhaps, when you return, you will have another talk with him. I shall write you. You may trust to that. But for the time being —"

Houseman knew enough to stand.

"Make certain you look up His Grace," Wykeham said by way of good-bye.

The evil rumblings in Houseman's stomach told him all too clearly he was going to be ill. He lurched down the aisle heading for the next car, only stopping a moment outside the lavatory. He rattled the handle desperately but the door was locked.

There are pieces which belong in the puzzle, their curious irregularity perfectly matching the oddly shaped hole in the left corner, their unexpected shading the exact color of sunlight on dark foliage, pieces which nevertheless are set aside at the outset and only rediscovered after searching and anguish. So Nora, who had begun looking for portents in dreams, had taken the ten-pound note from the drawer in anticipation of nothing, simply because she felt she had earned it.

She had never intended to follow him. When the letter had come, she had set out merely to discover whether the ticket was real and not a joke in cranky repayment for having asked him to pay once more for what had already been paid for. For if in fact there meeting had been destined, she had not recognized the first stirrings of the thought until, fleeing from the vulgar insinuations of the ticket agent, she had come upon the young man once again at the station. Without looking I have seen him twice, she had thought, as though twice was lucky and a sign. And so, even as near as she was to the beginning, she had missed the start. She had taken the ten pound note not knowing she would or that she would have need of it, but remembering perhaps that it was more than she had ever taken into the streets of Bodø. It was not until she had mounted the steps of the train that she realized that while ten pounds would more than cover the fare, it would leave her less for all the uncertainty that must surely come after.

The first time the conductor came through he collected no tickets. Nora stared out the window waiting to be certain he had gone, keeping her face turned so he would not remember it. But it was that face, before her journey had ever started, that Harwood had seen from the platform and would remember though the year was nearly over when he next saw her, running across the snow-covered lawn, down from the great house at Greenchurch, though her hair would then be golden.

Before the conductor returned she had locked herself in the lavatory. Later, someone had stood outside and rattled the handle frantically. She could hear little gulping sounds. But eventually whoever it was had gone away.

The train made its first stop at Stratford, which the Indians had called Cupheag, and the next at Metichanwun, whose name, for no more reason than they had rejected the other, the English had kept. They were small towns and few passengers either left the train or joined it. The conductor hadn't bothered to come through punching tickets until just before Bristol. Four miles out, when the train came onto the flats by the river, one could sometimes see the tall smokestacks of the factories. But the furnaces no longer burned at night. They made clocks in Bristol and the demand for clocks had diminished. Even at this hour there would be men on the platform waiting to board the train, workmen with their families, their few belongings packed. From up the river, from Devon, there had come rumors of work.

The conductor paused before Wykeham and asked for his ticket.

"You're the gentleman with the circus car," the conductor said, not quite making it a question for he had seen how the young man was dressed and now that he had been through the cars he had found no one else who looked likely to have been able to afford the expense.

Wykeham turned slightly.

"You wouldn't mind saying what it is you have in there," the conductor said carefully, not certain as yet whether the young man was being rude or whether he had been dozing.

The conductor rested his arm on the back of the seat.

"You're too young a fella to remember perhaps," he said. "But the circuses used to come through here quite often. Years back, when times were better. And, of course, they would stop at Bristol. Then on up the line to Ohomawauke. Queer name, Ohomawauke — Indian." He seemed to think of something else. "But then the circuses brought queer folk too. You're not, by the way — I mean you're not dressed like . . ."

Wykeham looked disinterested. "Horses," he said matter-of-factly.

"Rather a large car for horses," the conductor said testily, beginning to take offense.

"Large horses," Wykeham answered.

"The windows all boarded up."

" — And blind."

The conductor took Wykeham's ticket, punched several small holes in it, and, muttering, went hurriedly on. He had no intention of coming back to speak to the young man. Certainly he would not have except for the second young man in the car after who when he tried to wake him he found was dead. There was no need to go through his pockets. Unfolded in his lap was the rental agreement for the circus car. There were three names on the paper, one clearly that of the business agent for the circus and two others.

The train was held in Bristol for a little under an hour. Two policemen, who arrived at once, stared defiantly at the corpse rather as if it deserved most of the blame, turned its head, felt for a pulse and asked questions of the nearest passengers. A woman said that she had thought the man was drunk. She said:

"He kept on making little coughing noises. And mumbling.

Not that it made sense, you understand. I could tell he wasn't right." She shook her head with knowing sadness. "But don't his eyes look odd," she said.

The policemen were not distracted.

"Do you remember the words exactly?" the sergeant asked.

"Just foolishness."

The sergeant tugged at his belt importantly. "We shall be the judge of that," he told her.

"The world's coming apart," the woman answered softly. She was a small tense woman. She seemed about to blubber.

The sergeant stood in front of the corpse so she would not have to stare at it. "Yes," he said in a calming tone, not looking at her but at the other policeman. "These things can be difficult. If you would just —"

"No!" the woman said with a sudden fierceness. "It's what the poor man said. The world's coming apart, coming apart. Over and over."

It was the doctor who asked if anyone knew the man. So it was not until then that the conductor, who had already thought of it but who had not been asked, went into the other car and came back with Wykeham. A shadow of stern regret passed over his features.

"This is Mr. Houseman," the conductor said, guessing from the names he had read on the paper and introducing the young man to the policemen.

The policemen shook hands with Wykeham. They had not thought of that before either. They had sons who were older, but somehow, looking at the young man, you did.

"That, I am sorry to say, is Houseman," Wykeham corrected them. Something caught the corner of his eye. Wykeham stopped, fished under the seat and, retrieving a piece of paper, presented it to the sergeant. "We were traveling together from New Awanux," he told them. "He was only newly in my employ." Wykeham looked down at the collar buttoned firmly around the throat of the dead man. A fragment of straw clung to the starched white cloth. He brushed it off. "Understandably we rode separately." Only his eyes betrayed his grief. "I wish he had told me he was ill," he said.

The passengers kept edging nearer and had to be shooed away. The doctor had closed the dead man's shirt and was wiping his fingers on his handkerchief. Death, he told them, was the result of heart failure or shock, or perhaps both. Unusual in a young man but it happened.

There was not much else to be done. The body was taken off. Shortly afterward Wykeham himself left the train to telegraph the bank. He left instructions for someone to travel out on the next train and ride back with the body. At the funeral there would be a lavish array of flowers and a card signed in his own hand. Houseman, it would be discovered, to the surprise of his family, had purchased a generous insurance policy for which his parents, because there had been no wife, were beneficiaries. Death always leaves loose ends. But those which could be tidied up would be.

In something short of an hour the new passengers were permitted onto the train. In the confusion Nora came out of the lavatory. The window in the cubicle had been painted over and she had sat in the little space, her knees drawn up, unable to look out. Over the course of the journey persons unknown had banged at the door and wrenched the handle. To make matters worse she had begun to hear whispers about policemen. She had been frightened and she was now more than willing to pay the fare from wherever she now was. But though she sat in the open, no one thought to ask for it.

II.

The Hill and the Tower

1.

The error in the maps of that time seemed to arise both from the limitations in the knowledge of the world of the men who made them and from the limitations inherent in maps themselves. That man's knowledge of his world continues to be imperfect is perhaps widely enough accepted as to need no defense. The problem with mapping is, as it has always been, that each map is the surrogate of space and not the space itself. It is a problem familiar to poets: It is the heart, before a line is written, that takes the wound. . . .

At Ohomawauke the river bends, following the nearly perfect figure of an "S" tipped on its side. Along this broadly cursive pattern Devon lies both west and south. The figure is too huge to be seen from the hill at Ohomawauke which gave the town its name. The name itself meant owl's nest (or literally owl-place) once but owls stay deep in the wood where they can sit all night among the boughs. Crows fly higher but never high enough. Coming in from the moon you would have seen it, shining with the moon's reflected light. Even a thousand years before the English came to make their marks on the land, amid the illiterate vegetable scrawl of the naked continent, there would have seemed a sign, as if a vanished race had left a message for a god. Certainly it would not have surprised the Reverend

Mr. Longford if this were so. He had devoted many months to the attempt to reduce just this possibility to a few clear lines of proof.

He settled back easily atop the cart in the stationyard. He was gazing over the empty tracks to the place where the train, although he would hear it long before, would come into view. After forty years his whiskers were still the rich chestnut color they had been at twenty. His eyes were deep and with the years had seemed to grow deeper still. To the dismay of a score of women in a half dozen churches he had married young and fully expected to have his helpmate with him through eternity. It was a quarter of twelve already; the train was late.

Longford had come north from Maryland, from a little country church in Mt. Airy where at the request of his bishop he had spent three years. Longford had left in November and gone to stay with a sister in New York. In January, right after Christmas, he had been installed in the parsonage at Greenchurch. Before he had ever heard of Wykeham or the Will, he had asked for the appointment. While in divinity school, one of the numberless tiny colleges named after Wesley, he had been looking through an atlas and discovered, like a piece of ancient mischief, the figure of an "S" lying on its side. During the years that followed he had never quite forgotten it. When at last the bishop had offered Devon, although he was quick to point out that the post included certain added and unusual responsibilities, Longford had agreed at once.

There were three cars in the carriage house, two model A's and the Pope-Hartford, but all were up on blocks. In the first months, with so many more pressing matters to contend with, Longford had never had Charon Hunt, blacksmith, mechanic, drive his equally primitive Ford pickup along the dark wooded road which led to Greenchurch. The pickup itself was so old and so often fell into disrepair it needed both Hunt's skills to keep the relic just bolting along within the village. Then too,

the cars were probably not worth the trouble. Longford imagined that with Wykeham coming the time was not far off when
they would be replaced with a fleet of sleek new ones. Longford
had no illusions on that point. Wykeham after all was a boy of
twenty and could afford to do what he pleased. Longford, however, having no other choice, had backed the cart from the hay
barn, settled the horse and hitched him, then set off down the
long avenue toward the village. At the top of the green, behind
the feed store and the church, he had passed by the rambling
building that served as Hunt's garage. Parked to the side was
the dark green Dodge Longford had driven from Maryland and
then nursed patiently up from New York. It had waited since
January for a missing part. For three months Longford had
wandered past it several times a day, going on foot around the
village on pastoral visits. This evening, after dinner, he had
walked the two miles to the big house at Greenchurch to fetch
the cart and later, after Wykeham had been settled, whatever
luggage he had brought with him lifted to the porch and the
lights switched on, Longford would walk back. But when he
saw the car, the corners of his deep blue eyes rose in a smile.
It was much the same smile he would have given on this or
any night to shut-ins and invalid members of his congregation.
The pains of this world are temporary, it seemed to say, wait.

As the Reverend Mr. Longford turned the cart into the stationyard he was content. Wykeham, he hoped, would soon settle
the odd business with John Chance. There was more to the
old gamekeeper, he suspected, than met the eye but it was a
matter between the old man and the boy. What he really wanted
from Wykeham was permission to fell a few trees on the crown
of East Wood, above the house. The trees were giants and even
now, before the April bloom they blocked the view of the river.
If he could have them down, he was convinced it would open
up the clear line of sight he needed to make the final measurements. He was not unprepared. After months of planning
he now had ample chains and flags and while in New York,

scraping together the last of his savings, he had purchased a new brass surveying compass. He hoped Wykeham had remembered to drop by the booksellers before he left New Awanux. One of the volumes was particularly necessary. Longford smiled again as he thought of it: *Geodaesia, or the Art of Measuring Land Made Easie.*

The darkness by the river was lit suddenly by the one glaring lamp at the front of the train. As if smelling other horses, the cart horse tossed its head.

The Bristol men and their women, carrying all they had, climbed down first and looked around bleakly at the small station and the one empty street: city people in a country town. The stationmaster greeted them easily. There was a boarding-house, he told them, not far, just opposite Hunt's garage. And yes, there was work, for those who didn't mind long hours and were good with their hands. But, of course, it was already Sunday; they would have to wait over. The man in the cart, the Reverend Mr. Longford, was the man to see but not until Monday. Though it wouldn't hurt, the stationmaster added with a wink, if the good Mr. Longford happened to get a glimpse of them in the back pews of Greenchurch in the morning. The stationmaster studied their faces, then shook his head. Perhaps one or two would do, he thought; the rest would be gone in a fortnight.

No one remembered a slender straight-haired woman with no luggage. The surprise had long since passed from her face. She hurried across the platform only pausing a moment to stare at the horse cart. If she felt a blush rising against her neck and cheeks, in the darkness it attracted no notice. She looked back all at once and saw Wykeham step down from the train, saw him raise a hand in greeting to the man in the cart. The hand holding the reins lifted in turn, the greeting of strangers. For a moment she felt the same dark knot of fear she had felt as a child when she had dared herself over the edge of sleep. But she continued on into the stationyard and across the gravel and the darkness of the one long street received her.

Wykeham counted out a few shillings for the stationmaster. The man looked disappointed.

"For your boy," Wykeham said, "when he has unloaded the boxes."

The man brightened. "And the stable car?" he asked, a hint of authority restored to his voice.

"It's all in the shipping orders," Wykeham answered. "Though you might check them yourself to see if there is any added expense. The car stays here the night and goes back empty the first of the week."

The man dug his hands into his pockets where he kept a string of keys. "And the contents?" he asked.

"Quite safe," Wykeham said, "by itself. You needn't bother. Longford will have a gang of men by tomorrow evening to handle everything. I am sure we shall manage."

"You wouldn't know when?"

"Late, I should think."

The stationmaster watched Wykeham turn. "Mr. Wykeham," he called out suddenly.

The young man glanced over his shoulder. The stationmaster looked almost embarrassed.

"My grandfather knew yours," the man said. It seemed like a compliment and for a moment it silenced him. But then the man grinned. "Welcome home, sir," he said.

"There's something wrong with the mails," Longford complained when, the boxes loaded and Wykeham settled on the seat beside him, they turned up the empty street toward Greenchurch. "I had hoped you would have found me further along but I'm afraid the letter didn't come until this morning." Longford gave the reins a shake as though to hurry both the horse and his preparations at once. "I did carry up some fresh linen from the parsonage," he said. "Monday I'll see there is someone out there to begin airing your own."

"Tomorrow, if you wouldn't mind," Wykeham said, as though he had already given some thought of it, "after breakfast. A woman, just on trial, for the kitchen and a maid. Just to start. I shall be needing several. And in the afternoon, say at four-thirty, a half dozen men."

Longford pulled at his handsome whiskers. "William," he began, not yet insisting. "It has perhaps escaped your attention. But after all there can be no question . . ."

The cart moved against the shadows of the trees. Away from the last scattered lights of the village the stars burned fiercely. Longford hadn't noticed when Wykeham withdrew the package from his coat.

"You see I have brought your books," Wykeham interrupted him. It seemed such an artless and generous gesture, so meant to please that for the moment Longford let the abrogation die on his lips. He could afford to wait. The horse stepped lightly ahead of them. But as the young man chatted on about boats and his schooling, the right moment seemed continually pushed beyond reach. It was not until the cart had actually stopped before the porch of the great house and they were helping each other down with the boxes, that Longford, with the return of resolve, placed his fatherly hand on Wykeham's shoulder.

"About tomorrow," he said firmly.

It was dark under the eaves. Hedges that had not been trimmed for years grew up over the sagging porch railings. In the daylight Longford had seen the work that was needed here, like the Lord's work, a never-ending task of pruning and rebuilding, a labor before which, unless refreshed in Christ, even a man of persevering conscience must despair.

"One day in seven," Longford said. "Not in His honor only but because of the spirit of man . . ."

Wykeham walked away from him. Out of the shadow of the

house, Wykeham turned abruptly. Longford saw the tears streaming down his face.

"I am sorry," Wykeham whispered. "There was a man of my acquaintance. . . . He died this evening on the train." Slowly he straightened himself. Longford came down beside him.

"No," Wykeham said softly, rejecting his arm. "You go on home. I shall be fine."

"I hardly . . . ," Longford protested.

"No, honestly. I am sure to manage."

Nevertheless Longford lingered on for a quarter hour, ready if anything were needed. Under the circumstances he was not so ill mannered as to mention the Sabbath.

The doctor puzzled over the corpse. He had pulled back the sheet to examine its eyes and was surprised again at their help-less wonder. He had gone to his house and, without waking his wife, had returned through the quiet streets with his camera. His own dark eyes screwed up at the corners as he focused the lens. He had a theory that the eyes of dead men held, even some hours after death, the slowly fading image of whatever last they looked on. It was a phenomenon he suspected without the least sliver of proof. He arranged the lamps to throw a greater flood of light against the pale, almost spectral head. The irises were a brownish green, roughly the color of the earth at the edge of the wood near the fine gambrel-roofed house in Cambridge where he had been born.

The undertaker already knew all he wanted to know about corpses. "You'll lock up, Oliver?" he wondered.

"Yes — yes," Dr. Holmes said defensively. "I shouldn't be but a few minutes." He repositioned the lamp, for it seemed to him that the wide dead eyes kept on drinking the light. He hesitated, then pushed the lamp nearer.

2.

 In the same darkness, on a hill overlooking the river, old Okanuck knocked out his pipe. A few strings of tobacco curled with a moment's redness but, unsustained by his breath, they blackened on the ground. Only the fierce stars and the hearts of the Pequods, with equal fierceness, kept their brightness.

Outwardly he was nearly invisible, his wings held perfectly still, guarded and immune to the wind. It was the best sort of vanishing trick: turning the darkness within him inside out. Not even the owls had seen a movement or sensed a presence. And yet there were mornings in the world, the blackness running inward back through his veins, when he would have seemed as clear as a shaft of sunshine slanting down through the trees. In neither case would a man have seen him. But Okanuck was old and skilled. The boy was only a boy and he was gone.

In the towns along the river the English slept; the lights of their houses that earlier had been gorged with light were darkened now, the warmth gone without a fading spark or a memory. Walking on, he followed the path where the English road had been. But was not the road he was following. The hilltop regions where the English first took hold were the first to lose them. The roots of trees overgrasped the pasture walls; the cleared meadows closed with shade. Now to either side the big cellar holes of the once great houses were filled with elderberry and cedar. The scratches left on the rotting wood were made by thorns. Watching and remembering, Okanuck climbed among the moss-backed stones. "Oohoomau-auke," he whispered, giving back to the place the name it had never lost.

From across the river valley a glint of firelight caught his eye. Despite his uneasiness, Okanuck smiled. John Chance is awake, he thought. Even among the English there were a few very old men who, seeing all too clearly the rest that awaited them, neglected sleep. Okanuck went down to the bottom of the wood where the track became an English road again. If, as he feared, the boy had set out in anger to begin his own grim war against the English, Chance more than any other would have heard of it. Though in these last years he seldom went from the falling-down steps of his cottage in Black Wood, the young men of the towns still tramped out to talk with him. The young, not yet content to sit in their shops and houses, knew far better than their elders the back lanes and abandoned barns, the remote discarded edges of the towns where among the rusted implements and broken machinery of his enemy the boy might go to brood and plan their further ruin.

Okanuck skirted Paper Birch Farm though for a moment he had been tempted to peer in at the bedroom window of the old widow Birch and the three hounds which she now slept with and had since the night sixty years ago when after rather more thorn wine than he was used to Okanuck had floated down to the third-story window and waved at her.

Of course they were not the same hounds. Sometimes, in the long summer darkness, he had slipped into the side yard where they were buried, one generation after another, still keeping watch. Through the trampled earth he had renewed his acquaintance with their bones. At first, thinking he was a hound himself, come nosing and pawing, eager to disinter them, they had only whined mournfully. But in time they had grown fond of him and looked forward to his coming. Like Okanuck they had thought themselves well rid of the skinny young man their mistress had married and who had to be buried himself soon after, ten miles to the west and south in the cemetery at Greenchurch. The hounds, although they had no sense of human beauty, suspected nonetheless it was her physical attractiveness that drew Okanuck again and again to the grass-covered mound a hundred yards from the house. She is old now, they had told him. Unsurprised, he had nodded. Better than most he knew how these English perished. He had never gone back to her window. And yet sometimes he saw her face in the airy darkness, her red hair disordered on her pillow.

But though he skirted the farm, Okanuck came in sight of it. It took him only a quarter of a mile out of his way but then it brought him nearer the far end of the village than was absolutely necessary. Even at this hour there were likely to be men on the road. With a kind of wondering sadness Okanuck turned. He unfolded his wings. Their broad edges caught the air with a thump. Reaching out in a series of sharp, increasingly distant handholds, Okanuck pulled himself into the sky. Woods and fields wheeled away under him, their particular landmarks diminishing, even as the land itself swung more fully into his sight. In the deep evening air the little darkened farm slid far behind.

John Chance leaned back in his chair and regarded the cluttered yard beyond the rough front steps of his cottage. Because of his years he was not always certain where he was in time. It was far easier and, to his thinking, more to the point to keep watch of the seasons than to weigh his mind with the useless addition of dates. The years kept piling up no matter if he wished them to or not but between one and another there was never much to tell them apart. On the other hand, the seasons and the weathers that rushed along with them meandered and changed: gales howled in Black Wood, yellow leaves fell like showers of gold and under the crusts of rotted snow the green spikes of deer grass lifted their heads. Great things and small pressed themselves on his attention but the only firm conclusion he was willing to come to was that the winter advanced and receded and that the summer followed spring.

John Chance glanced out at the evening. He knew more or less it was April but he remained uncommitted as to whether it was precisely this April or some other come blowing from his memory. He had the impression, however, because he needed a blanket wrapped about his shoulders, that he was old. Very old, he thought with a deep, clear pride. For a second time the awakened breeze brushed his face and he looked up.

Okanuck grinned at him.

"Now it's the end of the world, is it?" Chance said, smiling back. "The impatient dead coming in from the hills, eyes filled with murder."

Okanuck went on grinning. They liked one another well enough to joke at each other's expense and gladly traded wounds, unharmed by an honesty that would have parted lesser friends. Though not the sort of thing he would have denied if pressed, Okanuck never cared to be reminded he was dead and so the old man never failed to find a way to mention it.

"I thought I'd find you dead as well," Okanuck answered.

"No. Not yet." A sly triumph showed in Chance's eyes. "I've made April and still hope to make one more."

Okanuck looked with gentle disapproval at the old man's crippled legs. "It's not the life I'd dream of," he said kindly.

"Hell, it's life," Chance said. Enjoying himself, he leaned farther back in his chair. "Besides, Wyck's come back again and I've a mind to see one last time what he's up to."

Okanuck grunted. "Which one is he now?"

"William — or so Morag thought, poor man. And he had, for he showed me them, a bundle of letters all signed with a great scrawl of a W, which might have been for William as much as Wykeham." Beside him on the steps was a half empty bottle. Chance reached down for it and when he had had a taste of the whisky he passed the bottle sociably into one of Okanuck's large clawed hands. "And the man, Longford, called him that," Chance said, "coming around not a month ago when there were still patches of snow in Black Wood, saying Master William this and Master William that, as though he knew him already. Wanted me off the property, he said, in William's name. It took me a moment or two at first to figure out just who he meant. But it's likely it's William."

"It would be," Okanuck said. "Leastways he's been a handful of Williams since the English came, since Bradford anyway." He drank the whisky. His eyes narrowed and he stared into the web of the branches. He was trying to remember the names that had been before. "They were usually Welsh," he said.

"Wyck?"

Okanuck nodded. "Names like Kyfarwydd or Gwalstawd. Hard to say unless you were used to them but then he kept hold of them longer, there being no need to pretend he was anyone but himself."

While Okanuck was speaking, Chance began to notice he was colder. The whisky warmed his throat and belly so at first he paid no attention. But gradually he felt a damp cold nosing about his feet. He kicked at it lamely. He was not yet frightened. But from now on, he realized, he would have to vigilant.

They both heard the crack of a rifle shot and they both started. The sound echoed between the cleft of hills. Chance jabbed the side of his shoe at the dark. What had been there had gone elsewhere, ignoring him.

"There are poachers in East Wood," he said.

Okanuck's eyes were wide open. He could see only the sky and the nearer trees. Somewhere in the dark men were running, their sides heaving, stumbling because they had not dared to carry a lantern. The paths were grown over or blocked with timber. They heard a man swearing, far across the wood.

"That would be Fred Norfolk for the mouth of him," Chance

said. "And Charon Hunt with him." The wind backed off, taking the sound of the men away with it.

In the stillness Okanuck let himself breathe again.

"You were worried," Chance said.

"For a moment." Okanuck gave him a sideways grin. "But Fred Norfolk never did hit anything." He spotted the whisky and sat down with the bottle between his knees. His toes dragged in the dirt. After that there was no moving him and he began to explain why he had come.

Longford looked up from the text of the sermon he was still writing and found his wife staring at him from their bed. It was early and the lamp at his desk gave a warmer glow of light than the little that came in the south window. Longford had begun the work alone, beneath the stairs, on the dining room table. But as soon as he had heard Plum stirring he had gone up, seeking her help with one phrase or another. He had just finished reading aloud a particularly complicated passage which she had already corrected twice.

"I shall go if I must," she said on another matter altogether.

"Dear Plum," he sighed, relieved, aware that he could not really have expected anyone else to do it and that even if he had, she would have gone anyway. "You will tell him," he said, "that this is a special case and not how things will be handled ordinarily." She looked preoccupied. He cleared his throat. "I'll admit I might have been more forceful. It is best to begin with a clear understanding. I've always said that." He looked back guiltily at his sermon, adjusting the spectacles he only wore indoors and away from his flock. He said: "It was just that I was caught unprepared when he told me about the death of his friend."

She waited to be quite certain he had finished. She knew he meant well but it was one of his greatest faults that he never knew when to stop.

"He won't think, do you suppose, you actually are the kitchen help?"

She met his eyes. "I shall be certain to tell him," she said.

Later he went down the walk with her and opened the gate. He had put his spectacles in his inside pocket. His arm wrapped around her, warming her in the morning's chill.

"You don't mind?" he asked again, assured now, needing no answer.

Beside her he seemed to grow taller, his shoulders a full foot higher than her own. Her chin was tucked down and he could not see her smile. At a point where the street climbed the first hill she looked back and found him watching. She waved, already missing him.

At the entrance to the estate, there were two broad oaks, already coming into leaf, one to either side of the drive. There was no sign. Its lack had never puzzled her for she had seen at once that the trees announced plainly, to anyone who cared to look, that this was Greenchurch. The church on the other hand — back in the village — though it shared the name and was in fact a church and had been painted a shadowed and peculiarly ancient shade of green, had a placard importantly out on the lawn. It was not hard to imagine which had held the name longer. The steeple in the village would have been dwarfed by these trees. She squinted up into their leafy branches, losing her sight among the clouds and countries, the acres and deep green seas of the mounting oak-wood. A kind of old-fashioned awe filled her. Going up the drive, her face dropped to a human height again, she saw another face, pale against the gray bark of the oak, and got a bewildered stare in return.

The woman, who had been reclining, stood quickly. There was a stain on the sleeve of her coat; her disheveled hair, darkened by the shade, half covered her neck.

"My girl," Plum Longford said breezily, though the other

was no child, "you look as though you slept in the wood." To Plum's surprise, the woman nodded.

"I'm not from this place," the woman said quietly, in a way that made Plum wonder if truly she had come from anywhere. The woman blushed. "I wasn't sure just where to go," she said, turning abruptly, taking a nervous glance up the long slope of the drive. "It doesn't feel right going up there."

"You mean it didn't" — Plum helped her — "last night in the dark?"

"Then too," she answered.

Plum noticed that the woman's small hands were clutching a paper. Plum had met most of the village women but there were always some, she knew, who hung back and now with the reopening of the estate there were strangers coming every day. Mostly they were men. But eventually, Plum decided, there had to be women as well, hired for the kitchen and house-keeping, though, under the circumstances, she knew Tim would have preferred them older and, well, more matronly. She found herself inspecting the woman's slender legs and laughed at herself.

"You'll be wanting to see my husband," Plum said, "for he is in charge of the hiring."

"I haven't —" the woman began.

"May I see that?" Plum interrupted her, for she was accustomed to being in charge. She reached out for the paper, expecting an employment notice.

"He gave that to me," the woman said but she let Plum take hold of it. Plum turned the paper over in her fingers. It was the steamer ticket to Bodø.

"I mean to exchange it," Nora said, smiling. "I will rent a box at the post office so I will have a place when they send the money back. I have it all figured out. I was going to go down to post it this morning but then I remembered it was Sunday. But I will go tomorrow."

"Who gave it to you?" Plum asked, astonished and trying to find the beginning.

"The young man who was come to live here."

"Why?"

Nora closed her eyes as though she were looking for something but wasn't altogether certain it could be found outside of her. "I am hoping," she said, "it is fate."

"And if it isn't?"

Nora ran her fingers into her cider-colored hair, trying vaguely to restore it to order. Among the brown strands, Plum noticed there were little flecks of gold. Nora opened her eyes and Plum became conscious again of their remarkable innocence. Somehow it touched her.

"I don't suppose he knows you have come," she said, in a voice that seemed unlike her, almost embarrassed. While she had mistaken practically everything at first, very quickly Plum was beginning to readjust her thinking. Tim, she knew, would have been scandalized. But her own view of life had always been kinder and more tolerant for she knew the world better. The truth was, she was eight years older than her husband. "Look," she said gently, "it is really none of my business."

"No," Nora said. "He doesn't know."

They had begun to walk up the drive. Beyond the sentinel oaks the light was brighter. Plum looked about. The broad trimmed lawns had long ago turned into meadows. The plantings of exotic trees, brought from Europe and the Orient, had been left to grow wild. Only an experienced eye would have marked them apart from the elms and maples. Yet Plum half sensed their oddity. Who can say she doesn't belong here? she thought. Though if she were wanted, Plum guessed, he would not have given her a steamer ticket. Bodø was in Norway, wasn't it? Almost the other side of the earth.

"I am Hannah Longford," she said, "though my friends call me Plum."

"Like the heavy thing —" Nora screwed up her face in wonder. "You know, the weight sailors use to tell how deep the sea is. Like that?"

Plum laughed. "That too! Yes," Plum answered, deciding she liked her without reservation. "And your own?" she asked, still smiling.

"Nora."

Plum waited for her to finish.

"Only Nora," she said after a moment. "Now at any rate. You see, I've run away from the rest of it."

"You have a husband?"

Nora looked blank.

No, Plum thought, I shall not let it matter — I have decided to be a friend to her. Plum began to walk a little more briskly, trusting her body to keep her mind from thinking. There was the good feel of gravel under her feet. Out in the morning, rising over the trees, a crow circled, eyeing them. It opened its black throat and cursed. Or perhaps it was only the cough of the battered Ford pickup, bounding around a turn in the drive up ahead of them. Nora climbed up the embankment and hid in the trees. But though she stepped into the grass Plum more or less held her ground. It was Charon Hunt, of course, driving and another man, his head averted, refusing to acknowledge he saw her or not wanting to be seen. Plum waved at them. The truck barreled past. There was a large canvas sack in the back. Whatever was in it was heavy. The truck bounced and swayed but the sack did not budge. The truck took the turn by the oaks widely, edging precariously near one of the trunks, rattling over the snarl of roots and, with a roar of its old engine, vanished.

"You needn't worry," Plum called out to Nora. "They didn't care to be looked at anymore than you. So I doubt they will be saying they've seen us."

Nora peered out from the brush. Her white skin was reddened down to her throat.

"It's just that I'm not ready yet," she said.

"Well, you had best hurry, my girl," Plum laughed; "the house is not much more of a walk."

Nora shook her head and stayed where she was.

"What will you do, then?" Plum wondered.

"When I have my money," Nora said, knowing that part, having begun her thinking somewhere in the middle, "then I will rent some place. I will live in the town he lives in. I will wait till he notices."

"Until then?"

Nora brightened. "Couldn't you," she began. "I mean, already you've been so kind."

But Plum knew she could not, not with Tim. Though she could get him around most things, she knew with a pang of hard feminine regret, this would not be one of them, knew, despite his tenderness for her. She remembered the warmth of his arm about her waist. No, she thought, until it was all sorted out it was best perhaps Tim did not learn she was here. But clearly something had to be done and, as she looked around, it was equally clear to her that it would have to be herself who would have to do it. She studied the paper, which with the sudden appearance of the truck she had neglected to hand back to Nora.

"I shall keep this," Plum said firmly. "It has the address right here on the top. I'll send it off myself tomorrow. You needn't go into town. In the meantime . . ." It really was a fine muddle, she thought. Who knew what had gone on between them? Or was likely to? Not yet anyway, she decided, not if she could help it. Certainly the woman could not go up to the house but neither could she be permitted to sleep under the trees.

Nora stepped out on the grass.

"No you don't," Plum said with the sudden fierceness of inspiration.

"Plum?"

But a small smile was shaping itself into the corners of Plum's mouth and she mounted the embankment with a sturdy, determined tread. "Turn around," she directed, coming under the edge of the wood. "Now walk straight ahead," she said, driving Nora before her into the limb-tangled darkness that even in the bold light of morning always made Black Wood seem like one of the straggling, spectral provinces of night.

An hour later Plum let herself into the Great House without knocking. The hall was empty. Nonetheless she made her way carefully, trying the doors at random, until far in the back of the house and down a half level of stairs she discovered the kitchen. It was the largest kitchen she had ever been in. There were a great many copper-covered tables and at least five black stoves. Off to the side there was a separate room for a pantry, another for the table service and a third, quite a bit smaller, with drying racks and sinks. A month ago the first of the groundsmen and the chief hostler and his boy had been let in to make their suppers. They had left, she saw, exactly the sort of disorder she had expected whenever men were let alone in a kitchen. Plum poked about impatiently. Now that Wykeham was here, of course, this would all have to stop. She began to collect the scattered plates and saucers.

The young man, in his gray tweeds, came in quietly behind her. Plum's first impression as she turned and found him smiling at her was that he was dressed like an old man. She had an armful of dishes and, becoming increasingly irritated, had just discovered a new hoard of messy platters wrapped in a tablecloth and hidden under a chair. Her breath came quickly through her teeth.

"I don't suppose you know you have a woman waiting for you in the wood?" she asked him angrily.

Wykeham held open the kitchen door. A crow hopped across the threshold. Its rakish black head was tilted up so it could look at him.

"The other one . . . ," Wykeham asked, seeming only mildly interested. He returned the crow's black stare. "Did you think she was pretty?"

3.

"You should not have asked."

"Would you have answered?"

"No."

"Then there could have been no harm."

"It is harm enough if she thinks you are heartless."

"She may think what she likes."

"She will in any event. That proves nothing."

"Then it little matters if I ask you questions."

"It was never the asking."

"Then what?"

"It was the thing you asked."

"Whether a shop girl was pretty?"

"Yes."

"And was she?"

"I am no judge. You all have fat legs and hair."

Wykeham grinned. "There! I have you," he shouted happily. With both hands he hauled himself up the last rungs of the ladder. His large dark face pressed against the small attic window, he stared, smiling, down at the lawn. "And on two counts," he said. "The first being that you are incapable of speech. And the second that, speechless or not, you are no fit judge. In neither case could she have thought I took my question seriously. Therefore there is no harm." Wykeham scratched the glossy feathers along the crow's neck but the crow turned away sulkily.

"You are wrong in both," it rasped. It hopped to the sill, holding its place with a sudden spasm of its heavy wings. It brought its head level. It blinked in the daylight. "For if," it continued, "I could not answer, then she could only have thought it was herself you meant to ask."

"And the second?"

"She was fit to judge."

Wykeham looked annoyed. "What can that matter? She is just an old woman."

"And therefore you are heartless," the crow answered. "And she knows it. Accordingly there is harm."

Wykeham reached for its neck. But the wary crow flew up into the rafters.

"Open the window and let me out," it said. "I have spent the whole night watching and now I am hungry." The crow looked Wykeham straight in the face. Wykeham knew he would not be able to catch it.

"There is a new-killed rat in the pantry," he said.

The crow turned its back on him resentfully. "In the drive there is a hare," it said, "run over by a truck." The crow picked at the underside of one of its long feathers with its beak. A little gust of wind rattled the window pane. It was already some hours since the woman had deserted the kitchen and the house was quiet.

"I had been meaning to mention it earlier," the crow said. "It appears, lord, that they have shot an Indian."

The wind had freshened all morning, tearing off small branches and throwing them to the lawn. In the afternoon Wykeham heard the wind prowling under the eaves and muttering among the loose bricks of the chimneys. He sat at his desk making drafts of a long letter to His Grace which, with each rewriting, grew shorter and shorter. The truth was he was agonizing over a verb in the very first sentence, struggling over meanings as a man will only struggle over a love letter, which, in a limited sense, this was.

Dear Callaghan, the letter began but his letters always started so and the salutation was essentially without content. *I regret that I must request* was what he had written first and the letter ran on to two pages. They both lay crumpled in a basket at his feet. He dug his pen into the inkwell, starting over. *I need your help once more,* the second announced bluntly. The rest came a word at a time, grudgingly. He folded the single page over and set it aside. The deepening afternoon sunlight came in through the window behind him and lit the edges of a fresh sheet. The shadow of his right hand lay across its middle. He wondered what thoughts would come into Callaghan's mind when he unsealed the envelope and began to read. Wykeham was desperately sorry about the death of Houseman. But there had been no choice. It was not the killing, though in fact he had never relished it.

He had killed before, both with his own hands and by proxy. He had never pretended, as men often did, that both cases were not very much the same, but he had been at it longer and had less reason to lie to himself. The wars in which he had taken his first heads and left the bubbling necks empty were no longer remembered; the lands over which he had fought were no longer lands, but ocean. Yet he had never failed to understand what it meant or what a powerful thing it was to take a life or to be less frightened by it.

He did not expect to be understood. He knew that not even the most rugged men now living could have lived as he had lived, gone where he had gone, or done what, to the horror of his soul, he had had to do. Nevertheless, for Callaghan's sake as much as for the young man himself, he wished that Houseman had continued.

I must call you again into service, he wrote at last. *Houseman,*

*failing, is dead and I shall trust no one else in this enterprise. I have
no other reward to offer you except my affection;* he stopped, then
added, *everlastingly.*

Beneath the tiny printed letters he set a large cursive "W."
For a moment he looked at it oddly. His hand must have been
unsteady. He had just about decided to make a second copy
when he heard the men tramping onto the porch.

He sealed up the letter in the envelope he had already addressed. Still, it was curious, he thought as he walked into the
hall. Tipped on its side, rather as if he had been falling as he
had written it, the one bold letter of his signature almost seemed
an "S."

He put it out of his mind. Walking toward the door, he pulled
on his coat.

The men looked shy when they came for work. It was the
first time they had ever seen such a big, queer house. Silently,
collecting on the porch, they waited for the last straggler to
remove his cap.

"Is there a man among you who has ever handled a horse?"
Wykeham asked them.

When he had come out, they had stepped back, crowding
against the railing, and looked puzzled. The wind, which had
been building up all day, tugged at their collars.

"There's work here he told us," George Tennison answered,
who for twenty-seven years had been a tool and die maker at
the Bristol clockworks. "Maybe we never asked what kind, but
Longford never said it was horses." George Tennison winced,
thinking he had walked a good long way for nothing. He was
about to put on his cap again, there being no further need for
deference, when his eye ran into an unexpected piece of mischief
in the young man's face. He smiled himself. "Though I could,"
he said, grinning, "manage to pick up after a horse." He con-
trived to wink at the man next to him. "And Sam here, he'd
be right good at it."

Sam snorted but after that they all seemed a little less miserable. One by one Wykeham asked them their names and in turn each man came forth to shake hands with him.

"I'm Jakey."

"I am pleased to have you, Jakey."

"Adam France, sir."

"Adam."

The others came forward. Despite the formality, as if their shared amusement at the thought of horse manure were bond enough, the curse lifted from the air.

"Mostly it is your backs I'll be wanting," Wykeham told them leading them off the porch and up the slope by the side of the house. "Though one of you, George I think, will have to ride with me when the rest are finished." He paused and there was a moment's dead silence. George Tennison seemed dubious. "It's the horse," Wykeham said, "that does the work. All you do is hold on to him." Wykeham smiled. "And of course, it pays double."

"I'm your man, then," George said.

Wykeham laughed. "That was just what I was hoping."

There were birds in the wood, blown along by the wind from branch to branch or simply fleeing ahead of them, it was difficult to tell which. But because it was East Wood there were breaks where the evening light yet lingered, coppery and brown-yellow. They could still see one another clearly. Nonetheless Wykeham had brought along lanterns. Although he was not used to looking at the sky, George Tennison thought that they had at least another hour of daylight. He clambered up on a stone and looked out through a dusky thicket of sumac. They were, he judged, a half mile or so from the house and climbing along the high uneven edge of a hill but Wykeham had yet to mention what they were doing there. With long, unbroken strides he kept on going and they tramped behind, dodging the ragged limbs, their arms already welted and their perplexed sweating faces smeared with the blood of small scratches.

Far below him George Tennison heard what he guessed was the river. We're high up, he thought and wondered whether he'd break his neck scrambling around in the darkness when evening came for good or they walked, as Wykeham showed every intention of doing, straight up at the stars. "Even then more likely than not," he mumbled under his breath, "he'll just keep on going." But at the top they came to a clearing. Wykeham waited at its edge.

"There," he said, pointing, though there was nothing in particular to see.

The wood merely came to a halt, leaving a rough circle nearly a hundred feet across. The undergrowth had stopped with the trees. There were a few blue flowers, of the sort without many roots that grow anywhere, and a crop of leprous white toadstools that grow only from decaying timbers. Otherwise the clearing was empty and flat. A tunnel of glowing light opened above it.

"Set the lanterns alight," Wykeham told them, "and later we needn't be bothered." He took a lantern himself, turned a knob at its base until the wick swelled with vapor. When it began to flicker, he put the lantern aside, his face looking curiously pleased in the fog of yellow light, and walking beyond the edge, began scraping the side of his boot in the rags of weed. Underneath there were boards.

"Pull up the planking," he said. "But be careful."

None of the planks was nailed and the wood, long out in the weather, was soft. It shifted easily and though it creaked, nothing staved in. Gradually the sky darkened. The last hour they labored on in the shine of the lanterns. We must look like a crew of devils, George Tennison thought, opening a pit. He could see the immense hollowness growing under him, the steep earthen sides falling into a blackness too dark to be reached by the lanterns.

"This a barn cellar?" he asked the man working next to him.

Adam France shrugged his shoulders. "Christ if I know. But it's deep."

"Why would any one put a barn so far from the house?" George Tennison wondered. Not that it mattered. Almost despite himself, he was beginning to enjoy the work. It was actually quite an adventure, he decided. He imagined coming back in the small hours to the boardinghouse where Mrs. Tennison would be waiting for him. She would badger him with questions. "Woman," he saw himself answering, "he's a madman certain." Then he would count out the pile of guineas, letting each clink in the darkness on the dresser. He was astonished and disappointed when the last board came up.

"That will do," Wykeham said, in a voice which seemed to say, Now off with you, the rest is my business only. But the Bristol men lingered about at the edge. Adam France was reaching down with a lantern.

"It smells like an open grave," Sam said.

"Much you would know of that," George Tennison answered.

"Take the lanterns," Wykeham said. And they did that.

George Tennison stood in the doorway of the stable watching his fellows walking away down the drive. He waved and got a wave back but the darkness took them and the wind muttered and he lost the sounds of their shoes on the gravel. He ambled around out in front and peered in at the door. A light had been clicked on and he could make out a large center room.

The stables had been divided. The left side, beyond the tackroom, disappeared down an aisle of wooden half doors behind which the beasts paced warily. To the right the stalls had been dismantled and the flooring replaced with paving stones. At the far end of the huge black shapes of several very elegant, very old automobiles, now dull with dust, waited uselessly on blocks.

It had been nearly forty years since George Tennison had seen the like of them.

With a stab of memory he recalled the busy streets of Bristol. Sitting on the curb in the heart of the market, his eyes filled with envy, he had watched the great cars pass. He had discovered then, for the first time, how bitter the part was he had been given to play in the world. As if no time had passed, with the same deep humiliation, he felt again his smallness and swore.

At last there was a click of a latch, a clop of hooves. For an instant the light behind him was blotted out by a shadow. Through the dim opening Wykeham came forth leading a mare.

"Hold the reins," he said.

"And mine?" George Tennison wondered, stepping aside awkwardly, for the mare was huge. "Surely for myself, a gentler . . ."

Already the mare was beginning to dance. Wykeham grinned. "Going out you will sit up beside me," he said. "But watch me carefully, for you will be riding her back." He laid his hand on the horn of the saddle, then finding the stirrup, hauled himself up. "I will have your hand," he said.

George Tennison made a tentative protest; but strong fingers closed on his wrist. All at once his thin legs were straddling the mare's wide back.

"You do remember the way out by the roads?"

"I expect so," George Tennison answered. "I walked them."

For a moment or two the mare trotted agreeably along the dark drive. But then Wykeham prodded her side and with alarming speed she bolted into the wood.

For all George Tennison knew the mare might have leapt into pure darkness. A menace of shadows surged past his head. He could hear the thudding hooves, each jolting step shaking him clear to the bone. He grabbed hold of Wykeham's waist. The young man laughed.

When George Tennison opened his eyes again, the mare was

trotting easily under the trees; the old trunks were distinct and separate against the sky's shining blackness. The metal of the bridle, even the leaves of the trees seemed as lustrous as mirrors. The older man drew a breath. Between the branches, halfway out to the stars, a flight of swans rose like an arrow aimed at the moon.

"This is South Wood," Wykeham told him solemnly but the man heard the note of eagerness beneath. Wykeham shook the reins gently. "The tree-cutters have been busy here," he said. "Yet their work comes to nothing."

They rode through the wood. Although he could only see the back of the younger man's head, George Tennison imagined he was smiling. The mare lifted her neck.

A long time after, or perhaps a short time, he never knew which, George Tennison realized that they were close to the village. Soon he saw the houses, snug behind their fences, and the top of the green and he remembered that he had not asked where they were going.

"It is not far to the station," Wykeham announced all at once. "You will leave me there. You might," he added, "tie the mare up for the night wherever it is you are staying. You could ride her out to the house, if you wished, after breakfast."

George Tennison hesitated but then in his mind's eye he saw Mrs. Tennison peering out from the window into the morning, watching him climb like a jockey onto the back of the mare. "I would like that," he said, suddenly grinning himself.

"Where are the men?" the stationmaster asked him.

"I have sent them to their beds. Well you might go yourself."

"I have stayed to help."

"You look tired," Wykeham said. But the stationmaster insisted on walking with him into the yard where the stable car waited on the siding. Nevertheless he found he needed to lean on a post or a gate, if only for a moment, holding his weary head nearly upright in the cradle of his arms.

The stationmaster awoke as the two A.M. train was pulling out of the station. The wind had dropped. An odd scent filled his nostrils. When he tried the doors of the car he found they were unbolted. He swung them open and poked in with his lamp. Its yellow beam ran along the floor and over the sides of the huge empty stall. His nostrils twitched, smelling the thick, unmistakable scent of oak-wood.

4.

"A tree?"

"At the crown of East Wood," Longford continued, pushing his cup away from him and into the assortment of abandoned luncheon dishes. "Up from the house," he said, "in the direct line of sight to the river."

Plum saw his disappointment. "Are you certain?" she asked.

"I have made the measurements a good half dozen times," he snapped, unaccustomedly cross with her for having doubted him. Plum folded her napkin. Her instincts told her to let it be. There had been no talk yet. She reached for the cup, seeking to touch what he had touched and restore whatever connection had broken. The mild brown liquid slopped unexpectedly over the rim. She watched the stain spread through the tablecloth and thought with gathering irritation, He might at least have drunk a little.

"But if it wasn't there yesterday," she complained.

"But it was," he persisted, "this morning." Indeed it had very much been there. He had come up the drive, having started out early to have his little chat with Wykeham, to invite him to dinner (after all, the young man was his ward and there were things to be settled), to mention, in passing, the matter of a few old trees he wanted cleared from the wood. As he had let his gaze drift over the familiar line of the foliage, he had seen the shocking new growth, brash in the sunlight, like an enemy standard raised overnight on the hill. He had still not gotten over his surprise or his anguish. Only yesterday there had been nothing but gaunt, dying trees. He had banged on the door. No one answered and he had tacked up a scribbled note on an envelope letting Wykeham know in the firmest possible way that he was expected at the parsonage at seven. On the way back toward the village he had met a man leading a mare. It was his habit to smile even at strangers, but he had trudged on past George Tennison sullenly, without looking up.

The box was surprisingly heavy yet the old man continued to lift it. For much the same reason once a week he limped into the village for whisky. To do less, even by the smallest measure, would be to admit finally that he had grown too old. He removed the box from the corner, sliding it first with the combined efforts of his feet and hands. It was a pretty box, he had always thought, compounded of a great many layers of lacquered wood and fitted with a pair of heavy brass hinges. For several minutes it rested on the seat of the chair. When his heart had stopped pounding and the whiteness had gone from before his eyes, he lifted the box onto the table. He would not let the woman help him. Not yet, he thought with sly cunning. The woman squeezed next to him; he could see her bosom rise and fall with expectation. He was not altogether certain he approved. Angels, he had been taught, were, or at least ought to be, sexless.

Nora reached for the lid.

"There is a lock," Chance said. He began to fumble in his pockets. Though it was difficult with her standing so close to him, he avoided her touch. He was still not frightened. But with Death's Angel come into the house, he would have to be careful.

Nora was happily unaware of his mistrust. Since Plum had brought her to his cottage, she had simply been waiting for whatever would happen next. She had not bothered to listen when the two had spoken. She may have wondered where she was but the sound of the wind, filling the treetops, reminded her of the great tidal race at Bodø, and the sound had distracted her. Nora had not followed when Plum made her way to the door. No other words had been spoken. The old man spent the night sitting out on his step; she had slept, without dreaming, in his bed. When she awoke she had made him breakfast which, since he refused it, she had eaten cheerfully. She hadn't the slightest idea what to do afterward. She had been sitting on the stool and humming when Chance came in the door.

"You'll not find me any easier prey than you've found him," Chance warned her.

Nora caught a glimpse of her face in the window glass and wondered at the wicked flush on her cheeks. The morning was warm. Breathing in the tingly scent of her own damp skin, she unbuttoned her blouse.

"Found who?" she asked, watching her reflection. The fabric of the blouse still clung to her. She wriggled and dug behind her back. Because he was only an old man and it scarcely mattered, she unfastened her brassiere.

"He you have chased forever," he said. "Though you ain't got him." He began to feel braver. "Nor is it likely you would."

She looked at him doubtfully.

"Could you tell me what you mean?" she said.

His gnomish smile widened; for he saw this as proof of his toughness. "Oh, better than that. I can show you!"

It was then he had gone for the box.

"Sixty — seventy years ago I made the drawing," he was saying as he placed the key in the lock. He pulled the lid open. "I was a lad myself then, running where he ran and near as fast if I'm not mistaken. Galloping off after hares in the wood.

Chasing foxes in and out of barns . . . and houses that ain't houses anymore, weren't houses then to tell the truth, just big old cellar holes." He put in his hand, touching the paper deep inside.

Watching his face, Nora had a sudden premonition. With that part of her mind that had always taken the pieces of her life and rearranged them until, however wayward, they seemed to fit into a single urgent tale, she thought: So my father would have mourned his youth. It did not matter that she had never known her father; she found the old man comforting. She glanced about the tiny cottage that was bedroom and kitchen and remembered the little room in Bodø and the ghost of the father who was not dead but gone. She would be glad of this old man's company. She would not let it matter that he did not care for her own. So Eve smiled, discovering her will was stronger, that it could change the face of paradise. With just such a smile, Nora took the faded paper from the old man's fingers.

"He wasn't pleased," Chance said. He crouched in front of her, trembling and holding himself upright with the butt of his stick. "Not one bit pleased when I told him I had done it. Hated the idea of anyone making pictures of him." Chance looked at her craftily. "But I kept it anyway. And he knows I have it. Told the same to Longford when he came around trying to chase me off. He won't send me packing, I told him."

There was a little twitch of a smile, a pause while he stretched out his arm excitedly and pointed. "See for yourself," he said. "Not a line changed!" He waited but she did not answer. "You do see?" he had cried at her.

But Nora kept her mouth shut. It was already too late to cover her breasts with the paper. She had simply stepped back. Wykeham stood in the doorway. He did not move but then he did not have to to make her heart beat faster. Not that she minded. But she wondered how long he had been standing there, dressed in his old man's coat, watching her nakedness.

. . .

It was fairly late, past eight-thirty, when Wykeham knocked on the door of the parsonage. Longford, who had fallen asleep in his reading chair, now stood bewildered in the middle of the front room. It was Plum who had gone to the door. Wykeham waited on the step. He was holding an envelope in his large fingers. Plum glared at him suspiciously.

"Forgive me," Wykeham said. "I do hope the dinner is not ruined." Before she had found the courage to answer, he walked past her into the hall. She hurried after, pausing to relight a lamp on a table outside the kitchen. At last he turned so that she could see the side of his face. The features were strong and roughly handsome. Except for the way the wind had tousled his dark hair, he did not look like a boy.

"It was only that I just found the note," he said in a voice blameless and contrite by turns. She was aware of his slow smile. She was not deceived. She thought, Something has happened.

Longford put aside the book and came forward.

Wykeham waved the note in front of him. "I am sorry if there has been any inconvenience."

"Quite all right," Longford said. "My mistake probably." He showed Wykeham into the parlor. There was a brief silence. "You have already met Mrs. Longford, I believe," he said formally.

Wykeham smiled. "Yes. Yesterday, very early."

Longford's lower lip turned ever so slightly as Wykeham took a seat in the upholstered chair where Longford himself had been reading. There was a longer silence. Longford blundered about the room. Settling at last on the edge of a sofa he had never liked, he crossed his legs uncomfortably. Plum remained standing.

"It was kind of you," Wykeham said to her, "to make a start on the kitchen. It needed a woman. The workmen, I am afraid, left quite a shambles."

"Men do," she said, watching him. So far she had told her husband nothing of her visit to Greenchurch. Tim had not even remarked on it, when after the service he had come back to the parsonage and found her already home and furiously cleaning her own kitchen. He had merely welcomed the sight of her in her apron.

"But as you say," Plum continued, "it was only a start."

"But a beginning has been made," Wykeham said cheerfully. "And I am grateful."

Longford uncrossed his long legs. He had completely forgotten to look for a housekeeper. It was this awful business about the trees. He thought, At least he's come and we can get that settled. But he was impatient with himself because he had not remembered.

"Tomorrow," Longford said apologetically, a little taken aback by the petulance in his voice. "There are women in the village who would be glad of the work." He turned to his wife. "What would you say, dear," he asked her, "to Mrs. Hunt?" Strangely he could not read her face. "Or Mrs. Norfolk?" he suggested more tentatively.

"That will not be necessary," Wykeham interrupted.

Plum's eyes were suddenly on his. Her color deepened.

"But I insist," Longford rumbled. "After all, I had promised."

"You needn't have," Wykeham said. "Quite by chance I have managed to find someone myself."

After dinner, while the men were still seated and Plum was out of the room, Longford put the question directly.

"What exactly do you know about this woman?" he asked.

"Do either of you want tea?" Plum inquired from the kitchen where she had seemed for a time unusually quiet. Longford murmured noncommittally.

"Yes," Wykeham said. "Thank you."

They both heard the water spilling from the tap. With noisy

efficiency Plum seemed to be clearing away, washing up and brewing the tea all at once. What's got into her? Longford wondered. He glanced at the open doorway as her shadow passed. After several minutes Plum came in with a tray.

"Nearly forty," Longford was saying. "I daresay that seems a safe age in a woman." But noticing the look on Plum's face, he added charitably: "Of course age is merely a state of mind."

Rewarded with a smile, he turned again to Wykeham. "Certainly," he said, "you wouldn't object if Mrs. Longford were to call on her." He looked to see Wykeham's reaction and added, although nothing more was needed: "Certain little formalities. You can well understand." Well satisfied with himself, he stood for a long moment in the middle of the room, smiling. Out of the corner of his eye Wykeham saw Plum look hastily away.

They carried their tea into the parlor.

The furniture, in large measure, had come with the parsonage. Except for a chair or two and a photograph of Longford's father, looking very much like Longford himself, the furnishings were in fact Wykeham's, having come down with the estate and passed along with the pulpit, for temporary use, from one minister to the next. There were pieces from a half dozen periods, English and Dutch, pieces elegant and droll, austere and operatic. Wykeham sank willingly into the stiff, horsehair sofa Longford loathed and seemed, Plum thought, almost immediately pleased with it. He balanced his cup on his knees in a way that made her think of an Oxford dandy. Yet, with his big hands and square shoulders, he would not have appeared out of place among the laborers her husband had hired on his behalf. Indeed, she imagined he was skillful at things that they were and her husband was not.

Plum glanced across the room at her husband. The questions about Wykeham's schooling and travels had been exhausted insofar as Longford had patience to ask or to listen. Wykeham had already promised twice to visit Black Wood and pay a call on John Chance. Tim ran his blunt fingers along the spine of his book. She saw he was preparing himself and wished somehow she were sitting next to him and could slip her hand into his. Then he could ask what he liked. Yet she blamed herself for having argued with him earlier. Nevertheless she dreaded the question. Only the strength of her deep affection kept her quiet.

Longford arched his wide brows. "I have the distinct impression," he said, beginning already well into his argument, "that there is a new tree in East Wood."

Wykeham waited.

"Undoubtedly it isn't the sort of thing you would likely have noticed?"

Slowly Wykeham finished his tea. He glanced at Plum before he set his cup aside. Finally, he shook his head.

"I didn't think you would," said Longford, disappointed. "Though I can assure you it is there now and wasn't yesterday."

There was a pause. Plum had such a strong sense of impending disaster she nearly stood. She was looking for an excuse to mention the hour, to remind Wykeham that he ought to be going. She was even willing, somewhat contradictorily, to offer more tea though she knew perfectly well none was wanted.

"You can imagine, I hope, my astonishment," Longford was saying. "I have paid extraordinary attention to the trees in East Wood. There are one or two matters about them I had planned to discuss with you. Trivial, some might think. But from my own point of view I should say they were most important." His handsome face tightened with seriousness. Plum saw him about to plunge once again along a path the young man, not knowing him, could not have expected to follow. She wished Wykeham were the gentleman she was now fairly certain he was not. Then he might have succeeded, where she admitted only failure, in diverting him.

"A tree?" Wykeham showed no expression but Plum knew very well he goaded him.

Longford nodded. "Precisely," he said. "A tree where no

83

tree had been." His voice made an eager, quivering sound, not at all like a clergyman's.

The curtains stirred dully in back of him. Plum could hear the whisper of the cloth as clearly as if it were the sly whisper of women in the parish hall. A half dozen churches in a dozen years. A sadness fell on her. During their last months in Maryland, as elsewhere, there had been talk. She was prepared as well for silence. But Wykeham turned his head.

"How did you first come to notice it?" he asked, without a trace of irony.

Longford thought the question over. "It is easy enough to see," he said at last. "But the reason I saw it, I believe, was that I so thoroughly hadn't expected it to be there." He drew a breath and eased himself up in the chair. "For a week," he said, "whenever I went out to Greenchurch, I had watched that little bit of wood. I was waiting to see, when the trees came to leaf, which wouldn't bloom and were dead timber. You see I wanted your permission, a favor to some studies I am pursuing, to cut a few branches, maybe a tree or two, so I could get a clearer view from the house to the river."

Longford leaned a little nearer. "You, William, would not have minded. It was old wood and scarcely a leaf . . ." He remembered the top of the hill. There had been a view over great stretches of bare limbs and, in patches, the pearly mist of the river. "It would not have done much damage," he said. "Dead wood and dying. I know, I am pleased to think, every inch of the timber. I had picked out the trees." Though he had just got himself going, he made himself stop. The night air moved the curtain. He was trying not to think of his wife, who was sitting very still, watching him.

"It's in this book," Longford said because suddenly he was beginning to discover that he had not the words for the turning of his own thought. "One of the two books," he said after a moment, "you were kind enough to bring up from New Awanux. You didn't by any chance happen to look through it?"

"No."

"Well, it's in here," Longford said. "Not the whole thing of course. I've seen the clues myself, followed them in fact for some time, until, quite independently, they led me here. Really the book is no more than the confirmation of my own work." He leaned farther out and gave the small volume to Wykeham. He waited while Wykeham folded back the front cover. There was the same plate of a naked Indian Wykeham had seen in the shop on Abbey Street. On an inside page he found the title: *The Celt and the Red Man: A Preliminary Discourse on the Old Welsh Origins of the Algonquin Language.* The book had been published in Boston in the middle of the last century. Wykeham turned past the table of contents. "Proofs," the author began, "must not be arguments, but testimonies."

Longford cleared his throat.

"I believe," he said rapidly, "that the first Indians, the true Indians, were Welsh." He forced himself to smile. "If you know how to look, everything points to it. Though I do sometimes wish I were an etymologist." Indeed it annoyed him that he could pronounce a mere fraction of the words whose embedded sources and branching histories he had followed in his reading. He suspected, because he had not mastered the sounds, that some meaning always eluded him. "Yet I haven't done badly," he said. "I have made astounding progress, especially in the relationship between topography and language. And yet," he said, "if only one had other lives. Time to pursue things thoroughly. Haven't you wished that yourself?"

"I thought they were Chinamen," Wykeham said.

"Oh they were," Longford answered. "Yes. Very definitely. Beyond dispute. But later." Suddenly he looked very grave. "It all sounds, I know, William, quite foolish. But it fits. Not perfectly by any means; but a sight better than any other explanation I've heard of. For one thing there are dolmens. Right here in the village. In Devon. Huge upright stones and root cellars. Though of course they aren't root cellars at all. And

writing on the bare rock! Not simple pictographs but whole
stanzas: battles and eulogies, clear facts of history. In deep-cut
Ogham letters!" An effervescence of spirit had filled him. He
leaned forward as though catching the breeze from the window.
Plum, for once, gazed at him without pity.

"I know," Longford said. "Certainly, I know what you think."
But his look implored Wykeham not to judge him too quickly.
"I can show you the proof," he admonished him. "And not
only in the stones and cellars of the village."

Looking away, Wykeham began to explore the pages of the
book. There were drawings of boulders cradled on smaller stones
and drawings of Indian sachems, spear-armed, alone by a pool
in a wood or surrounded by archers, Indians kneeling before
altars or standing under the open sky on the bluffs at Ohomowauke. But for the most part there were drawings of letters,
plate after plate of Ogham nicks and scratches, cut on squared
stone or wooden billets, the English translations marching sen-
sibly along underneath.

"Stones can be forgeries," Longford said. "I'm the first to
admit that. The farmers who first settled here were learned
men, university men not of few of them, reading Phoenician
and writing Greek."

Plum was looking out the window. On the far side, across
the darkened green, the lights were burning in Charon Hunt's
garage. She could make out a knot of men standing there. It
was difficult to see their faces but their figures, in the illumination of the garage lamps, had a dramatic and furtive quality.
Hunt himself had seldom been anything but polite to her. But
Plum had always had the impression, even when he wasn't,
that he was scowling. He was a large man, strong and angular,
of no certain age. He had masses of deep red hair crowding low
on his forehead. It was not exactly that she objected to the
man's coloring. Yet neither was it entirely unrelated, she reflected, to the brashness and anger she sensed was inside him.
He had as well, she knew, a habit of appearing where he was

least expected, like the morning she had watched him speeding recklessly down the winding drive from Greenchurch, too preoccupied or too guilty to wave. The breeze touched her face and she sighed, wondering for the moment less about her husband than what Charon Hunt and his cronies were up to. She was all but certain they were up to no good.

Wykeham's gray-black eyes held no hint of amusement.

Longford was explaining how the river, along the stretch that included both Ohomowauke and Devon, described, as though by a conscious act of will, an almost perfect letter "S." "Except," he said, "to my mind it isn't properly an 'S' at all. At least not any longer. You see I'm rather persuaded that over the last half century or so it's been changing."

He stood up. "I have," he said, "if you care to have a look, some drawings of my own." He went to his desk and pulled open the drawer. He was glad that Plum was there. He hadn't, so far, explained this to anyone, not in any great detail. It was time she heard it fully. He spread a large wrinkled paper on the desk top.

"Come along, William," he said. He looked back at his wife. Wykeham and Plum joined him silently.

Longford smoothed the paper with the side of his hand.

The map, to Plum's embarrassment, looked like a drawing for children. Devon and Ohomowauke were marked clearly enough, as were the greater towns and cities to the south, but not with the orthodox cartographers symbols. For Bristol Longford had sketched a ridiculous frowning clockface and for Ohomowauke an owl made of flowers. Devon itself was a ring on nine towers, black on the land, and quite a bit larger than the size of the village seemed to warrant. Presumably the wavy lines meandering among them represented the river. There were too many lines, however, and they wandered confusedly. Longford traced a set of lines with his finger.

"This is the old river," he said, "the river one can still see on the government maps of the region. Oddly, the surveyors weren't that far off. Quite surprising given their equipment. Less than a few meters error at any one point." He traced the lines again, his finger following a gentler curve which tracked north from Bristol, bent around Ohomowauke, then south until in a sinuous line, leaving Devon, it swung north once more along the far western edge. "But you would expect," he added significantly, "at least I did, a common error." He paused. "Well, there isn't." He gave a furtive glance at Wykeham, then turned again to the map. "Actually," he said, "the error changes rather wildly."

Wykeham examined the lines carefully. "So you assumed," Wykeham said, "that the error was common — because it should have been — and figured the difference."

"Yes." Longford looked startled. "Yes, of course." For the first time he broke into a grin. "Though, to tell the truth, I had some sleepless nights before it occurred to me."

"And the true measurement?"

Longford went on grinning. Indeed he couldn't help feeling flattered by the way Wykeham put it. "Yes," he said, pleased, "I have made, I think, a number of rather exact measurements."

Conscious of disloyalty, Plum turned again to the paper and found, even against her better judgment, her attention attracted to the largest of the nine towers scratched on the hillsides of Devon.

"The channel is straightening," her husband was saying. "The bends, I believe, have sharpened."

She bent over to examine the drawings more closely. At the base of the tower there was a sort of absurd scribble which she suspected must have been meant to be thorns. What an odd thing, she thought.

"All I need," Longford continued, "is the final measurement."

"Which is from Greenchurch?" Wykeham asked. "From my hilltop?"

Longford nodded.

"For which you wish my permission to cut down not only the old trees but the inconvenient new one."

"Tim," Plum said, not listening, her eyes riveted on a small dark square hidden among the crosshatch of lines which suggested the stonework at the top of the tower. It was hardly more than a blot, with just a fleck or two of white highlights. Yet there was a feeling of delicate roundness and a suggestion . . . though it was silly. "Tim," she asked, not aware she was interrupting him, her voice raised more than was necessary.

He broke off and, annoyed with her insistence, turned.

"What's this square?" she asked, pointing down at the tower.

He did not look. "Tell you later," he said for he was eager to hear Wykeham's answer.

She pressed her thumb on the undecipherable blur of lines. "Tell me *now*."

He looked straight at her and then at the paper. Half in anger, he smiled.

"Just a window," he said quickly, solicitiously, already looking back at Wykeham.

"I guessed that. But who is inside looking out?"

"Who?"

"Obviously there is someone. A face." But she saw all at once that he did not see it, that she was being foolish. It was only a blot. It was astonishing how much she read into things. She lifted her head. In a moment she was able to laugh at herself. She was thankful at least she hadn't actually mentioned she had thought that the face was Nora's.

Wykeham, who had pretended not to hear, studied the paper. He kept his square shoulders turned, excluding Plum. But even from the back she thought he looked preoccupied and ill at ease.

"This figure," he said, addressing himself to Longford, "the one the river is changing to."

Longford pointed to the lines again, ran his hands sharply in the air just above them. "Of course I cannot be positive," he said. "Not without the last measurement. But I believe it's a

'W' or will be when the banks have all straightened. And here."
He pulled the map edgewise so that Wykeham might have a
clearer view of it. "I don't suppose it means much of anything.
Though it is curious. Having found one letter, as it were, staring
out of the earth. Perhaps your eye just plays tricks." His finger
rested on a little slip of a lake, south of East Wood. The lake,
probably no more than a large pond, was curved like the paring
of a fingernail. "Of course the scale is different," he said. "But
they're both water and from a certain distance, seen from the
air, or on a map . . ."

Wykeham shook his head, either in disapproval or annoyance. There was a silence.

"It's a 'C,' isn't it?" Plum asked. Longford beamed.

"It is pronounced 'ku,' " Wykeham told her softly. He had
straightened his back. His face, now that Plum saw it, looked
odd. She had noticed it before, a hardness in him which showed
itself only now and then, but which somehow seemed more like
him than his smile.

"I didn't quite . . . ," Longford began.

" 'Cw,' " Wykeham said quietly. "Pronounced 'ku.' It is the
question asked by cuckoos and owls in the old Triads; the first
question that poets must master since there is no definite answer. It means 'where?' " He took his outsized hands from his
pockets. "I am surprised you did not come across it in your
reading," he said, "for it is Welsh."

Plum could tell from his voice he was leaving. "I shall think
about the tree," he said in a way that ended the conversation.
He shook hands with Longford, who, because he did not quite
know what to think said nothing. Wykeham left him standing
awkwardly by the desk. "Thank you again," Wykeham called
back. Plum went beside him to the door and opened it.

The lamps of Hunt's garage had been switched off. The green
and the surrounding houses seemed strangely malevolent. She
was still holding onto the latch. She hadn't realized, until then,
she was shivering.

Wykeham tilted his head.

"She wished me to ask," he said in a voice serious and not unkind, "whether you had managed to send her letter."

Plum wanted to cry out. But he had taken her hand. Her fingers which were not dainty or small seemed lost in the strength of his grasp and, although she had promised herself she would not answer, she nodded.

5.

Like Luther, His Grace thought, consoling himself, remembering that even the mighty theologian had suffered from the same disorder of the bowels. Humbled, he had endured the ailment more or less stoically. He refused to see his physician. He had his port and ate normally. Work generally set him to rights. With the beginning of each new week, within an hour after he had returned to his desk he felt a pressure building in his lower intestine. Then, with a gratifying urgency, he would head for the lavatory. This arrangement worked perfectly well. His Grace saw nothing greatly amiss. He had not fully considered, however, until it was already too late the effect of retirement on his bowels.

The corners of the Duke's mouth pulled down sullenly. In his house across from the park he had been sitting for a quarter of an hour, counting the diamond-shaped tiles on the lavatory floor. He had been trying to determine, without actually looking, the exact number of tiles hidden beneath a Chinese vanity. He had no particular reason for wanting to know this yet he had brought a small collapsible desk in with him. Already he had covered half a page with figures. Down below a young man from the bank began to knock on the thick, paneled door. The Duke, his head filled with calculations, took no notice.

The telegram announcing Houseman's death arrived at the bank some hours before dawn on Sunday morning. It had been received by the watchman, who, because there was no one to relieve him, had waited until the next man came on duty before taking a cab to the apartment of the senior clerk. By then it was nearly seven-thirty. The old clerk, although he had opposed Houseman's appointment, had been honestly shocked. He had seen to many of the arrangements himself and met the train bearing the body. He had even, after he had informed the chief partners, gone to visit the young man's family. Gently he had broken the news to the disbelieving parents. Houseman had always been neatly if somewhat inexpensively dressed so the senior clerk had been wholly unprepared for the deep poverty of the parents' quarters. The mother, a large, nervous woman, wept profoundly and had held onto his arm as though she had feared that he too, a stranger, might be taken from her. Putting aside his reservations, he had told her how fond everyone had been of her son.

It was left to the partners to inform His Grace. They conferred in the middle of the day. It had been scarcely two days since they had been lifted unto the top rung of power and not, they were uncomfortably aware, by any skill of their own but by the Duke's climbing down. Nevertheless they considered for several hours the consequences of withholding the news from him. They were not without certain grievances. By rights, a young man from one of their own departments should have been appointed master of the Will instead of Houseman. They had had, of course, their own schemes for getting around him, by taking a subtle control of the Wykeham trusts until for practical purposes they would rule them. Accordingly, although it had dramatically cleared the way, they had little enthusiasm for Houseman's death. They could not be certain who would be appointed next. Unsettled, they debated for some time the merits of installing, temporarily, a man of their own.

"It isn't a question of one being better than another," the

first partner said. "I daresay, the issue is who Wykeham is most likely to accept."

"Which leaves us," the second partner said, "with His Grace."

"The Duke has taken his retirement."

"Nor would I have him. I was thinking of him simply as an intermediary."

"Yet surely, as soon as he had one foot in the door again . . ."

"We could see to it that the door was shut."

"And if Wykeham wanted him?"

The second partner grinned. "It was Wykeham who sacked him. Too old, that's my guess. I think you will find, gentlemen, that we shall be fairly safe on that quarter."

The talk turned to other matters. On Monday, two hours after the bank had opened, a junior clerk, because this business should not be made to appear too important, rapped apprehensively on the door of the Duke's house. The butler left him on the landing where he waited, blinking unfamiliarly at prints of old-fashioned gentlemen dressed for hunting. The Duke emerged presently, engulfed in a roseate dressing gown. His face appeared similarly colored as though he had been engaged in some strenuous and, seemingly, unsuccessful labor.

"Your Grace," the clerk squeaked, "I bring dreadful news."

The ponderous brass gate opened. Within, the Duke pressed the elevator car's single button and heard, as though he had never been gone, the magical whine of its motors. Deus ex machina, the Duke thought mockingly but without embarrassment. The gentle lights fluttered, reflected on the walls of rubbed mahogany. It was then, reminded of opulence, that His Grace first realized that the world had been unfair to Arthur Houseman.

It was not the sort of thing which would ordinarily have troubled him. The death of a man, particularly a young man without accomplishments, while saddening, was not an event likely to be much remembered. Yet he had picked this one man out, though few had seen the worth in him. With disturbing clarity the Duke remembered the look on Houseman's face just as Wykeham sat down beside him. Houseman's face had had a look of extraordinary anticipation, a look which the Duke had resented bitterly until something of its eagerness had reminded him of himself. The lines of his own lips hardened. As well I had violated the prohibition, the Duke thought, had gone to the station, although the Will required there be no second meeting. He was acutely aware that he had entered by chance a world whose dangers he did not and, despite his skills, might never understand. After two days' absence the Duke stepped again into his office. Through the huge windows he looked out once more on the great tangled city of New Awanux.

It pleased him to stand again at the center, with the accumulating wealth of the Wykeham trusts passing through his fingers. In this place he had been a lord in fact as well as title, able at his word to send from the docks of Cardiff a fleet of colliers into the Severn fogs or by the mere scratch of his name to swell or shrink, as the times demanded, the crews of men who worked the forges and the precision shops in Bristol.

The brash sunlight glinted on the steeple of the center church. Without quite being able to chart the progress of his thoughts the Duke found himself wondering how it was that Wykeham, who might have ruled all this and more beyond imagining had with no agitation, no perceptible reluctance or doubt, left these matters in his charge instead. With an amazement which over the last days had only heightened, he wondered what Wykeham, his one life stretching out, might do if he wished. Or what he might have done!

There was a rattle of the gate behind him.

The partners walked in briskly. As they came into the room they saw the tall old lord by the window. They stood still and waited. From their places they had an almost equal view of New

Awanux yet they failed to notice either the color of the sky or the pillars of smoke rising starkly from the mills. They looked instead at each other.

"Your Grace," the chief partner said, "it is a bitter day for all of us."

"Please have a seat," the Duke said, his tone gracious, as though the office were still his own.

They sat opposite him, saying what is always said of sorrow and disrupted lives. Leisurely, and yet sooner than perhaps was fitting, the talk turned from death. They began to explain what they had planned for him, its temporary nature, its obvious usefulness to the bank. The Duke settled himself in his chair. His head was tilted ever so slightly so that he could keep watch out the window. Only half listening, he gazed across the rows of buildings as though face to face with a mystery. Even from this height, he could see no definite pattern. Grumbling, he put on his glasses. To the younger men he looked suddenly older.

"It need only be for a day or two," the second partner said. "Time enough for an exchange of letters. We have a list of candidates. You might, nonetheless, suggest whomever you like. Wykeham trusts you. And certainly the board would find any suggestion you would care to make acceptable."

His Grace was silent. He was trying to imagine the city from the air, to see it whole, but he found his eye dwelling on one detail after another. The partners were staring at him.

He knew an answer was expected; he was trying to think of one when once more the elevator gave a groan. The gate parted and the senior clerk came into the room.

"I beg your pardon," he said. He nodded to the others. "Gentlemen." He had an envelope between his thin fingers. "It was sent around from your house, Your Grace, and looked important. Of course I recognized the hand." The clerk set the letter on the desktop. Without waiting the Duke broke open the seal.

The letter was set down in the same small, precise hand he had expected. *I must call you again into service,* it began. For a second or two more His Grace turned in his chair. He seemed somehow heavier. Suddenly he gave a sly glance at the clerk, rose and went from the room.

The partners looked at one another in disbelief.

"I don't suppose you understand any of this," one said to the clerk.

The clerk was barely a month younger than the Duke and had worked for him for twenty years. He did not quite dare a grin.

Soon after, in a cubicle off the landing, the ancient plumbing roared.

"This will be your room," Wykeham had told her, pausing outside the door.

"And your own?"

"Above," he had said, not even smiling. When he had told her she must come with him up to the Great House and stay there, he had already been half out the door of the old man's cottage. She had gone after him, hastening through Black Wood, dazed but untroubled by the ease with which he meant to take her in.

"I have left my husband," she had said.

He had plunged through the trees. "It is time you were somewhere," he had answered.

In the wood it had seemed later but it had still been morning when they had come out on the drive. White moths had fluttered over the dazzling lawn. She had stopped at the edge of the gravel, quiet and at last rebuttoning her blouse. Finally he had looked back. "Tomorrow, if you like, we shall talk," he had said. "Now there are things I must see to. And this evening I must go into the village."

He had avoided the endless turning of the drive and had led her straight out among the larches and rhododendrons to a place where the ground rose to the top of a knoll. She had made him stop.

"He made a very strange sailor," she had said, not certain yet, although he was standing close to her, that he was listening. "For one thing he always carried a bag full of books. Even when we walked in the streets, with the people staring, he read aloud to me. But I didn't care. Sometimes he told me strange things about myself. Foolish things. The first time he saw me he said that I would marry him. He had been to Africa and Marseilles. He was an engineer on a ship named *Anna*. He told me how he sat down with his engines, drinking gin and water and reading through the gales. He had never, he said, looked at a girl until he looked at me." She stared down at her feet. "He does not share the blame. It was a cold, little town by the edge of the sea."

She hesitated.

"Truly, it was a wonderful gift," she had said. "But I will never go again to Bodø."

"One day you may have need of it."

She had told him then how she had slept in the wood and, meeting Plum, the thing she had given her to mail back to the steamship agent.

He had taken her arm.

The house stood above the great sweep of the lawn. Seeing it for the first time, she had held her breath. But he had been with her and she had not dared, had not wanted to loosen the touch of his hand. He had moved her up the steps, past the tangle of junipers and the thorns, into darkness. When he had closed the wide doors, she had stood perfectly still. She had made herself smile because her hopes had been so much greater than the worst of her dread.

The house was enormous. For a few hours she had been alone in it with him. From the start she had been aware of the quiet. She had gone carefully from room to room, knowing that whenever she heard a board creak or a door pull to, it had been

Wykeham. He had said no other word to her and when he had gone into the village, she had simply waited.

The room he had given her had a close, sweetish smell. Nora guessed it had been ages since anyone had slept there. Steeling herself, she poked into corners and knocked on the plaster. There were only cobwebs and silences. But there was slut's wool under the bed and grime on the windows. She had let in the air. A little breeze (here there was always a breeze, she had noticed, either blowing or just about to) made the dusty shutters creak. She discovered bed linen folded on one of the shelves in the closet. In a trunk there were blankets. Nonetheless she did not set to work. Instead she stood at the open window. The trees along the drive obscured the approach to the house. Yet, if she stood there, he would be able to see her when he came up from the gate. The window would shine like a beacon. She need show no sign of her presence. The lamps lit her face. In the light her skin had a gentle radiance. Although she was tired, she held her head proudly. Turned to the proper angle, the line of her neck, she knew, was inviting. That much had not changed.

She felt a strange giddiness. She thought of the long, glowing evenings when she had strolled through the streets of her village. After the bleakness of winter the world then had seemed unbelievably light. The brightness had touched the golden hairs on her neck. Boldly, she had walked under the eyes of the sailors. "Let us come with you," they had called to her. But though her heart pounded, she had looked ahead steadily. When they are old men, she had thought joyfully, and I myself am an old woman, they will remember this moment. Yet, when she had come to the end of the pier, she had realized that her beauty must vanish if flushed and out of breath she were forced to climb the street again past them. Gravely she had loosened her dress from her shoulders. When she leapt, it must have appeared to the sailors that she had plunged to her death in the sea.

While they had searched for her, she had scrambled up on the rocks. She had tied a kerchief over her hair and, when the last of the men had gone, had returned by another village to her mother's house. Seeing her, the quiet old woman, abandoned herself by a sailor, had said nothing. When Nora slept she would mend the tears where the dress had caught and torn on the rocks.

Her mother had clear dark eyes, like her own. Once a year, on her birthday, a man from the town would ride out to deliver a letter. Nora would stand by her chair as the old woman tried to decide whether she would open it. The letters from other years lay sealed on a table beside her cot. But always her mother would shake her head. For the briefest moment her eyes would flash with defiance. "No, child," she would say this time as she had said the last, "you are gift enough."

A door slammed. But there was no tread on the stair. Just the wind.

Nora gathered the bedding. When she had finished, because he had still not come, she climbed up and propped her elbows on the pillow. Staring down at herself, she saw how ludicrously little there was of her and, even beyond the kick of her feet, how much bed. I am as small as this beside him, she thought as if she were the child, passing lightly over the fact that while he had money to give away steamship tickets, he was a boy really and still in school. To her mind he simply did not seem so. He was taller, for one thing, than any man she had known; the directness of his look matched his bearing. Abruptly, without a young man's shyness, presuming an intimacy as though by right, he had reached out his hand to her.

Toward midnight she woke.

She had wriggled out of her skirt. Having no other clothing, she had not switched on the lamp but had found the stair to the upper story by tracing her fingers carefully along the wall. The air was cool on her skin. Somewhere other windows must have been open. She took the steps two at a time. She was excited by the prospect of his finding her, this time deliberately, naked. More immediately, she thought of his bed. She would be warm there, warm, safe and high under the eaves of his house. It was surely the best place to wait for him, the one place he was certain to come. She wondered whether he would be tired or if tramping about in the night would leave him restless. Either would be agreeable, provided he slipped in beside her. She could content herself with touching his hand or, should it please him . . . Nora smiled at the darkness. The door to his room opened with a reassuring sigh.

Wykeham cut across the dark meadow. He took the shortest path, passing quickly among the caretakers' sheds. The roofs had fallen. Vines and tendrils obscured the stones just as thick tufts of grass now grew in the best garden beds. Wykeham grunted without truly noticing. Long ago the roses had turned into lawn. Unconcerned, he vaulted over a wall. There was an open stretch for a hundred yards and then more trees. He ducked under the branches. At last, against the blackness of the hill, he saw the stables. He remembered he had not met the hostler Longford had hired. He knew he ought to check on the mare. He did not permit himself another glance at the house. She would be waiting in any case. He entered the tackroom hurriedly and took a brush from the shelf, disturbed that there was so little time now that he had need of it.

It did not matter that he had other lives. In each he seldom had the use of more than a dozen years. Too soon friends with whom he had no hope of lingering began to notice the remarkable preservation of his changeless face. Sometimes, unwilling to renounce affection, he had stayed. But there is no welcome for an ageless man among grown children and enfeebled wives. Now and then he had invented his own death. More often he had simply turned his back. The longest voyages, to Maui and around the Horn, even under sail, were short to him. Afterward there were other years on land, at Heidelberg, at Oxford twice, at Yale, nights in the crowded libraries and peaceful mornings in the empty lecture halls, brief years among young men who themselves were swiftly gone to other lives. He was well aware such moments were a dream, crammed with the kind of promise which came, by rights, to nothing. He turned aside advice, declined — kindly when he could — offers from old men who, startled by his learning, saw him as the heir to labors that had cost them, without conclusion, half their lives. He knew he was no scholar. He had merely read the books before. Under their tutelage he had begun a thousand things and finished little. When he came back to the old university towns, those men were dead. He went back less often. But the shallow trough of the Housetenuc drew him. Now, after barely fifty years away, still haunted by its miles of squalid woods and low gray hills, he had reentered the valley. I must get on to Devon, he had thought when he had finally set foot again in the harbor. And although for the better part of three years, kept to his studies, he had not gone, it had been the reason he had settled on the college. From his rooms, looking out over the court, there had been a perfect view of the river. Certainly, there had been other reasons. Callaghan, for one, had been getting old and would need to be replaced. Duties had lain ahead of him, as they had each time he moved the trust from one hand to the next. Yet he had waited for this moment, indeed had welcomed it and in much the same way he had welcomed the sight of the unkempt and empty house. It was not a matter of choice. Houseman was dead. Longford, though a fool, was proving less a fool than he should have been. His wife was dangerous. Charon Hunt, despite its evident impossibility, was killing Indians. Wykeham let out a puzzled sigh. He gave a perfunctory pat to the mare's dry rump and wondered, this time, how he would manage.

He closed the door on the stalls and set the latch. Tomorrow he must introduce himself to the hostler. Then too, the roof of John Chance's cottage needed patching. That at least was no great trouble. In the morning he would send George Tennison down with fresh pitch and shingles, a reward for keeping Nora from the wood while Hunt was in it. Wykeham smiled speculatively. He wondered what the old lame bachelor thought of her. It had not been something he would have asked with Nora standing, half unclothed, between them. In his own kitchen he had asked the crow. But he had got no useful answer. He hoped she was pretty. It made no difference that he found her so. His own tastes had been set too long ago. In the markets of Maracaibo or in the streets of Lyme he had too often turned back to stare at women whom the men walking with him, captains of her Majesty's ships and London merchants, found common or, at the very least, unworthy of the effort of looking back. It had helped, of course, that he had seen that face before. In profile there had been no mistaking it. He had not been more than a few moments in her husband's shop when he recognized the tilt of the head, the exquisite line of the neck. He had had no need to ask why she was so far from home. His idea of justice was clear and literal: given sufficient opportunity, all things returned. Life especially came back, even across cold tides and oceans.

He had come up onto the porch and through the massive front doors. It was late; the house was quiet. On the first landing he looked in at Nora's room. The breeze, still pouring in through the small window, had driven off some of the dust and dampness. Even in the shadows he saw that the bed was made and that she had gone from it. He unbuttoned his coat. Knowing more or less what to expect, he climbed the last stairs to his room. She was asleep on his pillow, the edge of her tangled hair curled around her throat. He tried to imagine how she had looked at fifteen or twenty. It did not matter. He was not disappointed.

For a moment he stood silently, unwilling to wake her. Her face had turned toward him, dreaming. Her dark eyes were open. He supposed there was sadness in those eyes but, although there was every right to be, there was no despair. Nora moved suddenly, driving her mouth against the pillow. He knew she could only add to his troubles, now when he had troubles enough. Yet he was comforted. He would protect her if he could.

When she had quieted, he retraced his steps. Reluctantly, the hour pressing him, with too many matters demanding his attention and too little time, Wykeham closed the door noiselessly, letting his daughter sleep.

III.

Faces in the Earth

1.

Dr. Holmes spread the photographs along the examination table in his surgery. The emulsion was still wet and he handled each print with a pair of small forceps. He had drawn up the lamp as he had when he had examined the corpse. Not that he saw much improvement. In the print's glossy surface he could make out little more than his own disappointed reflection. At one corner of the print, caught at the edge, there was a slender filament. Because of the magnification it might have been an eyelash or no more than the grain in the negative. There was honestly no way of knowing. He lay aside his pipe. Smoke no longer curled from the bowl. Muttering, he pushed another photograph under the lamp.

He had had such hopes. When he had set up his camera, Houseman's body had only just begun to stiffen. Such opportunities were in fact rare. He had attended a hundred deaths during the course of his practice. But nearly always there had been family. He had seen to the living. At such times they could not be expected to view his investigations with the detachment of science. Normally, hours later, he had had to prop open the taut lids in the narrow back rooms of morticians' chambers, had to focus his lenses on pupils that had already hardened. By then the image of whatever had held the sight at life's last

moments had gone. But there had been no one to mourn Houseman, merely his employer, who, although he had shown a delicate interest, had not interrupted his journey. Peering crossly
over his spectacles, Dr. Holmes edged the lamp nearer.

He was the same Dr. Holmes who wrote verses and sketches
for *The Atlantic*, the same whimsical sketches and doggerel which
in a universe not too far distant had earned him a minor but
respected place in American letters. But here (having been born
merely a decade, not a century, before the Great War) his
writings seemed only quaint, the easy Latinity of his prose an
impediment to popular acceptance. Instead he had made his
mark as a physician and would be longer remembered as an
anatomist.

Nonetheless, the outline of his early life was here not sub-
stantially altered. He had been born on the outskirts of Boston
and had spent the first years of his manhood on Montgomery
Place. After a dozen years of marriage, he removed to Bristol
and the house inherited from his maternal great-grandfather.
He knew Cornelius Mathews and James T. Fields but not Melville or Hawthorne, although assuredly their places were taken
by others. (For in one form or another both are indispensable.
A New World cannot be made without them.) Only his later
years pulled atom by atom away from his other existence. In
this world he would not die in his own bed and his oldest son,
with whom he shared his name and many of his sympathies,
would never become a supreme court justice. I will not judge
which life better suited the man. In either world there had
always been some who suspected that beneath the gentle satire
of the poems, the strained didacticism of the novels, there was a
pure vein of venom. It is certain that here that same bitterness
had quietly deepened, had given him an added astringency and,
when at last it was required of him, a sterner, more courageous
imagination. Whatever the cause, something was changed in
him. Perhaps there is no defense against doubt. At least it is
not as unusual as it may seem that a man who felt himself

nourished by the regard of an intelligent woman, buoyed and uplifted by the affection of able, caring children, devoted his private hours to the study of the possibility that all life, his own included, was without meaning. In any event, he did not dismiss the next photograph although at first glance it appeared much the same as the rest.

He was sitting still, deep in thought. After a while, with a weary swipe of his hand, he pulled the lamp nearer.

There was the same maddening configuration of light and shadow, blots more than squares. Yet the blots, by some as yet unfathomable arrangement, turned in rapid stages into squares. He shook his head. As easily it could have been the other way round, the pattern shifting, turning peevishly, automatically ungeometric. Either interpretation was possible. Between his lips his tobacco-blackened tongue flickered impatiently.

Behind him, from the cramped room that adjoined the surgery, he could hear his wife turning down the covers of the cot. He kept a small bed there, fitted snugly under the shelves of medicines. He could hear his wife humming to herself under the phials of laudanum, the tinctures of nightshade, and frowned. It was a rich practice. There were maids for such work. For that matter he would have done it himself. But Amelia's sense of duty required such small attentions to his comfort. She did not look in. He waited until the door squealed. Amelia's footsteps retreated into the hallway, turning back toward the main house where already the servants were in bed and the children slept. He shrugged his thin shoulders. He was thinking of death.

Taking the matches from his trouser pocket, he relit his pipe. The match flared above the photograph.

For that moment, enhanced by the spurt of flame, it seemed he was staring into a glowing blankness. Patches of light, jarred subtly, seemed suddenly to come loose. Unfixed, they began to squirm. He smiled slightly, fascinated by their curious mobility and yet knowing it could be no more than the temporary effect of the matchhead, that, or, because he was mortally tired, the crackling of the ragged circuitry within his own head. The match burned out and he blinked.

The brightness persisted. He moved and the brightness moved with him. He sat rigid, holding his breath. The brightness continued to fall into place. Squibs of light, turning cunningly among the blots he saw were bluffs and hills, joined link by link. The perception was so clear and definite that he moaned. The air rushed past. Beneath him, suddenly from a great height, he recognized the fiery line of the river.

Its brightness came down from the mountains.

Tipped as from a cauldron, it burned between hills.

He opened his eyes very wide and saw the distant towns, lurid and burning where the river itself was choked with flames. Some instinct made him wish to turn away. But the river blazed ahead of him. Lightly, luringly, at the bridge at Ohomowauke, where the river bent, it broadened, spreading in a widening crack as it reached the levels and wandered south.

He gazed over the earth. Across the southernmost horizon he saw the dismembered channels sunken into hissing silence on the coast. He bit his lip.

And, surprisingly, there was no river. Instead, the brightness suddenly reversed. A darkness — added as the light was added, link by link — changed over to blackness. Blots and shadows fused, became twisted limbs and climbed. He looked down into the maw of branches. Black leaves rushed about his head.

And yet, at the very same instant, he was certain it was still the river. He saw it then even more clearly. The only difference was in how he looked. His sallow cheeks reddened.

It was outrageous. He muttered something to himself. The words were familiar but it was not until he heard his own voice that he remembered where he had heard them.

He went in his bare feet to the closet. Old man's legs and old man's feet, he thought, feeling the prickly numbness of his flesh, the chill of the cold floor under his feet. Silence flowed

back into the room behind him. Methodically he began to ar-
range his coat on its hanger. He knew he ought to have slept
in the surgery. Yet by the time he had returned Amelia had
switched on the lamp.

"I did not mean to imply —" she started in once more. She
was used to him and had no need to listen to guess that he had
wasted his time. And yet, seeing him, his bare legs sticking out
from under his robe, she added more quietly, "I fear, Oliver,
I do not explain myself well."

He laid his spectacles on the bureau. Because of the light in
the room he could not look out into the garden.

"Forgive me," she said.

"I have." He spoke with absolute definiteness. "I have
understood perfectly."

Once again there was silence.

"You will let me see it?" she asked.

"In the morning."

He climbed in next to her, bringing the cold in with him.

As calmly as she was able she reached out, taking his hand,
waiting for the moment he would grasp her own.

"It is a photograph of the river," he said. "Only it is more
than the river."

Deliberately she tightened her hold on his fingers.

"Oliver?"

He went on implacably. "But it was what the woman said
that startled me. That convinced me that at last —"

Her breast rose. "A woman?"

"On the train." Then finally he had to look at her.

All at once she understood that something had happened.
Until that moment she had not honestly noticed.

She watched him carefully. "She told you something."

"It was the dead man really. She was simply repeating it."
Suddenly he pulled away. Both his hands were free and he
thrust them alongside his temples and into his hair.

She had made her voice soft. "Can it matter?" she asked.

The house was silent.

But now, when he opened his hands and she could look again into his eyes, she was frightened.

However inimical, the pattern had to be the same. He understood this, even though he was quite as certain he was dreaming. The blackness of the trunk, which even in his sleep was wholly separate, wholly distinguishable from the river, existed, nonetheless, because the river existed. Seeing one meant the other was not, not simply faded, but gone. Yet they shared the same space. They were, or at the very least must be thought to be, contemporaneous. It was this that troubled him.

He had not chosen which he would see. Had he been given a choice, he would have dreamed of the oak. Its leafy vaults were elegiac and sad, matching his thoughts. Their darkness consoled him. In an earlier age such a dream would have been called a prefiguration of death. The strength of his youth was behind him. The yearnings of his early manhood, which had once filled him with impossible anguish, were over. Now, although he slept with a woman beside him, it was many years since he had found her naked in his arms.

It was not his will or even his intention that determined which, for a moment, prevailed. In fact he had dreamt of the great sprawling branches and continued to dream of them, intermittently. But where he had expected their pattern to hold he found instead its odd symmetry broken.

His numbed feet paddled through the bright water.

Holmes pressed his nose into the pillow.

Because it was a dream it hardly seemed he was climbing. Slowly he made his way forward. Down the river went and then up again, its queer shining current spilling outward over the steep valley wall. The heavy branch swayed. Increasingly it became difficult to hold his balance. Caught between wind and water, struck by the real possibility of falling, he no longer looked down.

The river forked.

Rather like a passage in a book he had read twice without, until the end, noticing, he realized that he had made this same passage before. To the left the river tumbled into more vivid life. Its brightness reflected up into brambles, lighted the meadows won long ago from the wood. But if he blinked? He made no decision. He did not dismiss one or embrace the other. There lay behind him years of speculation and doubt. They made no difference. There were endless worlds, each with its own composition and laws, each waiting invisibly for summoning. And it was chance that called them forth. Chance only that mattered. His child-sized hands pressed blindly into the bedclothes. For the briefest moment his exhausted eyes flickered. . . .

Against his cold fingers he felt the harsh, scored bark. The great oak coiled away under him.

He awoke with an erection.

Except for the blood in his loins, there was yet no warmth. Dawn merely edged the bricks on the back garden wall. He lay chilled and motionless. To his nostrils came unmistakably the scent of horses. He moved his neck. Someone was knocking.

"Yes?" he called out. His voice seemed unusually distant. What was it he had been thinking?

"Yes?" he answered once more, uncertain whether whoever it was could have heard him.

His daughter did not enter the room. "Father," she called softly. "There is someone waiting down in the surgery."

He struggled into his robe. This at least was a world he knew. He looked down at the sleeping form of his wife. Her tiny fishlike mouth opened and closed noiselessly.

"I shall be down in a moment," he whispered.

His daughter went on before him. He had gone himself, more slowly, into the hall and had just finished buttoning his fly when she crept back. She looked at him hesitantly, her normally proud features suddenly perplexed. Somehow she had been found wanting. Not by himself certainly. Beginning to wonder, Holmes straightened his collar.

He padded in his slippers to the bottom of the stairs. He took a shortcut through the kitchen and, because he had gained a moment, paused, snatching a hopeful glance at the garden. The sky had not yet taken on enough color to allow him to see more than the roughest outline of the hedge. The barberry seemed pale and ordinary and failed to cheer him. In his mind he kept smelling the damnable scent of horses. He trotted down the corridor.

The man had been standing at the far side of the room facing the street.

He unfolded his manicured fingers. "Please forgive the inconvenience," he said.

Holmes took hold of the presented hand. The grip was firm and yet along the cool fingers he felt the slightest twinge of anxiety. His own small hand stiffened. Nearly at once Holmes placed the name that went under the large, well-proportioned head. "Rather, it is an honor, Your Grace," he said.

Without actually frowning the Duke conveyed the impression of a frown.

Holmes managed a look of absorbed seriousness. "Perhaps you would care to tell me the nature of your complaint," he suggested.

"I have been out driving," the Duke said.

"Do have a seat."

"Yes, of course."

The Duke drew up a chair.

"I was out for a drive," the Duke repeated. "Out quite early." He raised his eyes. His hands rested easily in his lap. He said: "Generally I have my driver go north. I am fond of the river." He looked to see if there were any reaction. Now that he had begun to speak, deliberately, in a low voice, he seemed utterly calm. Only his eyes were more intense. They moved across Holmes's face, watchful and yet deprecating.

"I believe that eventually I must have slept," he said. "When I woke I recognized the mills. It was at that point that I thought of you."

Holmes waited.

The Duke put his hand into his pocket. "I remembered that you had signed the death certificate." He paused before drawing it forth. "Since this arrived at the bank," he said, "I have carried it about with me." He gave the paper to Holmes. "You have a clear hand, doctor. The name is quite unmistakable."

Holmes did not bother to examine the paper. "But something isn't," he said.

The Duke was staring at him.

"I needed to talk with you," he began. "I have already spoken with the police."

Holmes remembered the two young policemen on the train. "I imagine they were of no help," he offered.

"He had never been sick," the Duke said bluntly. "Not even as a child. I spoke with the mother. In the family there is no history of illness. Even his grandparents are still alive."

"You came by accident?" Holmes asked dryly. "You were out driving, being driven —"

His Grace might have smiled then but did not. "The hour at least was chance," he said. "I was already in Bristol. In any case I should have insisted on seeing you." He drew himself forward. "Forgive me," he said. "I confess to impatience. I might at least have waited until you had had your breakfast."

Homes shook his head. "It is a doctor's life."

"But in this instance the patient is already buried."

Holmes noticed how for a moment the Duke's fingers dug into the arms of the chair. Holmes waited. "There was literally nothing to be done," he said. "The young man had been dead for some minutes when I was called to him."

"I have implied no impropriety."

"Then why have you come?"

In the hall outside the surgery there was a step. The door

opened. His daughter Amelia (named after her mother as Oliver, his oldest, was named for himself) pushed in with a tray bearing two white cups and a steaming china pot. She came and stood by her father, meeting his reproachful glare with her prettiest smile. He saw how trimly she had dressed herself, her mobile, flirtatious face clothed with impertinent cheerfulness. Rather as if in revenge, he thought. Somehow His Grace had offended her, probably by taking no notice. The man after all was at least as old as himself and, Duke or not, unless he seriously misjudged him, not the sort to have his head turned by a pink complexion and a new spring dress.

Holmes gave her a second provoking look.

"I listened," Amelia said, setting the tray down disobediently. "You were only talking. It isn't as if . . ."

His Grace had got to his feet when she entered. Standing himself, Holmes was struck, possibly for the first time, by the Duke's stature. The Duke made a vague gesture and Amelia extended her hand.

"My daughter, Your Grace," Holmes said.

"Your Grace," she repeated.

Oddly, that seemed enough. Having won or at least drawn even in a contest which remained to Holmes essentially mysterious, she poured quickly and with scarcely another look curtsied. As the door closed Holmes found His Grace staring after her.

"Undoubtedly," Holmes said, faintly embarrassed, "you have children of your own."

As if to banish some foreboding, the Duke laughed. "I am just an old bachelor," he conceded.

"Confirmed?" The question slipped out without intention.

It surprised them both when for a moment the Duke did not answer.

2.

 When Wykeham stepped onto the platform of
Bristol station it was exactly dawn. He was freshly
shaved; the air felt agreeably mild on his cheek.
His head turned expectantly. It was one of those
suddenly bright spring mornings, mimicking summer, which give the solid practical earth the appearance of a dream. Like all real places met in
sleep, the city below him seemed at once larger and more intimate. Wykeham smiled to himself. He went down the steps
and onto the pavement.

He was dressed with more than usual care in a light gray
suit which, although out of fashion, was on this occasion not
conspicuously so. Earlier, soon after rising, his chin lathered,
he had examined his face in the mirror. He had understood this
was foolishness. After fifty years she was probably dead. At
best she had gone off, as old unmarried women often did, to
live precariously and barely tolerated with her younger rela-
tions. She did have sisters. He remembered he had met them,
once, in the dining room of the King's Porter Hotel. He had
taken her down to the little seaside town on their last holiday.
How pale and injured she had looked then, her short black hair
tousled. Only moments before they had come from their rooms.
He had told her he was leaving her. As he remembered, a tiny

wave of sadness washed back over him. Her elegant sisters, there by chance, looked up from their table. Their husbands, being men and more tolerant of scandal, commandeered the necessary chairs. But her sisters sat coldly. They had seldom approved of what their older sister did, certainly not her work for wages at a second-rate preparatory school for girls of the middle class. They had approved even less of Joseph Wykeham, although until this point he was known to them only by rumor. It was not that he was beneath their station (as to that the rumors were both extravagant and reassuring) but even wealth could not bargain away the distinctions of time. Had the situation been the reverse, had Wykeham instead been indisputably twice her age, the sisters might have learned to ignore the difference. A husband, even a dull old one, would have provided at least the outward show of propriety. But it was their Willa, regrettably, who was thirty-seven, nearly old enough, it had swiftly come back to them, to be taken for young Wykeham's mother. After the introductions, the younger women maintained a grim silence. It was one of the husbands, turning to look at her more closely, who first realized that she had been jilted. Motioning to the waiter, he ordered her wine.

The scene had all the elements of farce. Even now as he went through the sunwashed streets toward the school, Wykeham recalled with a pang of regret her look of incomprehension, then fear as, easing the chair from the table, he stood. Beyond the windows of the dining room the sea had been bright; white gulls cried overhead. "Come walk with me," he had said, knowing that she would not. He had not looked back. He need not have worried. This last time she had not disappointed him.

In the park the trees were in bloom. Their fragrance drifted across to him. For the better part of an hour he walked past the deserted shops, through empty squares, until, as the first men came into the streets, he approached the few last substantial white Federal houses and, simultaneously, the foot of the one great hill at the city's northwest edge. Here on its renovated foundations Bristol Academy perched overlooking the valley. The school was a fine puzzling mixture of wood and stone, the amalgam of architectual pretension and the plain common sense of its carpenters and masons. Before the turn of the new century it had been the estate of a brewer who, as the clockworks failed, slid toward ruin. The main building at the top of the drive had been converted into a dormitory, the untended gardens and the west meadow into playing fields. Other buildings, either rehabilitated or put up through subscription, lay clustered about the slope. Wykeham looked up, his eyes coming to rest on one little window, tucked high up under the dark roof of the main house. There, winter and summer, Willa had had her rooms. There, she had once told him, she had often stayed up, all the lights of the school but her own extinguished, writing him letters.

She was a born letter writer and for many weeks had continued to fatten envelopes with sheet after sheet of grief and news even after she had learned that he had been married all the while he had courted her. She wrote with quiet gravity of her students and, surprisingly, without malice, of her sisters' lives. He had told her, as unlikely as it sounded, that he had a son, an infant, whose name, Sebastian, he had invented as cavalierly as he had invented child and mother, merely to insure the orderly progress of generations required for inheritance. But thereafter, as much like a fond aunt as a lover, in letter after letter she had inquired after the boy. She made him toys. She was something of a sculptress, and from her affectionate fingers came dwarfs and winged rabbits, mischievous goats molded cunningly from clay, and shy, smiling giants, long-armed and heavy-shouldered, carved from pitch pine. Only at the end of her letters did she speak of her loneliness. There had been one long last letter waiting on the table in the front room at Greenchurch on the day it was reported that Joseph Wykeham had vanished. He had picked it up twice. For a time it had even rested in his breast pocket. But the letter remained in the house when he left.

For another long moment Wykeham stared at the window. After a while he walked on and began to climb the hill.

In the old days, of course, he had driven, in a shining green roadster, not unlike the magnificent automobiles George Tennison had watched in quiet despair. It made Wykeham smile to think, now, how quaint and old-fashioned that car must seem to any but his own eyes. He stood in the middle of the drive, halfway up, remembering. He would, he decided, have to talk with Charon Hunt about getting at least one of the cars back into service. He had already postponed their meeting longer than was wise. Tomorrow, he thought; but his smile faltered and he shook his head irritably.

Down the steps from the main house a half dozen young women, dressed in short gym skirts and sweaters and carrying sticks, hurtled breathlessly into the morning. One was pudding-faced, the rest audaciously thin. From across the courtyard Wykeham caught sight of dancing patches of blonde and auburn hair and acknowledged, without actually banishing Charon Hunt from his mind, that the world's irritations were not altogether without compensation. Wykeham found himself hurrying; but when he reached the embankment, they had gone out of sight. He pressed on.

In his will Joseph Wykeham had presented a rather remarkable sum to the school. The endowment, ignoring delicacy, had been in Willa's name, with her as executrix. The gossips had been left to think what they liked. The trustees would have found, he had expected, some way of accepting the gift. He wished frankly to see what she had done with his money. But he had scarcely taken another step when he saw a new figure moving against the broad classroom windows. She strode briskly toward him, her dark head thrown back, intent on the stout branches of a high-crowned elm growing up at the side of the court. She had not, even at the last moment, been paying the least attention to what lay in her path.

"Oh . . . sorry," she said in a flat, puzzled voice. "I was watching . . ."

She looked up, to see Wykeham smiling.

"Really, I am sorry," she exclaimed, dismayed, realizing that he was no one she knew. "There was a crow," she said helplessly. Then, as though imagining how it sounded, she laughed. "An immense crow." She studied him for a moment. "As black as a man's trousers."

It struck Wykeham, irrelevantly, that her eyes were blacker. He saw as well that his first impression had been mistaken. She was no more than a girl, perhaps fifteen or sixteen. Her figure, while tall as a boy's, was yet mostly leg. Above her narrow waist her torso was only just beginning to emerge from the compactness of childhood. Only her eyes and her mouth bore full witness that childhood was past. Yet, unaware of any discord, she stepped back, now quite willfully, to get a clearer look at him.

"Are you anyone important?" she asked.

"I like to hope."

She gave him an appreciative grin. "I mean you're not a new teacher or somebody's brother?"

"No."

There was a fluttering in the branches. With a startling cough, the crow launched itself above the court.

"There it is!" she shouted. He turned but she was not at all sure what it was he was watching. The crow sailed away over the treetops. Spots of sunlight winked through the branches. On the still air they could both hear the faint cheering floating down from the playing fields. It was excuse enough if she wanted it. She might have gone. For a minute neither of them spoke.

A man emerged from between the buildings carrying buckets of ash. Ignoring them, he went down the path. If there were faces behind the windows of the main house, they chose not to look out.

She had grown up at the school. Her father, whom she adored, traveled most of the year. It had fallen to her teachers more or less by default to instruct her to be careful of strangers. They had advised her as strictly as was needed in a world which, except for the odd-job man, consisted solely of women. Once, unaccountably, there had been a male Latin teacher, an unhappy young man with cigarette-stained fingers and an untried degree in the classics, who, after less than a month, had fled back to his university.

She stood quite still. The expression on Wykeham's face, although well-intentioned, nevertheless had an extraordinary effect on her. She gazed at him frankly. Surely, someone would come to call her if she were at fault.

"It was perched on my windowsill," she said, remembering the cold eyes that had peered in at her as she awoke in her bed. "It was in the yard again after breakfast." Her voice, which had sunk to a whisper, communicated a delighted sense of alarm, as if it had been no ordinary crow but a creature she had, with a quiet, amused determination, summoned.

"Perhaps it is an omen," he suggested.

"Oh, do you think so?"

The sunlight was warm on her neck. She fancied she could feel it running between her shoulder blades, buoying her, covering and uncovering her like the waters of a bath. For no particular reason, she stretched herself and yawned. One of them, it was impossible to tell which, took the first step.

"What is your name?" he asked.

"Jane."

"Only that?"

They walked slowly, each seemingly afraid to outpace the other. "Jane Hawleyville," she said, looking down. "And your own?"

"Wykeham."

She stared at him over her shoulder. "Like the hall?" she said softly, thinking that she had found him out. Her smile darkened. But when Wykeham looked innocently confused, she pointed.

"Wykeham Hall," she repeated. But something was wrong with his understanding and she pointed again at a building at the far side of the court.

"We have our science lessons there," she added. "They have frogs and intestines in bottles." She made a face. "We have to cut open cats." She had turned her back on the hall and was watching him.

"I should like to go in," he said.

Jane shook her head.

"You needn't cut anything open."

"It isn't that."

He could hear for the first time a nervous tremor in her voice.

"No one likes to go there," she admitted. "Not unless . . ." She wanted to say something more but found she could not. Instead she put her hand on his arm.

He was conscious of her touch, half curious and half cross with her for her insistence.

"Why not?"

His indignation took her by surprise.

"There was a woman," she said haltingly. "Years and years ago. She was a teacher and had the hall built." She stopped.

A procession of pictures marched through her head, pictures she had made up herself because it had all happened long before she had arrived. Yet, from stories traded from one girl to the next, retold late at night when the wind blew dead leaves on the roof and, looking out in the moonlight and frightened, she could see the hall among the dark branches, she knew, knew exactly the awfulness.

"One day," she said, her mouth dry before she had half completed a sentence, "right after the hall was finished, the woman went to the top of the stairs. And before anyone had time to think or could reach her, she hanged herself. And so, sometimes —"

She saw how quickly he looked away.

She had made some terrible blunder.

All at once the excitement that had grown wonderfully inside of her was threatened. She pulled at his arm.

But his head was averted.

"You won't laugh," she pleaded.

But he was merely staring across at the hall.

The sun breaking above the tops of the trees began to blaze on the windows. Amid the faded ivy stitched to the walls there were a few sprigs of green. The stone itself, inert, darkened by the door and blackened under the windows, took on a warmer tinge in the sunlight.

Wykeham turned.

"Then you must show me the playing fields." His tone implied a command. Yet, before he had quite broken off, she realized that he had never let her hand go. Pressed against her palm she could feel the rough wool of his jacket and the arm beneath, tensed and leaning into her.

"Will you?" he asked.

For an instant, looking up into the strong sunlight she was blinded.

The same sunlight lay across the table in Dr. Holmes's kitchen. Holmes squinted. The day was already warm but neither man was as yet comfortable enough with the other to remove his coat. The cook, deprived of her kitchen, sat alone in the dining room, where, if her employer had had the least sense, he would have ushered His Grace. With a great affronted swelling of her bosom she drank herself the last of the coffee from a proper china cup. The little pinched-faced maid, intruding on the cook's misery, backed through the door. The maid's frail arms were laden with dishes she had been unwilling to set in the sink in front of His Grace. It did not occur to either woman that the kitchen provided the only uninterrupted view of the garden or that Holmes, having discovered that the world was far stranger than he had expected, needed urgently to look at a hedge. But when he turned back, the Duke was still sitting across from him. Holmes put aside his napkin. As if to show he was not hurried, he folded it twice. The death certificate rested on the table before him. Face down beside it was the photograph he had taken at the last moment from the surgery. He had meant to slip it quietly into his pocket.

"Of course the body had been washed," the Duke had been saying, describing the funeral. "The mistake, clearly, was in putting him back into his suit. It was likely his best suit." His mouth turned down at the edge. "I am afraid it may have been his only one." Remembering the room in the cheap lodging house where they had set the bare casket, the Duke paused. He thought of the wealth that had come into his own hands, that as easily would have come into Houseman's. In a month, even in a few days, he thought and as quickly cursed himself for thinking it. "The suit he had worn on the train was in any case all they had. He was a fastidious man. They had no reason to suspect. Although almost certainly, I imagine, they had taken a brush to the sleeves and gone through his pockets. So it is even more difficult to believe that they missed it."

"I'm sorry," Holmes interrupted, "but I don't —"

"The young man stank," the Duke finished with brutal simplicity, "like a hostler, as though not five minutes before he had been mucking a stable."

Holmes shifted his head.

The Duke glanced up. He did not initially suppose it was important. It was just one more thing which for the moment he did not understand but for which, like Houseman, he shouldered unquestioned responsibility.

Holmes was again staring out of the window.

"Perhaps," the Duke suggested, "when you examined him —"

Holmes shook his head. "It would have been fairly obvious. And it wasn't."

The words left a silence behind them. Without being able to say how, the Duke saw that Holmes was lying; not lying outright, perhaps. He had seen, he believed, the doctor's essential honesty. If anything, Holmes had been forthright and, given the hour, remarkably unresentful. Presented with a direct question, he could not imagine that Holmes would be other than equally direct. The distortion, the Duke decided, had to have been in the question he had asked.

"Yet you did notice," he persisted.

Holmes turned, as he had turned in his bed, his mind as well as his body seeking a new position. Nonetheless he found himself again staring over his spectacles into the garden. Disgusted, he drove a quantity of air through his nostrils.

"Not then," he said, "not at first."

While he had kept his eyes on the hedge, he saw, reflected in the window glass, the startling image of his own sharp features. Was it his own face? Holmes wondered, the face of a man who was frightened? Because he was frightened. And for no reason. Because he had taken a photograph of blots and shadows. But, of course, he had not looked at it in the morning. His hand trembled.

A moment passed.

Holmes looked away from the window.

"Your Grace," he said, "I should like you to examine something."

Without looking down he found it.

The Duke took the photograph into his left hand, turning it at once another way. With the other he half reached into his pocket, then he stopped.

"A horse," he said confidently.

But he held the photograph again at arm's length as if to be certain. He continued to stare.

"Yes," he said after a moment. "See, here is a leg. In fact." He counted four legs. But before he had finished he had counted four more. The Duke shook his head. "A rather peculiar horse, I admit," he said, "but a horse indisputably."

3.

Olivia Tennison, who for the better part of a fort-night had been assistant housekeeper, half-scullion and full-time drudge, scuttered into Nora's bed-room without knocking. It was the end of the week, for there was washing. Her little wren's face was darkly flushed. Her eyes had been glaring. She advanced in fearless little hops like a bird on a wire. She had already stripped the master's bed, having removed a heap of books, a tablet of writing paper, pens and a hunting cap. His sheets, which were muddied and would cause no end of trouble, she had bundled into a pillowcase, which, with an air of injured dignity, she had placed by the door. By now she was accustomed to his thoughtlessness. More than once she had found his trousers, with most of a swamp still clinging to the cuffs, under the covers, where — weary, she supposed, after half a night's wandering with her Georgie through fields and ditches — he had kicked them. He threw his clothes every which way, more than likely still talking, his head swimming with plans, with innumerable tasks, changing every minute, which her Georgie, staggering after him from one place to the next and even up the old back stairs to his bedroom, must somehow see to as best he could. Olivia brooded. As if there wasn't enough to do, she thought, and only a few women for

the inside work. She would have her Georgie speak with him. After all, they were thick, those two. Her face went completely blank. She had left the door open.

Nora sat at the end of the bed. Bars of dusty light fell across her bare legs. Because she still had only the clothes she had come with, she was dressed, as she had slept, in one of his shirts. She stretched her arms and yawned. The shirt hitched up on her thighs. Olivia's pale eyes hardened. She stood before the bed, staring at rather more of Nora's rounded legs than she approved of seeing.

"I'll trouble you for the sheets, Miss Barnacle," Olivia said.

Nora reached for a brush and began on her hair. "He doesn't call me that," she said evenly.

"Oh, I've heard him, miss. Like a barnacle he says to Cook. Like those little things that attached themselves to ships . . . and no one knows how they got there . . . and they don't come off."

From where she sat Nora could see out the window onto the drive. She became aware of a figure, standing in the gravel, looking up at the house. As the face turned toward her window, she saw it was the stableboy.

"He wouldn't," she said.

"You'll suit yourself, I'm sure." Olivia began to tug at the sheets. "Though it isn't for my own good that I mention it."

Nora climbed down from the bed. For a moment her fingers lingered on the carved pattern of the walnut post. He hadn't, she was certain, even if he had said it, meant anything of the sort. Nobody could tell her what he thought. She had listened. More and more she was convinced that he spoke in a language which was only incidentally directed to those around him.

There was no sound in the room, only the crunch of the stableboy's boots from outside the window. Nora reached across to the chair. She took the skirt and, stepping into it, drew the heavy woolen over her legs.

"I hold my own here," she said coolly, sweeping out of her the last particle of doubt. "I work as much as anyone." To keep her long yellow hair from her eyes she had bound it back with a scarf. "But I get up when I want." She walked to the closet and began rummaging. But after a moment she turned back empty-handed. They were both looking down at her feet.

"You haven't by any chance . . ."

"No, miss."

On an impulse Nora went out into the hall. Her shoes, tipped on their sides, were in plain sight on the carpet. She slipped them on, knowing all the while that she had not put them there. Finished within, Olivia, a new bundle in her arms, came through the door.

"You've found them, miss," she said with pretended surprise.

"He is thoughtful, don't you think?" Nora answered steadily. They could think as they liked. The truth was he was innocent. Often enough she had waited in his bed; but he had on those occasions slept elsewhere or, for all she knew, slept nowhere at all. And what she had left of her presence, shoes or a scarf, the hairbrush (she had so little), he returned without comment.

Nora stood in the hall until Olivia trotted along down the stairs. Then she followed. Below a door opened. There was a faint sound of women's voices from the back of the house. She could hear the cook, old Norfolk's wife, complaining as she did regularly when, the men already come and gone, the last pan scrubbed, Nora came late to breakfast. "I see how it is," she announced in the abused tone she saved for those moments she had an audience. Yet Wykeham could come in without warning, in midmorning from wherever it was his jaunts had taken him, and Lizzy Norfolk, her heavy jowled face bent over the silver, was up in a moment and the kettle began singing.

"I can readily imagine . . ." The voice drawled on with accustomed resentfulness.

Nora took a small breath and went out onto the porch.

The stableboy was waiting. He turned on her with a brief bitter smile.

"He is gone," she told him. "I don't know where."

The boy's eyes fell. His demeanor was intense, almost desperate; yet it seemed to her that he had no one to blame but himself. It was the fourth time he had come seeking Wykeham. She had watched him for as many days, in the morning, pacing up and down in the gravel, looking uncertain, uncomfortable out in the open before the house. He had never come up the steps, never knocked on the door. It was as if he waited for her instead, waited to be told over and over that Wykeham had gone.

"I shall come tomorrow," he said.

She gave him an oblique look. "You might try after dinner." The boy stared back sullenly. She felt a sharp redness come into her cheeks. She had meant to be helpful but it seemed instead that a distance had opened between them. His grave small features were watching her. She realized suddenly how hard it was to look at him.

She had an impression of dark, haunted eyes, a plain lean face. Spikes of black hair fell in several directions across his forehead. But if she averted her eyes, what was left of her memory of him? She started to turn away.

He threw her a tortured look.

"Tell him," he said quickly, "that it is time he spoke with me."

As if he perceived as well some danger of vanishing, he thrust his thin shoulders forward.

"If I see him," she said. Nora hesitated. "If I do, I will ask him to come to the stables." Something else occurred to her and she turned, staring at the roofs, now partially mended, of the workmen's cottages. "You will be there? You do live here somewhere?"

His eyes had run past her. He was looking instead at the house, at the wide uneven porch where she waited. The old railings were threaded with thorns and buttressed with vines, just now beginning to flower.

"He can find me," he said.

There was a long moment. Then he went back down the drive, heading, it seemed to her, nowhere in particular. Later in the day she saw him again, shuffling idly along the edge of the hill. It was one of the last days of April; the sky was extraordinarily distant. He was standing out in the open without even the shadow of a cloud to cover him. She watched him as, unconscious of any immodesty, he relieved himself in the grass. It struck her then that probably he was ignorant of indoor plumbing. Looking out from the house, which now she seldom left, she found herself wondering where he had come from. Not from this place. He is like me, she concluded, feeling the tender stirring of sympathy.

There was a movement in the room behind her. Her heart rose to her throat.

The crow hopped onto the carpet. Shamed by her disappointment, she met its stare.

"Pretty girl, pretty girl," the crow rasped consolingly.

The voice, however, because it was the first time she had heard it, only made matters worse.

In the darkness, looking across the valley, George Tennison rubbed his right hand, acknowledging with a sense of good fortune and prodigality the thickness of his calluses. There was a little mound of folded pound notes in his pocket and more coming at the end of each week as long as the work lasted. And the work, he assured himself with a private wink, was sure to last longer than he did. He grinned. The shine of many twinkling stars winked gaily back at him.

He went across the field and through the gate. Over the black hill he recognized — or might have, he thought, had he not been brought up in the smoke of the mills — the striking array of fixed stars. They were pictures, he had heard, of men and beasts, of impossible deeds. A strange excitement filled him. With the pleasure of Adam, because there had never been anyone to teach him, he named them for himself. Cunningly, among the splendid luminaries, he distinguished the labors of which he was now master: George Tennison (those three bright stars were his arm, the fourth was a hammer) restoring breached walls; George Tennison, just to the left of the moon, climbing over slick acres of slate to repoint the chimneys. Deep in reverie, he leaned back his head.

Floating in front of him were innumerable stars, great stars for the great labors while his back was still strong, lesser stars, their configurations as yet remote, for the lesser tasks awaiting his old age. He patted the lump of folded notes in his pocket. His men would be waiting in the village, drinking away their salaries in the front room of the Royal Charles. It was only sociable that he go and have a beer with them — his fine bunch of Bristol stragglers, laid-off clocksmiths, men like himself, craftsmen made over into common muckers and gardeners and lucky, he knew, for the chance. Once or twice before he made up his mind to join them, but Wykeham had always needed something looked into and needed it right then. Indeed, this was the first evening in over a week George Tennison had had his liberty.

He shambled out of the margins of South Wood. The Royal Charles was still a good few minutes' tramp down the road. He walked stiffly. There was a bit of arthritis in his leg, which he had got, he suspected, from wading most of the afternoon in an ornamental fish pond, trying to unstop the drain. Nevertheless, passing along the dark shut-in corridor of branches, he found himself quietly whistling, glad of the work and gald, at least for an hour or two, to be free of it.

A light burned steadily in the bedroom of the parsonage. George Tennison turned down the cracked walk under the trees, passing within a dozen yards of the house without noticing. He did not know these houses yet; they were simply houses. He recognized the feed store because he had been sent there once and Hunt's garage because it was a garage and because Fred Norfolk, with whom he had spent a day shingling the roof of a cottage in Black Wood, had kept muttering and laughing to himself about Charon Hunt without ever once quite coming to the point. It had merely strengthened George Tennison's conviction that Devon folk were an odd sort, not actually a mystery but crackbrained and out of touch. Like their church, he thought, coming abreast of it in the darkness. It was an ordinary church, with doors and a steeple like any church, except, of course, they had painted it green. Painted it once, and every fifty years or so it looked, kept repainting it, not out of some prankish habit, not because they liked it, but because (it had been Wykeham himself who had told him!) they believed a green church would never be burned by Indians. It just makes you wonder, he thought. But, in truth, he did not. Instead he mounted the two broad stone steps of the Royal Charles.

"George!" someone called out.

"Mister Tennison," Adam France added loudly, because, after all, George was foreman now.

"Ten-thirty," Jakey shouted, examining his watch. "Well, you have a bit of catching up to do."

"A beer," George Tennison said, passing the counter. He stopped and, reaching into his pocket, uncurled a pound note and laid it out on the dark, polished wood of the bar. "And a whisky."

With a glass in each hand he wandered back among the chairs and tables where men he had never seen sat quietly absorbed in their glasses. He glanced abstractedly from one to the next, taking little notice until Fred Norfolk stood up.

"Come in at last, have you?" Norfolk said. He looked as though he wanted to shake hands, which, unless George Tennison put down a drink (and he had no mind to do that) was impossible. Comrades, nevertheless, Norfolk's lopsided grin seemed to announce, men of common understanding, both working up at the great house, their wives too, for that matter.

George Tennison looked for a way around him.

Norfolk saw it but did not move away. He whispered:

"You come along with old Fred."

He seemed to realize the Bristol men were watching him. He winked conspiratorily. "Later," he said none too softly. "Been waitin' a million years. Been waitin' forever." He winked again, the model of patience. " 'Keep till you've had a wee drop with your friends."

Norfolk sat, or rather his big legs folded, compelling the rest of him to follow. Seated, although undoubtedly the world wheeled ever faster about him, he held himself still, his huge elbows propped up on the table. His bleary eyes, undeterred by the chairs and tables circling past him, tracked George Tennison until he sat far back in the corner and brought a glass to his lips.

Jakey moved over. He still had his watch cradled importantly in his palm. It was too big and expensive a watch for a man like Jakey, but then, he had made half the innards himself. It gave him exquisite pleasure just to hold it.

"Things aren't what they were," he said mildly, not exactly sad but slightly perplexed.

"And what is?" asked Adam France. He lifted his glass.

"It's the bankers," someone said.

Jakey smiled down in a fatherly way at the watchface and nodded. "Bloodsucking capitalists," he muttered. "Squeezing out the last penny. One mill closing after the next."

"Yet," George Tennison said, the whisky warming his belly, "Well, you know, this is something too."

And they nodded, for his sake if not for their own. Jakey examined his watch ruminatively and sighed.

When George Tennison came back from the toilet, where he had stopped perhaps a moment longer than he had intended, the table at which he had so comfortably passed two hours was empty. I'll be goddamned, he thought, disappointed but without hostility. They had their work and morning came early.

In any event, if he hurried, he would probably catch up with them. He considered the last little bit of whisky in his glass but, pricked by a barb of conscience, left it regretfully.

In his pounding head there was still a small cold corner of sobriety, enough so that he recognized the hulking shape of Fred Norfolk climbing unsteadily to his feet from among the confusion of tables. Regretted it later — although he explained carefully to Olivia that he had been too far gone to remember. In fact, however far he had got, it was not quite far enough since, afterward, he remembered a great deal more than he liked.

Preemptively, with an apelike arm, Norfolk covered his shoulder. "You see who your f-friends are, G-Georgie," Norfolk announced. His grin was more lopsided than it had been before; his large smug face was whiter. "You c-come along with ol' F-Fred."

Somehow George Tennison eluded him. He made his way erratically to the front of the bar, through the door whose latch, incomprehensively, was either too high or too low but which, found, submitted at last with a groan. Only out in the street Norfolk was again beside him, looming suddenly out of the darkness, dark himself and swaying without the benefit of a wind. Once more Norfolk's arm secured its place on his shoulder.

"J-Just across the green," Norfolk whispered.

There were no eyes to follow them. The dogs that might have howled had already been whistled for and lay curled indoors on their carpets in the houses of the Browns and the Underwoods. The Reverend Mr. Longford, his sermon — by his own lights — finished, dropped his head to his pillow and was instantly asleep. Slipped in beside him, Plum clutched his broad arm contentedly, reviewing the few minor changes she would make in the morning before he woke. In the pocket of the apron hung over a chair in the kitchen was an envelope, barely remembered, addressed to Nora but delivered to the parsonage. The first of the week would be soon enough to run it up to her. She had meant to pay her a call, poor child, to see how things stood. But there was time for that. Her hand found Tim's elbow. Nothing to worry over. With half the village coming and going from the place, working inside and out, she would have heard anything worth listening to. She smiled at the darkness. With amusement and an ecstasy she knew was foolish but never minded, Plum listened to her husband's rough snores.

George Tennison was listening as well. But all he heard were silences.

"No one home," he said timidly.

"Don't matter," Norfolk said, pushing in with his shoulder.

"Up them stairs," he said, unmindful of any difficulty. "Him and me t-together in this. W-were from the s-start." His loud slurred voice trailed off into a snigger. " 'Cept, of c-course, hiss s-start was a little before yours t-truly."

George Tennison grunted. He tried to make his legs follow one after another. The stairs wound off into darkness. Unable to negotiate the steps and exasperated beyond measure, he began to swear.

"Y-you'll d-do al-rright," Norfolk called back encouragingly.

At the top of the staircase was an even darker hallway. At the end of it, when Norfolk had managed to discover the light, there was a door. Norfolk pressed his disordered face next to George Tennison's. "H-here we are!" he whispered. With a constricting hug he drew him back under his arm. With his free hand he pawed at the latch.

All at once Norfolk's vigorous grin faded. He shook his big head slowly.

"Y-you ain't f-frit?" he demanded.

George Tennison made a rueful noise. But to Norfolk one answer was as good as another. He pawed again at the door until it opened.

The light flooded in from the hall, illuminating a spare but otherwise ordinary bedroom. Charon Hunt was sitting beside the bed, a length of rabbit wire between his brown fingers. He was a large man, even larger than Norfolk. He was dressed in a blacksmith's burned and patched trousers. Despite the warmth of the room, a great coat covered his shoulders. The coat, like his face and hair, was red. Indeed, the man and his clothing gave out a ruddy glow. Even his great fingers, which were patiently tightening the snare, seemed to shine with an odd radiance. But however extraordinary, Hunt was a man, or nearly that. The other was not a man so clearly. George Tennison's mouth, soured by whisky, fell stupidly open.

On the bed, what might have been a large quilt made of feathers shifted suddenly. In the glare from the hall the feathers, which might once have been vivid, even defiant with color, appeared lifeless, a dull brown muddied here and there to a dark sepia. Moving under them, a lump of a head opened its mouth and screamed. It was not a sound a man would have made, although a boy, bitter, unrepentant, even in the face of an inescapable destiny, might have.

"Not even his death keeps him quiet," Hunt said glumly. He let the clawed fingers, now skillfully rebound, fall from his lap.

Once again the young Indian bellowed.

"I care nothing for your bellowing," Hunt bellowed back. "Burn what you will when the High King comes. But until then, by Duinn, you shall damn well wait like the rest!"

George Tennison stood gawking. Because there was nothing else he dared look at, his stare fastened desperately on Norfolk.

When Hunt rose, it was like a hill rising. His shoulders got in the way of the light.

"Whose soldier is this?" he asked coldly. "Whose side will he fight on?" Norfolk went right on grinning.

"H-he is s-solid behind us," Norfolk answered. "W-works at the h-house, w-works for W-Wykeham."

Hunt moved. He placed himself firmly in front of George Tennison and stared hard at him.

"Whose side?" he said.

His voice was louder and colder and yet, in an odd way, it was sadder as well. George Tennison stumbled backward. If his mouth would have worked, he would have uttered a cry.

It was Norfolk who answered.

"W-Wykeham's," he said unhesitantly, without a twitch of concern or apology.

From the bed, as if that as well were an answer, there came a high-pitched wail.

Hunt's lips curled at the edge.

"What makes you think," he asked, "that this time, after so long, Wyck has chosen?" His voice, now softer, was colder still. "Tell me," he said, "is the Sea-Road open? Have the Stone Kings put aside their sorrow?"

Hunt dropped his head.

The questions were addressed to no one in particular.

When George Tennison staggered alone into the street, he couldn't remember if anyone had answered. But he knew the green was in front of him. In the whirling space between the trees he could see the great burning stars, now greater and brighter because of drink. Disgusted, he turned away from them.

He wasn't altogether certain what he had heard or seen, but he had heard and seen quite enough. Like the stars, they were somebody else's business. He pitched himself forward. At the very least he knew the dark street climbed toward Greenchurch, that the hard grunting breath, very close at hand, was his own.

His head was swimming.

On the margins of South Wood, he failed to notice the clop of too many hooves, never felt the thick hands that lifted him onto the broad white back. Yet the wind did seem to sail more swiftly through the fringe of his hair. Under him too many haunches and shoulders rose and fell.

"How many legs?" he asked, despite himself. But it was a foolish question. Wykeham only laughed.

4.

There were really two kitchens at Greenchurch. The grand kitchen, with its five stoves and too many copper-sheathed tables, Lizzy Norfolk, although she did most of the cooking there, thought of as the men's kitchen. It was where the men sat for breakfast and dinner, pulling their bread with fingers that were never sufficiently scrubbed. Invariably they left their plates and their cups on the tables. Lizzy much preferred the smaller kitchen in the back with its one frugal stove and its single oak table. There, the men gone, she could sit with Olivia and, on rare occasions, with Nora. There she could keep a good lookout on the yard, on tradesmen, and, most particularly, on Fred Norfolk, who had a habit of slipping off. And there, having from the side door window an unhampered view, she presided over the house, over its routines and its schedules. Without regard for her failures with her own husband and with something less than the formal support of Wykeham, she had gathered about her not unsubstantial shoulders the sober cloak of authority; and, like an empress surrounded by savages, she felt it her given duty to chasten and instruct.

"It's a pity," Lizzy said that morning before Nora, carrying her own cup, had quite found her seat by the stove.

Nora detected a guilty look in Olivia's eyes.

"What is?" Nora asked blandly.

"Why, George has missed his breakfast."

"It's his leg, miss," said Olivia.

Lizzy folded her fat arms. "Funny things, legs," she said. "Your Fred —"

Lizzy smiled triumphantly. "My Fred had his breakfast!"

Olivia examined the narrow front of her dress.

"Well, it was Mr. Wykeham," she announced, "he came home with."

Nora's head turned up suddenly.

But it was Lizzy who saw the face at the door, or rather the chest and the hairy arms first, and the face a moment later, pulled down uncomfortably to the window and peering. It was an alarming face, ruddy and thickened like the sun just poking over the ridge.

"That man!" Lizzy exclaimed. "Now what can he want?"

But although she went to the door, she opened it no more than a crack. Nora could see one leg and one great shoulder and the grotesque half of a face, grinning. Nora examined the face with a curious stare. Something was missing. It was, she thought, as if another face, balancing the first, a face darker and less ridiculous, lay just out of sight. Nora put down her cup. She could hear the rumbling of the man's voice but she could not make out what he said. Lizzy shook her old head.

"No, Mr. Wykeham isn't here. Went away this morning. Down to Bristol, I think. Couldn't say why." Her voice had grown petulant. She wanted to be done with him.

"No," she repeated, taking a deeper breath, "I wouldn't know which car he wanted worked on." She was about to shut the door.

"It would be the Pope-Hartford," said Nora.

Lizzy turned.

Looking straight back at her, Nora repeated it. The astonishing thing was that her tone carried an unqualified air of conviction. Lizzy screwed up her own broad face.

"The Pope-Hartford," Lizzy said to the man at the door.

Charon Hunt grunted. His footsteps went away. In a few moments they could each see him lifting his long toolbox from the back of his truck. When he disappeared into the barn, Lizzy moved again to the table. But at the back of her mind a new and startling thought was forming. She was all too aware of Nora's talent for woolgathering. Right or wrong, she realized, it would be said it was at her direction, not Nora's, that the work had been started.

"That is what he wanted?" she snapped.

"Yes."

"He told you directly. You weren't by any chance," she improvised, "listening to little blue birds or —"

Nora smiled composedly. "Not little or blue," she answered.

Her confidant, in fact, had been neither. That it had been feathered, she imagined, was nobody's business but her own.

The May weather was sultry and electric, filled with the delayed promise of thunder, and got on his nerves. Grown desperate, George Harwood went one last time through his lecture notes, finding among the scraps of paper and torn index cards the Duke's letter. It was to be today, he realized, shocked with himself for having forgotten. Not two days before, on the very morning he had received the letter, he had sent a message back to His Grace, agreeing (I shall be honored, he had written) to meet with him. On just what matters the Duke had been vague. Something, in any event, to do with Will Wykeham. His memory jogged, Harwood unfolded the paper. But he put is aside on the desk. The lecture first, he thought and felt a mounting sense of alarm.

What he sought, what, in fact, he had spent three quarters of an hour unsuccessfully seeking was the source of a quote and, if possible, the precise language, describing the moment of synthesizing imagination when the ordinary tangle of human thought converged dramatically on a single compelling abstraction. It was to be the climax of the term's last lecture. In the fall, in another course altogether and relying strictly on memory, he had used it. Unaccountably his students had cheered him. In a dozen years such a thing had not happened. He still basked in the glory.

Only, of course, he had misplaced it.

Harwood fussed with his shirt. He was perspiring. Nonetheless, fearing rain, he took the greatcoat under his arm and switched off the light. On the stairs he turned, went back to the door and locked it.

Halfway up the street he remembered.

For a moment the coat, which had grown heavier and more awkward than it had ever been in April, no longer troubled him. His strides became longer.

"Imagine a table," Harwood commanded. The crowd of young men, bearing sluggishly along, took neither notice nor offense. Scores of backs, all of them coatless and damp, milled in front of him. With gentle but well-directed prods he steered past them. Just as the rain began to splash on the sidewalks, he went through the doors of the lecture hall and climbed to the podium.

He was early. Except for a pocket of stragglers from another class, the room was empty. A smaller group stood gossiping in the corridor. Yet slowly, driven in by the weather, the young men began to fill the hall. Their sleeves rolled up like laborers', they drifted down the aisles. A few anxious scholars, their notebooks already open, sat in front. But they would have sat as anxiously and as still and would, when he started, have begun to write with much the same ferocity and panic had he lectured on the *Encyclopaedia Britannica*. The windows along the sloping sides of the hall were opaque and emitted an uncertain light. I might as well lecture in a cave, Harwood thought; yet, in a way, it was almost pleasant, the air grown heavy and quiet. The world was shut out. Harwood felt a little flutter in himself.

"Shall we begin?" he asked. His voice, like the voice in a cave, surprised him. He opened a book and then for several minutes did not look at it.

"Even the smallest details are conserved," he said, now in earnest. "However minor and distracting, I shall expect you to remember. I have prepared a list . . ."

There was a groan.

". . . of birthmarks and certain articles of clothing, birds seen at midnight, objects as simple and as serviceable as china, isolated in aspect. And yet, gentlemen, reiterated. Infinitely recombined. Characteristic, I should think, of the obsessive nature of literary imagination." His voice became louder. He had forgotten his usual embarrassment. "But today," he announced, "I shall ask you to take a broader view. I shall ask you to stand back and to see, if you can, the beauty of the underlying pattern. . . ."

The Duke, who had come in before the lecture had started, sat in the back. On the wall directly above his head was a painting of a clergyman, most probably one of the Mathers, giving a Bible into the hand of a muscular Indian. The plaque beneath it read *Ansantawae, by the Grace of God, Receives the Book.* The clergyman, his features hardened into a look of moral belligerence, is imbued nevertheless with a kind of wooden glory. But it is the Indian who is bathed in light. He stands under it as unnaturally as under a lamp.

It is the light that gives the painting its essential falseness. Its anemic shining reduces the ragged hills to a few cultivated fields, the bend of the intruding river to the ordinary flatness of an English pond. Harwood, who each morning faced it squarely, had often wondered what purposes were served in presenting a Pequod chief with a Christian testament. "They could not speak together," he had once told his students. "Ansantawae understood only Algonquin." In fact, in this detail alone, the painting preserved the delicate relic of truth.

It had been commissioned by Benjamin Church, who at the head of a militia of farmer soldiers had driven to their deaths the last remnant of the Pequod nation. Captain Church himself had supervised the final slaughter in the Fairfield swamps. He had shot three young men trapped between the water and the wood. Because of the cumbersomeness and delay in reloading, he had continued the killing with the stock of his gun. The corpses were muddied. It had been difficult to tell them apart. Nevertheless it had been the general opinion that Ansantawae was among them. It was this victory that the painting commemorated. The artist had been given a free hand. The captain, being well acquainted with John Bunyan, saw nothing amiss when a purposeful Mather was depicted in his place. In the darkening pigment of three centuries, his only contribution is now scarcely legible. Yet it is the one detail based on observation rather than religious bigotry.

Almost from the first, Captain Church had felt a deep affinity with the Indians. The entries in his diary describe how, before he turned to murder them, he had lived in their villages and made expeditions with their young men into the Dutch territories across the Hudson. He had admired their bravery and their wisdom. "They know this Dark Land better than we ever shall," he had written. As sympathetically as any of the English he had learned their ways and he had insisted, although now one must stand up very close to see it, that the Bible, its pages folded back to a passage in Genesis and given from the hand of a clergyman who clearly had not been there into the hand of an Indian who only may have been, be written in Welsh.

The Duke leaned into his seat. His head pounded. The outside world was hushed. The windows were whitened by rain.

"Reality —" Harwood was explaining when he stopped. His tongue, as though waiting inspiration, pressed on the edge of his teeth. It was, he felt, his most potent effect. It gave the illusion of spontaneity, the impression of a mind poised on a knife-edge and conjuring with darkness. Harwood smiled with excitement. "— Is a Protean fog —" he continued, "— into which we read —" He paused. "— Not so much what is but what we have been led to expect." He waited.

"Consider, if you will," he said, "the pre-Copernican universe: the earth at its center. Devils beneath."

There came into his mind's eyes a picture of angular little creatures with drooling mouths and leather wings.

"Very real devils, it would seem," he went on, "for they had a very real place — the vast basement of the universe — and could and therefore did tempt us to perdition. Only Nicolaus Copernicus —" He seized the book he had put down, from which in a moment, although it had nothing to do with Copernicus, he intended to read a long passage. "One man," he said, "one man learning to look some other way, feeling, though none before him had felt it, the apparently fixed and solid earth, our oldest foundations, begin to slip, to slide beneath his feet, to —"

Someone coughed.

Harwood could feel his words creeping cold and friendless over the hall. No more than a handful were still listening.

The lines deepened on the Duke's forehead.

"Truth, gentlemen, particularly literary truth," Harwood persisted, "must be encountered suddenly." He opened the book.

There was only the ignorant murmur of rain on the windows. The Duke tapped his long fingers. He considered the old woman buried on the grounds of the school in Bristol, the young man dead in New Awanux.

"Imagine a table," George Harwood was saying.

The Duke rose quickly and went to wait in the corridor.

There was a moment's hush and then the clap of spring seats snapping shut. The young men pushed past him. The Duke scowled. Harwood gathered up his books and his coat and came up the aisle. Until he saw the coat the Duke had not truly recognized him. His clerk had made certain inquiries of the Dean. In the space of a few hours the Duke had learned that Harwood had been Wykeham's advisor, the one man at the college with whom, if it could be said of anyone, Wykeham had been intimate. The Duke had written straight off requesting a meeting. He had not troubled himself to think who the man was. He had cared only to discover what Harwood knew, what, if anything, he could explain about Wykeham's behavior. He had not stopped to wonder what effect Wykeham might have had on him. The Duke had only half listened to the lecture. Perhaps it had been clever. He was no judge. Certainly there was little else to recommend him. Harwood's figure was stout, his face without delicacy. Ordinarily, having learned what he could, the Duke would have left him abruptly in the emptied corridor. It was surprising, and even foreign to his nature, that instead His Grace had taken the man by the shoulders.

"I shall need two hours of your time," he had said. "If you can spare it. Afterward, my driver will drop you wherever you like."

He felt the perspiration on the man's heavy shoulder.

"I hope I can drag you away," he continued, though now he had not the least doubt. He had seen the expensive coat Harwood carried. He remembered the little lighted windows of the train into which Wykeham had vanished, leaving them both on the platform, both stranded and, for a moment, unable to walk away.

The street was mobbed with students running to get out of the rain. It was several minutes before the college towers slipped grudgingly behind. For the better part of a mile they crawled beside the long snaking wall of the First Settlers Cemetery, past the statues of Protestant saints, centuries old, crumbling back toward the shapelessness of the original stone. It was not until East Bridge, after they had emerged from under the railroad trestle, that they were able to pick up speed again. By then the unfamiliar street had narrowed. Between the poor row houses they caught a glimpse now and then of the river. Backed up by the wind, the estuary had swollen and was flooding the weirs. The traffic had thinned. The wipers thudded dully on the windscreen.

"He told you something of his travels?" The Duke asked finally.

Uneasy in the Duke's presence, Harwood rearranged his coat. "Very little," he acknowledged. "I gather he had seen much of the empire. Certainly wherever there were any number of English." Looking out at the river, Harwood was reminded, unhappily, of all the places he had never been. "Though who can say," he added deprecatingly, "what exactly he remembers. He was, I believe, Your Grace, quite young."

The Duke watched Harwood carefully.

"He isn't," he said.

Harwood turned.

"Isn't English," the Duke said.

This one point, at least, although he had been slow himself to see it, was indisputable. The ledgers, of course, had been in the vault. He had devoted his life to them, to records which in themselves were a kind of history, repeating not only Wykeham's existence but, in a sense, his own. Yet strangely, until the past evening, he had not brought them all, not one after another, to his desk. And even then, knowing them too well, he had not known where to start and at first he had looked in all the wrong places. He felt his heart sink.

"It is, I should have thought," Harwood protested, "the most English of names."

"Yes. Yes, of course." The Duke nodded. Somehow the topic had gotten away from him. His head still ached. He had been thinking of women.

It was not the first time. More than once he had found himself worrying over a mere few hundred invested yearly in a Norwegian bank. But the amounts had been so trivial he had let them pass. Nevertheless, he had gone on his own to visit the young women's academy. He had been a young man himself when he had walked over the lawn, stopping at the edge of the open pit where the new building would go up. The woman had trailed behind him from the house. He had not conversed with her. At the time he had not even been troubled. Surely there would be women. He had expected that. The trust could well afford the expense. His own habits were regular. He was not himself much given to foolishness.

It all seemed so long ago.

In the morning he had awakened at his desk. The ledgers had been scattered in front of him. On the borders of sleep he had seen her, a dark-haired woman in a blue dress, sweeping across the green lawn. She had almost stumbled. The brightness had been in his eyes. Until she was quite close to him he had not noticed that she wept.

His head still pounded.

"You shared, one would imagine," he said quietly, "certain confidences." He tried to calm his mind, to remember that the dead woman, however he felt bound to her, was Wykeham's. "You were his teacher," he said.

"Yes."

"And you talked?"

"We traded books." Harwood smiled. He meant to be honest. "I may have given him one or two," he said. "He gave me dozens. Late in the evenings he would come to my rooms and we would talk."

"Of?"

Harwood thought he had been clear. "About books," he said. He was puzzled. The Duke was watching him strangely.

"He may have mentioned acquaintances."

"Your Grace?" Watching him in return, Harwood realized

that the Duke was drunk. Not alarmingly so. But there was a gauntness about the Duke's eyes, behind his deliberateness, the clear possibility of panic.

Harwood frowned.

"Did you gather —" the Duke continued. "Forgive me, these questions are necessary." His large, veined hands shifted uncomfortably in his lap. "There were women," he said. "I know for a fact there were several. Not that I find that astonishing. But afterward."

For a moment he was unnaturally conscious of the sound of the rain. He waited until his head had stopped buzzing. He said: "There had always to be something new, don't you think? To distract him. Something to worry over." His eyes shone. "Something," he said, "to stir up all the wells of thought and feeling at once —"

His head tilted awkwardly. A strand of his dark, parted hair fell abruptly over his forehead.

The Duke sank again into his seat. He was tired. Since he had seen the photograph, he had barely slept. He had been drawn up short, suddenly, without reason. He knew that much. It was no help. Reason, he had decided, was of no help.

"May I ask," His Grace began once more. He stopped. It was all too long ago. When Wykeham had abandoned Willa Brelling, Harwood had yet to be born. "There were others," he said. "Probably more than I know. You are quite certain he never —"

"Your Grace?"

"Women," the Duke said, a bit sharply.

"No," Harwood answered. "Not to me."

On the outskirts of New Anwanux there was more open land. Grimly, the Duke stared at the patchwork of meadows. Harwood kept his gaze resolutely forward. Still His Grace was not without hope.

"Would you remember," he asked, "if Wykeham ever spoke to you of horses?"

Harwood shook his head dismally.

Crossing the trackbed, the car jerked twice. The driver cut the wheel sharply. A cluster of blurry shapes appeared out of the rain. At the end of the lane there were five rectangles of gray stone. Two of the mossed roofs had already fallen. The house itself was set back and to the left, its few small windows broken, its side porches rotted. The Duke felt an immediate twinge of displeasure. It was no longer a working farm. That it had been preserved at all was due to the rent he paid one year to the next, at Wykeham's direction, for the use of the barn.

Beyond the rusted front gate the car halted. The rain went on clinking on the hood. The sky, which until that moment had held a slight glow, had darkened. Harwood could see little but the two phosphorescent circles the headlamps cut in the fog and, even less perfectly, in snatches, the track that went up to the doors of the barn and, seemingly, under them. He rubbed at the glass.

The barn was unusually large, perhaps three stories. Its high eaves appeared and disappeared in the mists. Harwood peered up at it doubtfully.

"Is this what you wished me to see?" he asked.

The Duke did not answer. Without a word, he swung the door open. Suspicious and yet not wanting to be left behind, Harwood followed.

The yard, blocked up against the foundation, spread before him like a deepening pool. Harwood ran. But by the time he had reached the old, closed doors his shirt and trousers were soaked. Sheets of water rolled down his face. The Duke grunted. He was trying, unsuccessfully, a set of large keys in a padlock. For what seemed a very long time Harwood stared at his back.

The air was much cooler. The rain was so heavy that neither heard the splash of the tires on the stones.

The cab ran onto the gravel and stopped. The small man who climbed out unfolded his umbrella. He looked up at the barn. After a moment, quite likely by accident, something brushed Harwood's arm.

"Your Grace," the man said.

The Duke looked around silently. There had been no introduction.

The little man returned the pipe to his teeth and, maneuvering his umbrella, lifted a small dry hand toward Harwood.

"Holmes," the man said.

Mistrustfully, Harwood held out his own. "George Harwood."

"So His Grace wrote me." There was a slight movement behind the man's eyes. "Professor of —" he started.

"Assistant professor," Harwood admitted, "of Awanux."

Holmes looked at him oddly. "You realize, I hope, that you couldn't —"

"No." This time, overcome by dejection, the Duke had not bothered to turn. "He doesn't. And I haven't told him."

No one, in fact, had told Harwood anything. "Some one had better," he sputtered. Just then the Duke gave a heave to the door.

A wedge of murky light was cast suddenly into the distant rafters. His Grace gave a second great push. The door rumbled and he stepped over the track.

Harwood walked ahead stiffly. The barn was quiet. At the far end, past the stalls where the track ended, he could make out the barest suggestion of another door. He lifted his head. It was Holmes who saw the indignation in his face.

"For the love of Christ," Holmes whispered, "hadn't it ever occurred to you that you should be? That you are," Holmes corrected himself.

Harwood glanced down resentfully. "I fail to see."

"Details," the Duke couldn't help saying.

"What?"

"English," the Duke said, more bitterly than he had intended. "Shouldn't you be a professor of English?"

Harwood only looked blank.

The Duke scowled with vexation. It was obvious once he started to look. The problem was to see it in the first place. Without Holmes, he knew, without seeing the photograph, he would have been just as stupid. Nonetheless he was nettled.

"We live," the Duke said with patronizing coolness. "We live, I am afraid, Mr. Harwood, at a very peculiar moment in history."

By then Holmes had left them and was scuffling alone through the hay. A channel for removing urine and excrement ran at his feet. He found a stick. Leaning sideways, he thrust it into the channel. But the stick encountered only dry stone. Unsatisfied, he wandered among the stalls. He rubbed his hands on the posts and, becoming less squeamish, poked into barrels. The walls were hung with straps and bridles. Advancing, he took each one and examined it. At a loss, he looked back. "There is nothing," he shouted. Under the rafters his small reedy voice echoed queerly.

Away from the door, in the brownish haze swarming with motes and the dust of hay, it had become increasingly difficult for Harwood to see anything clearly.

"What details?" he repeated uncomfortably.

"Names."

"Which —"

The Duke compressed his lips. Yet there was nothing to do but go forward. "Which are not," he said bluntly. "Although they should be. And were before the world started changing."

It scarcely mattered that he had struggled with it himself.

"Names," he continued, "like Awanux, which are but should

never have been. Since they are logically quite impossible. Like New Awanux particularly. The first English would never have called it that. They would have called it New Holborn."

At the far end of the barn Holmes was opening the door.

The Duke felt his voice stiffen. "Or New Kingston more probably," he said. "Or New Thames."

They had both stopped.

The barn was filled again with the urgent beating of the rain. Holmes stood up ahead against the sky's blackness. He was straining into the wind.

"You had better have a look at this," he called back.

The Duke stayed where he was. "Are you certain there is nothing inside?"

The little man turned. "It is not like that. All those years . . . Someone was certain to have looked." But there was a sparkling flash. The barn was suddenly rocked by thunder. "Not in here," Holmes cried, trying to be heard. But the thunder blunted his words and the wind blew them back in his teeth. "Just to be loaded," he shouted. "Only that."

"What?"

"Not inside!"

The Duke cupped his ears. Hearing only a buzz, he lurched forward. As his right leg pitched in front of him, Holmes caught his arm.

Beyond the door the yard vanished. At his feet an immense pit opened. Its sides were a nest of roots, thick as a man but blasted. On the bottom the slippery wood was cracked, torn through as though something of astonishing girth had been wrenched from the ground.

The Duke knew what he saw but his mind rejected it. "It was a horse," he said obstinately.

Holmes shook his head. "When you looked. And apparently when Houseman did. What I saw was an oak."

But it was Harwood who, no longer caring to look, saw their peril. He was tired of their gibberish and wanted merely to return to the college. He looked over the rim without interest. He saw the tangle of wood. There were stones as well, he noticed, halfway down, boulders really, gripped between the gross fingers of the wood as though by pincers. He did not examine them closely. The pit was black and the boulders merely outlines. But at the same moment there was a searing light. For an instant, as starkly as in the woodcut that hung in his study, he saw against the bands of wood the perfect whiteness of the stone. It was enough. Before the darkness closed again and there came the hideous boom of thunder, he saw the chance that what was stone might also be a thing that watched him. Shadows became eyes, cracks reproving mouths. Legs, that seemed too thick to move, bent their ponderous knees and climbed. Five tall figures rose, cast before them the carnage of the tree, and clambered up. Beneath, three others were advancing.

He saw their crowns, fire-gold and gleaming. But as he saw them Harwood blinked. And then they were no longer kings but eight bare stones. Black clouds rolled overhead. Halted on the brink of the chasm, the huge blank stones, now silent, were slathered by rain.

5.

"But when we came down upon the carcasses,"
the crow said, "Duinn drove us away."

"The dead are his."

The crow fluttered down beside Wykeham's
shoulder.

"Ah, but what I wished, lord, was so little,"
the crow rasped. "I might have been satisfied to
pick at a bone."

Wykeham stared into space. He was accustomed to the crow's
bitterness. "You will find no comfort," he said. "You are always hungry."

"One small knuckle," it said. "Where is there harm? In Black
Wood there are dead enough."

Wykeham frowned. "They are Duinn's."

"To the least strand of hair?"

"Yes."

"And the nails?"

"Even nails."

"And memory?"

He was being drawn into the old argument, and on the wrong
side. "All that was given," Wykeham said softly, mouthing the
words he had ceased to believe.

They had crossed the boggy meadow into the wood. The storm that had come up from the sea in the evening had gone before dawn. Despite briars and the dampness, he was dressed in one of his better suits. But though she was the cause of this attention, for the time being, he put Janie Hawleyville out of his mind. He thought instead of the Pope-Hartford.

Through the trees he could still see the roof of the old stable where the car waited. Wykeham grinned. He imagined himself hurtling down steep roads into the morning. He could almost hear the roar of the engine, almost feel the roughness of the rain-washed air prickling into his eyes.

He thought, it is the nature of crows to grumble.

Looking back over the yard, Wykeham felt his heart lifted. He was in love, now, after nearly half a century.

No, he would not listen to the crow.

His house and his grounds, the green meadows and the deep woods of Greenchurch, lay all around him. Changed but unchanging, they provided the background before which, one life to the next, he moved. They would pass. One after another they would vanish. Everything vanished. But something always sprang up in its place. Under the trees the dark air flickered. Spots of sunlight seeped through the foliage.

Wykeham smiled.

Always there was something new to touch, something new to see and feel. He thought, not even an ageless man can hope to live long enough.

On the spur of the moment he decided to take Nora with him.

He owed her that much. Twice already he had promised to take her to Bristol. It would not greatly matter if she went along to the school. Her presence, although it meant the dress shop first and alterations done on the spot, might even reassure the headmistress.

He had been to a shop. He was trying to remember just

where among the streets and alleys he had found it, when he saw the loose, weedy slabs of stone, tumbled down from the tower.

Wykeham looked around uncomfortably.

He had not intended to go into Black Wood. Yet he had only himself to blame for that. Out of habit, he went to bed late and rose too early.

While it was still dark he had washed and dressed. He had polished his own boots in the empty kitchen. Finding his solitude unnerving, he had gone to his desk and begun a letter to the Duke of West Redding. Ostensibly the letter was about the cost of ladders and scaffolding, a request for advice on a fair price for roofing the rotted patch over the library. In fact, he had written at the beginning of the month, a more necessary letter, which after rather longer than was customary the Duke had somehow not as yet answered. It had seemed untidy. Perhaps His Grace was simply getting older. Nevertheless, it paid to be certain.

The last drops of rain had skiddered across the window pane. At the edge of the world the bold light had risen. Light flooded into the valley, drowning the hills and farms.

His mind had been restless and he had found himself staring idly at the paper, daydreaming about the girl. He had put the unfinished letter aside and had gone onto the porch and then down the steps into the yard. In his mind he had been rehearsing his speech to the headmistress.

Fortunately, Janie's father was to be detained for some weeks by his business. He had already advised the school that his daughter would need to stay on at the academy for part of the summer. He should not, therefore, provided the headmistress agreed, prove overly difficult.

Wykeham had entered the meadow. The crow had come down to him and, together, they had drifted into the wood.

With an almost palpable sense of regret, Wykeham realized that he was not where he wanted to be.

He was less than a mile from the house. Yet when he came under the trees, the little path shriveled. The oak boughs, meeting overhead, thickened, turning the underwood moldy and dark. He was not surprised. The darkness had been deliberate. He had planted the grove himself, back in the sixteen hundreds, on the folded slope of the hill to conceal the huge stones. Even then the shoulder of the hill had closed around the base of the tower. Only the last heap of stones had risen above the ridge. Now, in less than four hundred years, whole new sections had fallen.

Wykeham went up to it. What was left of the tower leaned drunkenly. Unhappily, he lifted his neck.

Once there had been rooms without number, chambers and high vaulted halls, cocklofts and armories. The passages twisting between them had run out onto the walls. On the walls themselves there had been heralds and, under the open sky, yards filled with horsemen.

He had been a boy then, eager and dissatisfied by turns, frightened and waiting for something to happen. Like a child's, his eyes had flashed open with wonder.

Once the fair land undersea had been shining.

When he had ridden into the city, Lord Duinn beside him, all the colors of the harbor had danced on the stone. But the whiteness of the Great Horse Duinn rode had been more dazzling. Stunned, he had turned his head. He had looked very hard at the walls and the towers. He had looked everywhere except at the Stallion. Still his boy's fingers had ached to touch the white mane. In his heart he had already been a thief.

Out of a long pale face Duinn's deep sea-black eyes had watched him cunningly. He knew, Wykeham thought, even then.

It had been another time. Except for the scattered islands, all the West had been ocean.

Wykeham surveyed the rock. The great door, high above the ground, and the many shuttered windows were now no more than a few ragged holes. The flights of broad stairs, after years beyond counting, were merely a jumble of stones.

The old griefs boiled up in him. He waited for the crow to speak, knowing it must and not wishing to listen.

"And the Horse?" the crow said.

Turning aside, Wykeham began to climb up on the tower. He struggled over the boulders, for the handholds were gone. Blackness gave way to grayness. He grunted. The crow flew up to him easily. Wykeham pushed on through the branches and dug between thorns. At last he came out of the shadow and stood on the head stone, looking over the drive. The house and the stables were below him. In the distance, obscured by the green of the wood and the green of the meadow, there were two other towers, two more of the nine. But their rough mounds were broken, their stones carted off by farmers for back steps and cellars, remade into foundations and dry walls.

The crow settled down beside him and tilted its head.

"Since the world began changing, I have kept it," Wykeham said with conviction.

From where he stood he watched the women come out onto the porch. It was his porch. He had set the posts. He had planted the hawthorn whose branches wound into the railings.

"Well, perhaps nothing will happen for a while," the crow said.

Wykeham considered all that he had made and done. Now more than ever he did not wish to part with it.

"I am going to marry," he said.

"Do you not fear him, lord?" the crow whispered.

"Always."

"He will come for her."

For a little while Wykeham was silent. "There are other worlds," he said.

The crow laughed. "And he has gone into all of them."

Wykeham stood in the sunlight and thought. Before him, in

the lines of the walls, the squares of the meadows, he saw the spare ordered beauty of his own hand. The wide, windless landscape, the large country house at its center, was a picture he had fashioned, had marked with his longing and fixed with his thought. What had been before, what was Duinn's, eroded, was now nearly lost. It did not matter he had come to the tower. It was passing; all that had been, the ancient, violent warring world, would vanish.

Wykeham looked out, almost seeing the world that would be.

"With each day I grow stronger," he said. "Soon there will be a new land, a land which he never entered."

The crow looked at him.

"Indeed, lord," it asked quietly, "how will that be?"

Wykeham reached down and scratched it under the beak and along the left side by its ear. "I shall see it," he said, smiling, staring over the valley.

The stone moved beneath him.

Wykeham turned, too swiftly perhaps to have noticed.

Pressed by its own enormous weight, the stone never felt the weight of the man. There was nothing to be felt. (It was not as yet aware of the difference between one thing and another, certainly not between a man coming into the wood and a man, after a time, leaving it.)

It seemed only a moment.

Old R'gnir reeled back, rising from the unspeakable darkness, from the choking stench of his blood. . . .

It had seemed like forever.

Stupid with fatigue, he had pulled himself up the rough tower stairs, away from the battle. He had expected the pain. In his heart he had known he was dying, was perhaps already dead. He pushed the monstrous thought from him.

In the end he had only been crawling. Yet it had been too much to crawl and to think, too much to listen to the pounding of boots gaining behind him. It had been enough to know that he must not die trapped in the rock, in the darkness.

At the top, before the high windows, he looked at the waste of the city, at the world that was gone.

The blow had come at his back. . . .

R'gnir moved his thick neck. The live, bitter fragrance of oak-flowers filled his nostrils.

He looked up at the blue shining sky. He looked down. At his feet there was a solid mass of trees and beyond it the green shut-in valley. Loping across the field a dark-haired young man lifted his arm. A crow fluttered out of the sunlight.

R'gnir blinked. It did not matter that everything shifted. There was a white bird now and a black field. It was all much the same.

The young man, his hair pale as the ghostly blankness of a photographic negative, continued to raise his long arm.

Nora drew back the thick curtain, on the chance of getting one last look at the diminishing figure, in a print dress, striding heavily away from the house. Instead she saw the stableboy digging his boot in the gravel in the shade of the drive. Wykeham had come into the room. He stood silently just inside the door.

Nora pulled her hand back.

Her face, she was convinced, was scarlet.

Deliberately his eyes did not rest there. Rather he looked where she was staring. A single branch, growing close to the ground, swung idly in the breathless air. Deer perhaps. Even in daylight, the deer, wandering among the bracken and the May-bushes, often came quite near the house. But the hearts of the deer were gentle. The least gesture caused them alarm. Wykeham held his head still.

Whatever had been there had gone.

"Is there some trouble in the village?" he asked.

Before she turned to him she had tucked the letter in the waist of her skirt. "Only women's talk," she said mildly, certain that this would not interest him. She ran her delicate fingers along her neck.

He would not let her see he was smiling.

"Put on your shoes," he said. He did not have to explain they were going to Bristol.

Her breasts jiggled.

The Pope-Hartford, which was higher and grander than she had first imagined, gave a second alarming bounce. Nora held herself tightly. The river winked in and out between the dark trees. The car swerved, pulling her away from him.

She had been caught off her guard. Somehow the letter had slipped down under her skirt.

She gave a wriggle, trying to draw it back. The letter, unmoved, felt satisfyingly thick against her.

It was an immense sum, nearly three hundred pounds. Undoubtedly the steamship agent had sent a cheque. Somehow Plum had managed to cash it. Not that Nora had exactly asked her; under the circumstances, ignorance had seemed perhaps safest. But, however it had been accomplished, Nora was genuinely glad.

She was free, or could be, if she wanted.

Now, in the streets of Bristol, or, passing speculatively along the aisles of a shop, she could, if she dared, walk away from him. He would miss her then. Nora smiled. He would be in a panic. But when he returned to the house, she would already be stepping out of a taxi she had hired herself, wearing a dress that was already bought and paid for. She teased herself with the thought. It was as lovely as the feel of the letter, sharp-cornered and snug, pressed into her thighs.

Only it made her blush more deeply.

"I should like a blue dress," she said all at once.

The sides of the car, like the sides of a carriage, were open and her hair blew all over her face.

Almost tenderly he drew a strand away from her mouth. "A half dozen blue dresses," he said. "But there will only be time for one fitting."

163

"Are we in a hurry?" Her voice sounded odd because she had been holding her breath.

For an instant his eyes left her. "I have been thinking," he said. "It is a big house. You and Olivia can scarcely be expected to keep up with all of it."

For a moment he seemed not quite to know what he wanted to say.

"I have engaged a maid," he said quickly. "Or nearly that."

"Is it so difficult?"

He touched her arm.

"Is that difficult?"

He gave a little bark of a laugh. "Not so that it matters." He held his head still. He said: "Yet, in one or two things you might be of help."

She tried not to look at him. She did not want to know what was expected. It was only because the sky was so bright, she thought, so huge and so empty, that the tears came, squeezed out almost invisibly from under the lids.

The dressmaker fussed about her with pins. The woman was old and bent. Her own dress brushed the floor, covering all but the tips of her slippers. Nora shifted. In the glass she caught the woman's shrewd eyes watching her.

"You must hurry." Nora insisted.

"Don't you worry, dear," the dressmaker said. "He knows well enough how long this takes.

In the hall outside the fitting room a chair creaked. Nora was silent a moment. "How would he know that?" she asked.

The dressmaker said nothing. Her crooked fingers stirred lightly on Nora's back, straightening a seam. She felt the quick movement of the younger woman's breath.

"You look lovely," she said reassuringly.

Nora watched her reflection in the glass. Her eyes were gray black, hard and shining, like the eyes of a crow.

"What is she like?" Nora asked her.

"Who, dear?" the dressmaker said.

Nora moved. Her image moved with her. Faced with the inexplicable, Nora smiled shyly. I am a country woman still, she thought. The dressmaker lifted her shears.

"Myself I have a shop," Nora told her. "In New Awanux." Her voice was strained. Without knowing why she began to cry again.

6.

At first Willa Brelling behaved as though nothing had happened. Her deepest instincts told her that this was wrong, that some explanation was due her. But it was no good wishing for one. She was dead. It was impossible to question that. She remembered the details too clearly. She had been wholly resolved on suicide when she climbed the stairs. She had loved him. Because she loved him still, she was not revengeful. He had deserted her but he was also dead.

Had there been no bequest, no money, she would have followed him more quickly — with a knife over the thin bones of her wrist or a pistol at the forehead. (She had never been squeamish. It was not her own blood she feared.) Sometimes she wondered if the money were not a form of blackmail. It was as though, awkwardly and as unprepared as any of her girls, she had carried his child.

Nightly, the money swelling within her, she would turn away in the darkness. But he was stubborn and would come to her in her sleep.

You must care for this for me, he would say, softly, drawing the covers over his shoulders.

Tortured by longing, she would put her mouth clumsily against his and feel, instead, the dry woolliness of the blanket. She knew he was only pointing out to her the gulf between the dead and the living.

She did not wish to listen.

"I shall find you," she would say.

He would lie in the darkness of the bed, still shaking. He would be so cold he would hunch forward, hugging his chest with his arms. He had a real child and a wife.

"Let me come to you," she would plead with him.

No, he would whisper, your task is not yet over. The words were hard. She had given him everything. He had no right to claim more.

She would press her face into the pillow. Closing her ears to him, lulled by his silence, she would sink deeper into sleep. But long after, when he had left her bed, she would hear his footsteps by the window. She knew he was waiting.

"Yes," she said, once, quietly, unreconciled.

She lived on. She built the hall.

She hired the architects herself. She visited a dozen firms in Bristol and New Awanux, interviewing not only the principals but the plain draftsmen before she made her choice. Afterward she sat on the lawn among the confusion of carpenters with the plans rolled out before her. She was interested in everything; details great and small kept her awake at night. During the day she plied the workmen with questions. She mounted the scaffolding and stood up so close when the men were lifting the stones for the chimneys that at last they had to make rules about where she could stand and when she could shout to them. It was beyond their comprehension that a woman could spend day after day contentedly watching. Yet at the close of each day, as the warm dusk was deepening and she rose to return to her rooms, out of respect they stood themselves. They waited until she had departed before they left the hill.

"Well, that is settled at last," she said on the day the hall was finished. She put on a white dress and a veil. She shut the door behind her carefully and carried the rope to the top of the stairs. She did not cry out. The immensity of her love made her shy. "You see I am here," she told him and very quietly she broke her neck.

The moment should have passed.

Instead she felt the stone and the wood of the hall entering into her. She was astonished. Day after day through the huge arched doorways passed books and laboratory tables, jars of specimens pickled in formaldehyde and brine, glass retorts and Bunsen burners, until, finally, the last room was filled and ready and the first girls marched up the stairs. In the beginning she was silent. She simply hadn't thought of death in these terms. Impatient with the living, she could hardly bear to hear the lessons going on inside her. Hungrily, she waited for eve- ning. The long autumn nights were velvety and cool. The rain trickled soothingly on the tiles of her roof. She listened to the sounds of the school. The hall was at the farthest edge of the court and quiet. An acre of lawn separated it from the main buildings. After evening chapel when the girls returned to their dorms and the last sounds ebbed into silence she waited for sleep, waited to extend to him, however desperately (and if only in dreams), all her unused emotions of love and longing. But she never slept, and now that she was dead, never dreamed, and the severe young man who, once, when she was needing love, had sworn it, never came.

Was he not also dead?

They had told her that.

There had been lawyers and bankers and papers to sign. There had been no casket, no grave. She had a sense of a cavernous ocean beating silently beneath the thin crust of the earth. His death had burst through it. But it was she who was going to drown.

Now, when the sun rose or was setting, the hall would be pervaded by a cold miasmic dampness, by the cool smell of oceans. Darkness lapped in the corners, sunlight danced on the ceiling, intermittently, unhurried. But now always the rooms were full of the slow, mournful sound of the sea. The sound settled on her, came in with long and sharp whispers, possessing her. Her throat, which had been closed by wonder, by longing and fear, suddenly opened. It was then that she had begun to scream.

She was only wood, only stone, only a blurred mist by the stairs. No no one heard her exactly or saw, beyond question, her presence. No ropes were found miracuously dangling from the banister. The beakers boiling in the laboratory never darkened vulgarly with blood. After a decent interval the whole affair lay generally forgotten. Within the year the headmistress, because it was the newest building, removed her office to the second floor of the hall, not a dozen feet from the stairwell. When in a span of years she retired, the new headmistress kept the same office. The death, like so many deaths, was put aside. The girls who had been taught by Willa Brelling turned wives or scholars and went their ways. It was the new girls, daughters, then granddaughters, young women born decades afterward, for whom Willa Brelling was merely a figure in a perplexing tale, who in fearing the hall preserved her memory.

Somewhere over the playing fields a crow sounded its harsh, mocking call.

The Pope-Hartford stopped at the side of the court. She saw him at once. Out of twenty windows simultaneously she watched him climb down. She did not move, for she could not. Though she was burdened and numb, her ardor reached out to him. He was still distant, yet she felt herself spinning. Overcome with amazement, she began to weep.

Please God, she cried, let him come.

He walked to the other side of the car, walked as she remembered, moving casually in a world of his own interests. He was not a phantom. He was so much like himself she knew at once he was not dead, could never have been.

The woman tilted her neck. Willa saw her, a plain, rather unremarkable woman in a blue dress.

She watched him lay his hands on her waist, watched him lift her, solicitously, as one might an invalid. The woman appeared to be trembling. His hands still supported her. He spoke to her quietly. But the woman was frightened. Murmuring softly, he looked toward the hall. For the first time her upturned face fixed on him. There was a question in her eyes. Nonetheless, when he turned away from her, she followed.

Willa was not prepared for the touch of his hand on the door. Across the doorposts and along the beams of the ceiling there was the faintest twinge of alarm. Suddenly he was inside her, could be felt walking, one direct step at a time, along the polished boards of the floor.

There was an odd, joyful smile on his face. The woman, hurrying next to him, weighed the look. "Must I really say I am your sister?" she asked.

The smile had not faded. "It would be helpful."

"It would be a lie."

"Perhaps not so much of one."

"I do not understand," she said simply.

"We live in one house," he told her, "chastely, like brother and sister."

He began to climb the long stairs. Willa found the sound of his footsteps confusing. It should not have been so. In death she was so much larger. Truly, he was no different now from the other small creatures that invaded her rooms in daylight and went away in the evening. Except that he was himself. Should that matter? She had known him but four or five months. In all the years of her life that was so little time. In the years of her death it was less.

He moved quickly to the top of the stairs, to the place where even now some part of her, entrapped, was still lost. He paused, staring blankly. His hand, the hard blunt fingers, clutched Nora's arm. It was scarcely an instant. His attention turned.

"Yes," she told him, speaking swiftly so that she would not change her mind.

He was about to answer.

"If you wish," she whispered, unwilling to be interrupted. "But I shall remain in the house."

He watched her for a moment.

She waited as he opened the door of the headmistress's office.

Wykeham smiled, at her perhaps, or at the florid woman looking up from a book at the receptionist's desk.

"Mr. Wykeham?" the woman asked.

Wykeham nodded.

The headmistress came away from her desk and gave him her hand and shook his vigorously. She made a scrupulous effort to avoid noticing his youth.

"I am pleased you could see me," Wykeham said. "My sister," he continued.

"Miss Wykeham," the headmistress said charmingly, steadying her gaze on her. She was a woman of forty, athletic and handsome. Her hair was cut close to her forehead. She wore a white blouse, a purple scarf, tweed skirt and great brown riding boots. She took Nora's hand firmly. Pressing it, she ushered them both to a set of black chairs arranged starkly around a small table. A very elegant little table, Nora noticed, on which there rested a vase and a lamp. Nora looked around silently. The office was large and well proportioned, with two fine long windows looking out on the court. Yet somehow she got the impression of darkness. There was a strange smell, stale and disturbing. Nora found it vaguely menacing and she caught her breath. Perhaps she was not, even now, quite accustomed to expensive things. She turned a little. The woman was watching her.

"What a wonderful room," she said suddenly.

The headmistress smiled. "Of course we have your family to thank," she said evenly.

Wykeham's eyes darted toward Nora.

"You are kind," Nora answered. But her face was glowing. She took a seat quickly at the end of the table.

The headmistress selected a chair across from her. "Not kind at all," she said crisply, "simply honest. It was a most generous gift."

Wykeham frowned. "It was long ago," he said.

For the first time the headmistress looked at him directly. She became aware of his solidity and his quiet and was puzzled. She knew well enough what she thought of old money; she was less certain what she thought of young men. Although men, the trustees had the good sense to absent themselves from daily affairs. Having more pressing concerns, they hurried through the accounts and passed on, thankfully, to the brandy. After a few tedious hours, they were gone. Wykeham, on the other hand, had been seen lingering on the grounds of the school on six separate occasions.

On each he had spoken with the Hawleyville girl. He had spoken as well to several of the teachers. They had the impression that he was a student of provincial architecture. In any event he had asked a good many questions about the hall. It had come out eventually that he was a descendant of the school's great benefactor, that he had, in a sense, a proprietary interest. Word of his presence had come to her. If by the third visit she had detected a delicate situation, the headmistress allowed herself the benefit of a doubt. A renewed acquaintance with the Wykeham fortune would be advantageous. She had not acquiesced yet she waited.

His letter had arrived in a fortnight. If she had hoped to prove to herself that the situation was not really delicate, the letter put an end to it.

She let Wykeham see her look when she glanced down at the letter she had carried away from the desk when they entered.

"It was good of you to come and explain," she said.

"It is naturally a concern of yours," Wykeham answered.

The headmistress smiled. "I took," she said, "the precaution of writing myself."

"To the father?"

Her smile lingered a second or two. "He has concerns himself," she said coolly. "Regrettably, his business keeps him away. So it has been left, as with matters of her welfare generally, in the hands of the academy."

"She will be disappointed," Wykeham said.

"Do you think so?"

"Not to see him," Wykeham added, "now with the term ending and the summer ahead of her." He looked across at Nora. "It is with that in mind," he said, "that my sister and I have proposed an alternative."

"You are not actually acquainted with the family, I believe," the headmistress said.

"No."

"You, in fact, only just met her."

"Only recently, here at the school. I had come to look at the hall."

He was not looking at her but at Nora. He continued to stare, frowning slightly. She stared back at him, uneasy, knowing more was expected but too uncertain and too nervous to venture anything. She knew she should leave this place, leave him as well almost certainly. Only there were moments, few and rare enough, but moments, like the instant on the stairs when he had taken her arm, which she saw as proof of his feeling for her. It could not be, must not be, without reason. Did she not, sometimes, fill his thoughts? He had taken her in. He had kept her since. She was conscious, by the steadiness of his gaze, that she filled his thoughts now.

She lowered her eyes. She had no doubt that she disgraced herself. But the whole morning, coming in from Greenchurch to Bristol, had been shameful. She had not meant to weep. Though she had told herself over and over she understood him far better than anyone, she realized that she had entirely misread him. Even the old woman in the shop had seen him more clearly. How often had he gone there? she wondered. With how many women?

So as not to cry out she stopped herself from thinking.

The headmistress reached out her hand. "Miss Wykeham?" she inquired.

Nora moved away from her. The envelope, tucked up where it should have been safe, fell at her feet.

Nora froze in her place.

Unhesitantly, Wykeham leaned forward. Between his fingers he could feel the envelope's thickness, could see along the torn edge as he lifted it the large bundle of pale green notes. Without a change in expression he placed the letter in front of her. She did not move to reclaim it. He saw that she was strange and ill. "Nora," he whispered.

The sunlight, pouring in through the windows, lit her face.

She counted her heartbeats, waiting for the woman to turn on her. The envelope lay face up and accusatory on the table, the name typed in clear bold letters by the steamship agent: NORA BRELLING C/O LONGFORD . . .

Not Wykeham, she wanted to scream. Not his sister, not even his lover, only a harmless lonely woman in a blue dress, a stranger with no right to be here and no claim on him.

"Nora," he said.

She struggled helplessly, trapped by all the things she was not.

The woman sitting across from her did not appear to notice. Yet her keen blue eyes watched Nora thoughtfully, looked down at the letter and looked back. Again the woman's gaze met hers, swiftly, but without incrimination.

"I am tired," Nora admitted. But she realized, her thoughts unfolding violently, that it could only be the room's dimness that made them so stupid and blind. In the court beyond, the trees caught the day's pale illumination in their branches; their long shadows, cast into the room, fell wrinkled, light and dark, on the table.

"If only you could see!" she exclaimed. She reached across for the lamp.

But just as the light increased, she was distracted. For a breath's space she stared, seeing not the letter but the table under it, its plain surface glowing suddenly as a thousand tiny scratches caught the light.

She saw the hair first, saw in the nest of serrations the flat tongues of hair licked down and touching the face. The head itself was floating. Nora turned. The face turned and she thought with relief, It is my reflection. For an instant she wanted to throw back her head, wanted to look at them boldly.

It is nothing, after all, she thought thankfully.

Then the eyes opened. With a shock of alarm they caught sight of her own startled eyes staring into them.

"Oh, my God," Nora murmered.

He slipped his arm around her. Both of his hands were touching her; he was searching her face.

She continued to stare at the head.

"I'm all right," she told him, nodding, watching the head nod.

But her eyes were unfocused, as though she were not in the room but somewhere close by, looking back.

"It is a big house," Nora said all at once, a mere whisper. "Day after day, I am alone in it." For a long moment she was silent.

She could see the head clearly, its poor haunted eyes straining to look up, to be sure she was there. Such sad eyes, lonely and watching. Its lips moved.

"My brother," she said. Her voice stopped.

She looked up and found the headmistress's baffled face watching her.

"My brother," she went on quietly, "is often gone. It would

be a comfort to have someone. Someone . . ." She extended her hand toward the envelope.

It was a moment more before they understood that she did not mean to take it, that she was only pointing.

"I would be grateful," she said, speaking so softly she could scarcely be heard. "The family would be grateful. Would be generous."

They sat motionless.

A soft rustle came from the outer office and then the sound of a knock at the door. It was the girl. Nora was certain of that. Still she did not move. She did not wish to see her, not before it was over, not before it was paid for.

"Please take it," she whispered, her gray black eyes watching them imploringly. It had never occurred to her that it would not be accepted. The head wanted it done; she wanted it herself. Even her mother, she remembered . . .

"It is not a gift," she said distinctly; "it is owed."

IV.

Indians

1.

 The letter lay for a moment on the desk where the Duke had tossed it. At last it was dawn. The sun, rising out of the harbor, cast a ruddy glow on the paper. Even the faces of two of the men, His Grace and Harwood, their defiant voices carrying into the bank's deserted corridors, were tinged with red.

The Duke shifted his weight in the chair. He adjusted his spectacles. The river, to which he had turned to avoid looking at Harwood, winked between smokestacks and steeples. Holmes's face alone was without color. He had kept his back to the windows, watching both men. Wearily, he took up the letter His Grace had discarded.

"He wrote something," Holmes said. "We accept that."

"As you might," the Duke muttered. He was drinking, had already drunk too much to be quite certain of the use of his reasoning. Yet surely some things were beyond question. "I have had a hundred letters," he said. "Since he was . . ."

"A boy?" Holmes asked ironically.

The Duke scowled, recognizing that this was, in fact, just what he had meant. He had already told them of his discovery.

For a moment he recalled Wykeham's face as it had looked

on the train, the same face that had greeted him here in this room nearly forty years before.

He had explained it all carefully, how he had walked out onto the platform of Water Street station, how in the window of the passenger car he had seen the young man, who, after four decades, was as he had been, exactly.

But it was the face of a boy that was set in his mind, a lad of seven who had written the very first letter that had come, signed with William's name, from Egypt. For two months he had known it was a lie. But it mattered.

The Duke sat very still. He looked down at his own blunt fingers.

He said, "It is in his own hand. Isn't that enough. Do you question that?"

Harwood moved to the windows. "It's not that it isn't," he said too loudly. "The point is that it needn't be. Not any more than at the pit . . ."

He did not continue. Each man knew what the other had seen. Hours afterward they still felt the thick hands reaching up from the roots and the gravel, still saw the grotesque legs, bending what should not have bent, begin to climb.

It all had lasted through the space of counted heartbeats.

Then they had heard the gale scream once more, felt the rain beating down.

Harwood turned again, wandering. "It's just that it might have changed," he said. "It needn't be, word by word, what he sent." He walked out into the middle of the room. "I know it's crazy," he whispered. "My God," he said helplessly, "I thought you were both crazy."

The Duke poured another whisky into his glass.

Harwood glared at him. "It was you," he said doggedly. "You brought me out there. All the way out you kept badgering me, kept asking me questions, telling me how everything I thought I knew was changed." Harwood shook his head ruefully. "Well,

I believe you now. Every damn thing's changed. Or could change. Anything might."

"Almost anything," the Duke said.

"Is that it?" Holmes asked, surprised.

"Is that what?" Harwood wanted to know.

Holmes stared again at the letter.

"Anything," he said calmly.

The Duke set his glass on the desk.

"Something has to be fixed," he said.

"And that one thing . . ."

The Duke nodded, relieved, and at the same time not caring. He alone knew the immensity of Wykeham's strength and his cunning. Knew more, at least, than Holmes, who, although he had gone to the train and examined the body, could not have spoken more than a dozen words to Wykeham.

It was now morning. All night they had sat together in this room, talking, trying to think through the puzzle they were caught in.

The Duke glanced blearily at Holmes. He was aware of the small man's good intentions. "Since he was a boy," the Duke said, "he wrote me letters."

"He was not a child," Holmes reminded him.

"I know."

"It was you who explained it," Harwood said.

Harwood's insistent voice interfered with the progress of the Duke's thought. He lifted the glass.

They were not responsible. Holmes was merely the doctor called by chance to the death. Harwood, although he had known Wykeham longer, nonetheless shared no common act with him, no offense.

The Duke sighed.

Wykeham's life, he was certain, must have touched without consequence a thousand such men. He was not himself so weak and neutral. He had taken hold of what was given him, coldly perhaps, he knew that, and half in ignorance. But no matter what he did not know, a man was dead because of him.

"It was not an accident," the Duke said. "I will not accept that it was an accident."

"Men die," Holmes said.

Harwood's eyes moved from face to face. It had been his argument, but he had lost control of it. "What are you talking about?" he asked tensely.

The Duke dug his hands into his lap. For a long while he was quiet.

At last he said slowly, "Two months ago a man died on a train. He was a young man who worked in this bank. I had put him in charge of the Wykeham Trusts."

The Duke looked down at his fingers. "He was a man like myself," he said quietly. "No better, perhaps, yet no worse, not above doing what had to be done. He was supposed to meet Wykeham only once. Only talk to him once. It is written right into the Will, was written, over three hundred years ago. Surely that never changed. But Houseman . . . Did I say the young man's name was Houseman?"

Harwood shook his head.

The Duke studied his fingers. "Well, it was Houseman," he said.

"There was a young man," Harwood repeated. "And he took a train."

"And he should not have."

Harwood's eyes clouded over. "Does that matter?" he asked.

"Wykeham was on the train," Holmes said evenly.

"And there was a prohibition against that," said the Duke.

Harwood threw up his hands.

"The man died," Holmes said.

"He was murdered," the Duke added quietly.

Holmes's eyes darted up. "We don't know that. We cannot be certain."

"You might as well be," said the Duke. "You took the photograph. One of us, at least, should admit it. And you told me about the woman. I never saw her. Never heard what she said."

"What woman?" Harwood demanded.

Holmes turned to look at him. "There was a woman on the train," Holmes explained, "with the body." He waited, but Harwood only stood staring miserably. Holmes rested back on his arms. "A wretched, stupid woman, I think. She believed, quite inconceivably, that Houseman was drunk."

The Duke watched Holmes carefully. "It was what she said."

"What Houseman said really," Holmes corrected him. "She was simply repeating it. Saying it over and over. As he did."

"Which was?" the Duke insisted.

"The world's coming apart," Holmes said, each word measured and spare, but the meaning fell heavily.

The Duke nodded, content. "That was the first instance."

"Of what?"

Almost in spite of himself, as if enjoying Harwood's confusion, the Duke grinned. "Of anyone noticing. Seeing the world pulled two ways at once, literally ripping apart. Everything he knew and he trusted dividing inside of him. And not stopping. Never stopping."

The Duke tilted his head. He squinted at Harwood's round face. "You saw it yourself," he said, "for an instant, outside the barn."

Harwood would not look at either of them; he was trying to think. But all he saw or could think of was Wykeham. "Maybe he was a little stranger," he said, "a bit quieter. But he was kind."

Harwood felt his mouth tighten.

"He would smile, I remember. Never much of a smile, as if things he knew amused him. But he never spoke of them. Three years and I barely knew him. Then one day he brought me a letter."

Harwood paused. He seemed to be listening to an inner voice. "The next day he was going. I went down to the train."

He heard his own rough sounds of grief and looked away.

From the windows he saw across the green the bleak college towers jutting into the morning.

All his adult life he had spent cloistered in private rooms with the Dutchman, with Austen and James, believing each word added wisdom. And it was nothing. In a wink it could be replaced.

"There was a crowd," he said. "I never . . ." He lowered his head.

Holmes returned the letter to the desk.

The four sheets of white paper lay in front of Harwood.

In that instant he knew.

It made no difference. He had abandoned any plan of action. What action is possible? he wondered. Yet it was abundantly clear. He had already read the letter. Not this letter, of course. But he had sat, with Wykeham beside him, at his own desk with such a letter, staring into the morning.

Harwood looked across at the desk. The events of his life, all of which he had thought chaotic, whose scattered moments he had always found bewildering, fitted, he realized, row on row, in a line of cunning duplicates. He did not look ahead. The world was behind him.

He reached back and unfolded the sheets of paper.

"My dear Martin," he said, reading. He looked up. "That is your name, Your Grace? Your Christian name."

Martin Callaghan, the Duke of West Redding, moved in his chair. "Yes."

Harwood nodded, returned to the paper. "My dear Martin," he repeated, his voice clear and precise and a little too loud as it always was when he was excited. The sun had lifted well above the harbor; the room, although it had been garish, was filled with an easeful light.

"In a little while it will be night again," he read. "I have done what I could yet the war is near. I have a daughter. Before too much longer you must come for her. . . ."

* * *

Michael Morag was having trouble adjusting his eyes. The breasts for one thing, though they were certainly breasts, seemed to bulge and lean without a normal regard to the stresses and strains of flesh, without respect for the sensible laws of gravity. For another, they hung so near to his face, were each so amply capable of filling his sight, that from one moment to the next he could not decide which to stare at.

He moved his head sideways. The breasts swayed, tugged asymmetrically, as if he watched them in a distorting mirror.

I'm afraid this won't do, the Reverend Michael Morag thought. Reluctantly, he allowed them to vanish.

The world became gray again.

He had a sense, at least, of grayness, of a place somehow betwixt and between. There was a light but he was outside the range of its radiance. The shadows lay at a discreet distance, drab as a monk's habit and as unremarkable. He took no notice.

What was needed, he imagined, was something plumb, with corners at right angles. Something boxlike and square, he thought, like the cottage in Black Wood. For an instant the thought was so sharp, so familiar that it made him homesick. But a cottage, he rather suspected, could be tricky. After all this was new to him. He might as easily arrive under the porch steps with old John rocking senselessly above him, too deaf and, as likely as not, too impaired by his whisky to heed. And he had no desire to be stuck under the joists, a fool of a dead man, hollering, banging up at the boards. So in the end he resisted the temptation.

Nonetheless he was by nature much too cheerful to be subdued by mere inexperience. It must be, he became suddenly convinced, that one begins more modestly. Perhaps with a table, he thought, encouraged.

He happened to glance up.

Plum was staring across the dinner plates at him. Her generous bosom, which had become agitated, bounced up and down with alarm.

The old minister mopped his bald head. "Ah me," he sighed appreciatively. He smiled at her. Altogether too broadly, he recognized, but death, he hoped, had its prerogatives.

He tilted his head and was astonished and more than a little pleased to discover he was sitting, in fact, in his own parsonage. He looked around at the heavy plates and thick glasses, at the starched white linen, relieved that they were not much changed.

"I hope you don't mind," he said, aware that, as far as he knew, he was now quite powerless to undo his existence. "I imagine this is distressing."

"Who's this?" Longford asked, coming in at just that moment from the kitchen.

Plum breathed again.

"He was simply there," she whispered. But she had almost said nothing. Morag bestowed a slight gracious bow and a provocative grin.

"Dear, dear," he said. "The husband, of course. I might have thought of that."

Longford stared. He fancied an unaccustomed pink now suffused Plum's cheeks, but her head turned from him.

"Who are you?" Longford asked. "How did you get here?" He was agitated himself and, although both questions had been directed at Morag, he continued to look at his wife.

"Name's Morag," the other man answered. "Though I've always thought just plain Michael sounded friendlier." He spread his hands across his stomach and clasped his thumbs. "I know I haven't been asked," he said thoughtfully, "but there are a few bottles of porter down in the cellar. Boxes actually. I laid them in myself. And if it wouldn't be too much trouble . . ."

"You're Morag," Longford murmured, his voice grave.

The old minister clasped his thumbs tighter; his kindly face wore an expression of honest bewilderment. "Didn't I just say so?" His large bald forehead wrinkled. "Yes, I'm quite certain."

"The Reverend Mr. Morag," Longford told him.

Morag stared at an empty glass. "Michael," he said.

An odd flicker passed across Plum's face. "The Reverend . . ." she started.

Old as he was, Morag's dark eyes filled with laughter. "No longer, I think," he chuckled. "Not much use. Even less opportunity."

He unlaced his brown fingers and reached for the glass. "Of course it comes as something of a shock," he went on, patting the crystal. "Thirty years in His service. But they don't let you know beforehand." He gave a good-natured shrug. "I don't know. Maybe it's not what it seems. Perhaps He is somewhere."

Morag was suddenly quiet, wrinkling his forehead and staring at the glass as if he saw two conflicting shapes in the reflection and was not quite decided which was wanted.

"Though hereabouts," he declared, "for the most part it's Indians."

Almost as soon as her head touched the pillow Plum was asleep. Longford, still dressed in his shirt and his trousers, lay beside her. From the moment he had succeeded in getting her off to their bedroom he had wanted to talk. But she had gone about her preparations with unaccustomed privacy. While she undressed, he had caught her watching herself in the mirror, the very lifting of her head, the smallest turning of her mouth as she smiled, excluding him. It had seemed to him then that she was half a stranger; indeed it had seemed so all evening. She had filled a plate for Morag with her own portion and, with a maternal absorption, watched the old man devour everything greedily. Later, on her own, she had disappeared into the cellar, thumping back up the stairs shortly with four dusty bottles of porter tucked under her arms.

"They're his, after all," she had whispered, passing her husband and seeing his frown.

Morag had poured out two glasses for himself. The glass he

had poured for Plum she accepted readily. Longford's, untasted, remained in the middle of the table. In a few minutes Morag had reached for it. He had smacked his lips happily.

"It's a pity, don't you think," he had said, "to have wasted so much life wondering if there were delight both in the world and out of it?"

Longford had turned. He had expected to be frightened by the old face. He would have been, he realized, had Plum but showed the least alarm. There was a dead man at his table. For twenty years he had preached the certainty of resurrection, but he was not, lacking her, prepared to meet its confirmation without panic. Lazarus rose and so did Christ. He believed in miracles, but only in a far-off time, or in the world to come.

In their bed, watching Plum sleep, he understood how thoroughly he depended on her being near him. Every now and then her breast rose and there came from her lips a faint and barely perceptible moan, the sound distant and yet profound, as if something far beyond his reach had shaken her.

Unable to calm himself, Longford went down stairs. Morag was sitting where they had left him. The old man had brought up four more bottles from the cellar. Already two of these were empty.

"Don't you sleep?" Longford asked impatiently.

"Perhaps a little," Morag answered. "Though just from habit. No point in it."

Longford stared at him foolishly. He had wanted to rail at something. Death had entered his house. Yet there had been no outcry, no horror. He desperately wanted to be driven against something else, something more clearly appalling and obscene. He wanted, at any cost, to save his wife. But the ordinariness of the old man had robbed him of the usefulness of his anger.

Longford looked down at his feet. He had forgotten his shoes.

"You might join me," Morag said amiably.

"How are you here?" Longford shouted.

Morag raised his glass. "Because," he said, "I find it difficult to imagine women." He held the glass out at arm's length and gazed at it thoughtfully. "Have you ever noticed how difficult it is," he asked, "to call their faces to mind? Or any part of them? Not the general idea. That comes easily. But the specifics. The precise turn of shoulders and noses. The exact shade of their skin."

Morag's large splotched face looked a bit sad in the gleam that came from the lamp in the parlor.

"Of course geography's easier," he said. "The hills above the old towns stand out sharply. And the river certainly. From high up, coming in from the moon, you can see . . ."

Longford gasped. "F-from the moon?" he stammered. He was struck by a sudden vivid image of the river, not as he had mapped it, not even as he had imagined it would be from the hill above Greenchurch, but from an airy distance away from the earth. For an intolerable moment he saw it, a ribbon of cold-blooded light, turning among the hills and the towers, imprisoned, wriggling back on itself.

Their eyes met.

"Like a serpent," he whispered, "its tail in its mouth."

The old man smiled at his innocence. "Like the living," Morag corrected him. "Like the dead."

2.

Jane spread her long legs, enjoying their naked-
ness. Though he was gone, the pillow still smelled
of him. More than likely she smelled of him herself.
You wicked girl, she thought gazing contentedly
at the tumbled sheets. Her new dress lay over a
chair on the other side of the room. She remembered that she had been faintly surprised when
looking down from his bed she had seen it there, without her.
They had not, she knew, exactly agreed on any of this.

They had gone directly into the great room after dinner. For
a quarter of an hour she had sat beside him under the odd old-
fashioned woodcuts of horses, on her best behavior. Through
the half-closed door there had come a sort of listening silence.
The cook had been introduced at the table. But the old woman
waited with the others gathered now in the hallway, anticipating
a more formal introduction, at the head of the line.

"You'll do fine," Nora had told her. Yet the hand which
had reached toward her was trembling.

Jane thought at first that his sister meant simply to give her
a pat, the fingers unheeding and as perfunctory as the questions
about her schooling. But the hand which dropped into her palm
was cold and, when Nora straightened, Jane felt the small weight
of the ring she had left there.

His sister glanced at her slyly.

"Heaven knows he will not have thought of that," she whispered.

Wykeham, paying no attention, was watching the door. He was dressed for riding in a suit of brown corduroy and long black boots. An old cloak hung from a peg on the mantel behind him. Its clasps were bronze; its hem, if once stitched with care, now was torn. Somewhere a window was open. Assailed by a gust of air, the ancient fabric turned restlessly, first one way, then another. Wykeham lifted his head.

"Is Mrs. Norfolk here?" he asked.

As if on cue Lizzy appeared in the doorway. She had washed her hands and abandoned her apron. Her heavy gray hair had been pushed into a bun.

"Lizzy," he said, "this is Miss Hawleyville."

Jane felt in that instant somehow different. Wykeham, his mind elsewhere, scarcely looked at her. Yet she knew unmistakably that the situation which should have been awkward would not be and that, curiously, he was the cause of it. She had been conscious of this oddity from their first meeting. Nothing directly happened and yet always something was set in motion: slowly, with an almost casual inevitability, everything she expected, all that she had been taught to expect, changed.

The mountainous old woman bent one huge knee, curtsied.

"I hope you will be pleased with us," she said. Though she did her best to smile, her eyes, Jane thought, were more suited to fierceness. Yet a charm seemed to hang on them. They jerked to Wykeham's face, suddenly, fondly, and then back again. The woman took a step forward. There was something knotted in her hand.

"It is but a token, miss," she said.

"Oh I couldn't," Jane protested, not even seeing what it was.

Wykeham laughed. "Then you must say no to all of them." His voice had become a deep chuckle. "And to me as well."

She had thrown back her head to look at him, when he kissed her. It was the first time they had openly kissed, there in the great room, in front of the women. He was still holding her, his hand pressed quite deliberately under her breast, when a second figure edged the door open and came into the room. She had not even a moment to collect herself or to savor her feeling of wonder.

The man was tall and stoop-shouldered, his large horse-teeth stained. But his wild hair had been combed and he had been fitted out in a jacket that looked as if it had been borrowed.

"My lord," he said softly. He moistened his lips.

"Say what you have come to say," said Wykeham.

Fred Norfolk pulled his big hands from his pockets. He turned what he had brought over in his fingers.

"Lady," he said slowly, seeking courage, "it is well you have come. A woman is a prop for a man in times of great trouble. In such times . . . In these times . . ." He moved a little, uneasily. Because he had come into the light she could see his face struggling and guessed that he had rehearsed the words. Norfolk took a great breath. "Lady, it is well," he began again.

Without looking she knew that Wykeham was smiling. It gave her a mysterious pleasure to feel how easily she had come to read his moods. The man had grown pale. He loomed over her, clearly trembling, his practiced words tumbling over each other. With a part of her mind she listened, trying to discover why he stood there and what he wanted. But the other part, detached and unpuzzled, felt Wykeham's hands pressed hard above her waist.

"On this night of all nights," Norfolk went on solemnly, "I am honored to greet you . . . our little sister . . . our mother . . ."

Lizzy hissed at him.

Norfolk turned red. Quickly he gave what he held into Jane's hand and drew back.

The room became quiet. The only sounds were the one the

little breeze made and the rustling of the cloak. Jane's eyes moved between them, uncomprehending.

"L-lord, I never," Norfolk stammered.

"There is no harm," Wykeham answered, "only eagerness. How could I fault eagerness?" Wykeham smiled at him. "On this night of all nights?"

Jane was sitting up stiffly. "What is he saying?" she asked.

"Hush," Lizzy told her.

Once again the door opened.

One by one they entered now, making their way in from the dark hallway. For a moment they hesitated before her, watching her, lingering as long as they dared: George Tennison first, then Olivia. Adam France and Jakey pressed in close behind. Then suddenly the room was filled with a great cheerful company, nudging and laughing. There was a line coming in from the kitchen, small farmers and their wives who now and again did a job or two at Greenchurch and a man who had walked the ten miles from Ohomowauke, though the moon that night was only a sliver. By ones and twos they came forward and presented their gifts. But along the wall a woman, afraid her child would cry, kept back timidly until Wykeham saw her and called her out. Beaming, he took the child and let him crawl in his lap while the woman approached, curtsied, and pressed a small parcel into Jane's hand.

Jane was left staring blankly.

"I was hoping you didn't mind," the woman told her.

The child was quiet, respectful. His little face peered at Wykeham, then at Jane. He grabbed at her hair.

"Ah, lady," the woman whispered, "I just couldn't keep myself away."

Jane was trying to listen, but the words seemed irrelevant. Without giving up the child, Wykeham had slipped his hand down and was loosening her dress. Then once more he kissed her. In the merest fraction of a second, before she could make up her mind what she thought, two dozen voices laughed and cheered.

She rolled over on his bare shoulder. It was not quite morning. They had not slept. She was certain that she had not, not that she remembered precisely all that had happened from the moment he caught her up in his arms. She had opened the door to his room because he could not have. His hands had been filled with her and the small, unopened presents she had borne away in the folds of her dress, presents which with his fumbling and fiddling had seemed ever in danger of spilling. And they had spilled, finally, onto the bed, falling all around her as she fell, drawing him after.

The cool morning air played about them. It swept behind her and snatched one end of the coverlet. With feigned modesty she tugged back and, by chance, touched the edge of one of the little parcels. Inexplicably, it had not been scattered by their lovemaking. She moved her fingers over the tightly wrapped paper and into the loops of the ribbon.

"What are they?" she asked.

She could not see his face, but she believed he was watching her.

"What is usually given," he said.

She let her fingers rest and snuggled into his shoulder.

"It's customary then?" she said, grinning to herself. "A poor girl's deflowering?"

"It's been done before."

"Not to me." It was but a small demonstration of her independence. But the old memory awoke in him and he caught himself staring at her, looking at her as if for the first time, as if, even now in his bed, in his heart as well, she were a stranger. She was a child, after all. The feel of a man inside her was new to her. He drew his finger along her thigh. There were so many things she did not understand, too many things he had not told her. And he must, despite the enormous difficulty of explaining.

And he would. He was determined that this time it would be different. Listening to her breath, he remembered how, on a thousand other nights, he had been haunted by the terrible knowledge that the arms he held, that held him, would soon wither and grow old. The round flesh that bound him and would be bound by him gladly, would swell and rot. No, he thought, no longer.

He lay back in the darkness.

"They are wiser, love," he said. "They knew what was expected. They brought what must always be given."

He felt her head turn.

"What must be given," he repeated, "for a child to become a woman. Whatever there is to be wished for: beauty by one, the second virtue, the third cleverness . . ."

He stopped because she had squirmed.

The grayness grew a little, widened, and he could see the small line of her breasts.

"You treat me like a child," she said.

"No," Wykeham said.

"It is a story for children."

She was shivering now. This time, when she hunched over, he did not touch her.

"Tell me," she whispered, her face set, only her mouth working. "One day do I climb the attic stairs to a door? Do I say 'Good morning, mother' to the old woman waiting inside with her spindle?"

Agony was filling her.

"Do I prick my finger?" she asked.

He let her go on. Because she was beyond comfort, he did not try to comfort her. She had grabbed at the bedclothes. He knew that it was his body that she knotted and twisted. Her tears, when they came, were heavy and splashed down on his arm. He did not hurry her.

The window, as it would be winter and summer, was open. The air was thick again with the smells of morning, hawthorn on the wet porch railing, damp hay, mist from the river. Morning always came so, he knew, the earth raw and dripping, as it first rose, from the sea. In the new light he cast a long strange shadow over her.

So Duinn first saw himself whole, he thought, recognizing the man-shape — in the world before mirrors — in darkness.

He began to speak, so quietly that she had to lean forward. Thus, in spite of her hurt, she was again drawn to him and felt, next to his ribs, his heart beat, unexpectedly.

"What if it were a story for children?" he asked. "Would it matter?"

"Yes."

"They are all children."

"I am not." Her eyes were wide open now, staring.

"Everyone . . ."

"Once," she insisted. "But it changes." She had put out her hand, not to him, but he had clutched it. What she had reached for was not there. For a moment she had not even thought of him.

Her mother was dead. Her father, who when his knees were stiff and his legs unsteady she would help up the stairs in the drab little hotels where she had been taken on holidays, whose visits she nonetheless cherished, had been kept away, the headmistress had said, by his business. She was his only daughter. Without shame, ignoring the smell of his whisky, she had cheered him and had comforted him in his loneliness.

For a vivid moment, in her mind's eye, she saw his stooped shoulders, his sad grizzled head.

"You don't see," she cried suddenly. "But it changes. We start off. We have parents. We are their children. But it stops."

"And if it did not?"

He had pulled aside the coverlet and she could see almost all of him. Except for his face and his arms, which were deep-tanned, the rest, the lean muscled back and the long hard legs, although equally dark, were, in a way she could not quite place, unblemished. Unused, she remembered thinking afterward, protected, like the smooth inner wood under bark.

The sunlight flooded in through the window. He was sitting up in it.

"What if there were a man," he said, "in the very beginning of the world —"

The light, and the words as well, because they had the sound of another story in them, annoyed her. "Like Adam?" she said suspiciously.

"No," he said. "Just a man." He leaned back and seemed to take a long look at her. "Not even a man," he said. "Not at first. A boy. But he grew. He turned into a man and, like other men, he met a woman. And, after a time, there were children and the children grew, as children always have. But one day the woman, because finally she was an old woman, died. The man mourned her. He waited to be dead himself. But he was not. For something had happened to him. He did not die. In fact, he had scarcely changed. He was still the young man he was when he stopped being a boy. But he was alone, mourning the woman. So in time he found another woman. Perhaps as beautiful and as kind. Perhaps not. As before, there were children. But this woman also grew old and, like the other, also died. And the children, though themselves parents, also died. But the man still was."

She was listening but she was not looking at him. She was watching, as the light turned more gold, the faint variations in the shabby plaster on the bedroom wall, the blistered paint on the door. In the rooms below there had been new paint and fresh plaster. She had seen that when he had brought her into the house. On the ground floor there had been hammering and men in overalls. The workmen, in fact, had been everywhere. At intervals, through the first afternoon, she had counted over a dozen. But she had lost count altogether, when after dinner they had trooped into the great room. It was like a small private army. Coming into the room, she remembered, they had bowed to him.

"They called you lord," she said in astonishment.

When he was up and gone, she went to the door and looked out. Sunlight dappled the landing but the top of the house was empty. Sounds drifted up from the kitchen. She closed the door, and, because she was still naked, locked it.

"What if a man kept on having children?" he had asked her. "Not only for a lifetime but for a hundred lifetimes? For a hundred times a hundred lifetimes? For longer?" He had paused.

It had seemed to her like one of those unsolvable problems they gave you in school. If Adam had two sons and each, in turn, had two sons . . . But that hadn't been right either. Not Adam. He had denied that. But some man having children.

She lay again on the bed. Absurdly, feeling where he had been, she uncrossed her legs. They had argued. But her recollection of the argument was muted, was mixed with the slow warmth of the sunlight and the touch of his arm on her neck, his hand on her thigh. Now that it was done, she was much less frightened than she had expected. He had wanted it but all the while she had known she might have stopped him and in the darkness it had been she, though he had been everywhere, who had found him. "I have never been happier," she thought. "Nor has anyone," she thought more grandly. Perhaps it was that that made her remember the argument.

How many people were there in the world? she wondered.

"If one man, the same man, kept having children," she had asked, incredulous, "for a hundred lifetimes?" She had given a little gasp.

"Longer," he had said. "From the beginning."

"Then . . ." The word had almost the sound of a conclusion but he had interrupted her.

"Everyone," he had said, "or nearly that, given time."

His eyes were black, his hair blacker, like her own. She could smell the scent of his skin. "No," she had said furiously.

Long after she could hear the sharp hooves of the stallion on the gravel below. She was hardly listening; instead she had pressed her nose into the pillow. By the time she had gone to the window he was already halfway across the lawn. He was walking the stallion, its legs and its shoulders deep in the hay.

Clouds had come up but there was still a patch of blue sky over the top of the hill toward the wood. On the nearer slope, before he turned and went from sight, she saw him stop and unbutton his trousers. The pressure of her bare flesh on the windowsill awakened a hint of delighted wickedness in her body. With a tinge of surprise she watched him relieve himself in the grass.

She had been raised chiefly by women. "He is a boy after all," she thought, smiling. As she went on smiling, her face lost the least trace of wickedness and she went back, for a moment, to being a child herself. She turned quickly and with the unconscious morality of children, knowing herself naked, began to put on her dress.

3.

 In the books they had read together, books which for the most part Wykeham had given him, the women were pushed off until the end, a reward presumably. But here, Harwood thought, they were, his wife and his daughter, inconveniently in the middle. The Duke, of course, could come and go as he pleased. Holmes was married. All the same, Harwood did not think it greatly impeded him. Doctors' wives, he was certain, were accustomed to having their husbands called away unaccountably.

Harwood thumbed through his wallet, counting the few notes, and threw them all down on the table. "Twenty pounds," he said unhappily, realizing that His Grace would have to pick up his share of expenses.

"We can look after ourselves," his wife said with dignity. The girl, playing on the floor before the woman's feet, had not lifted her eyes to look at him.

"Just a few days," he said in despair.

The woman let herself be kissed. Behind her the little kitchen was hung with laundry. She had washed his one good shirt, straight from his back, when he had come home that morning. It lay starched and expertly folded in the bottom of his suitcase.

She had packed it herself with his underwear and his second pair of trousers.

"I would like to wear it again," he explained and she nodded, distracted. Through the open window, hours before, when he had only just arrived, she had caught a glimpse of the old gentleman climbing into the limousine. If he were anyone important, her husband had not mentioned it.

"I cannot say what will come of this," he had told her. He lifted out the shirt she had folded carefully, put his thick arms into it. "But the details have to be the same, I think. Or nearly so."

He was taking the overcoat.

"What do you want with that?" she asked.

She had the uneasy feeling that he was already gone. "It's summer," she put in scornfully.

Harwood looked past her.

"That first night I had it," he said.

It had also been April — or March. He had forgotten which and wondered now if it mattered.

"I must be going," he said, gently, and stepped out the door.

She watched him go down the walk. She did not know how long she stood by the curtain. It was not until she had turned back that she saw the suitcase open on the table.

Harwood went along the High Street and through the park, as he had come before, without luggage. As he crossed the intersection, cars with stone-faced chauffeurs hooted imperiously. Let out from shops and offices, men and women pressed into buses or, retracing familiar routes, melted anonymously into pubs and houses. Harwood trudged on doggedly. His Grace had been prepared to drive them all, Holmes included, out by the river road to Greenchurch, but Harwood had protested.

"You and I must start at the station," he had told him. "Please understand."

But he had not. "And Holmes?" he had asked.

"I must get on at Bristol, Your Grace."

The Duke had sat with his back to them, overlooking the city. During the night it had seemed clearer; but now, the whisky deserting him, he had not been able to think.

"How will you get there?" he had asked.

In fact, Holmes had taken a taxi.

"It seems a foolish expense," the Duke said, meeting Harwood by the information booth. Under the great dome of the waiting room his voice did not sound angry but humiliated. But he was not thinking of the money or, indeed, of Holmes. A daughter, he thought. It seemed impossible that Wykeham had not told him.

Except for the one secret, he had been told everything. He had earned that trust. He had worked indefatigably. It was he who had always been summoned to deal with lawyers, with loose ends, with death. But the one thing that counted, a child, the passing on of the inheritance, had, until the very end, been kept from him. It wrung him to think of it.

He walked stiffly beside Harwood. Because the evening was mild, the doors to the platform had been left open. They could both see the train.

As they neared the gate, Harwood stopped, shocked by the clarity of his recollection. His eye crept along the line of car windows.

"There ought to be a woman," he said.

The crowd of passengers, already boarding, were finding their seats. No face peered down at him.

He had not wanted to look this far ahead, to visualize anything too completely, as if all their lives had been plotted. But at bottom he had kept a list; he was checking against it.

"She was staring out of the train," he said, almost desperately.

For the first time the Duke noticed that Harwood was carrying the overcoat.

"There were two women," he reminded him. But Harwood had forgotten the other.

It depended, the Duke realized, on who had been watching.

And three men, he thought. Four, if he counted himself. But he did not think he should be added; there had been nobody watching him. Harwood, he remembered, had walked ahead but he had stayed where he was. There had been no part for him. The Trust, even his office in the bank, had been given to Houseman.

The Duke was looking up at the train.

The sky, because it was summer, was tranquil; its lingering brightness glowed a soft reddish gold. In the cars the lights had been turned on. The faces of the passengers, illuminated in equal measures by the sky and the lamps, shied first one way, then another, nervously.

The engine expelled a cloud of white steam. From behind it came the bark of horns, the sound, almost lost under them, of ships' bells in the harbor. In the first car, by the window, a man took his seat.

Harwood looked and saw nothing. He glanced sharply around.

"Perhaps I was wrong after all," he admitted. "We could just as well have driven." He paused, looking back at the station. "I thought that if we could just repeat everything, one thing after another, as it happened, something would change. But it hasn't." Dejected, he walked away. "Are you coming, Your Grace?" he asked.

The Duke's eyes were fixed beyond him.

The face staring from the car window was printed indelibly on his mind: the thatch of dark hair and the high forehead, the deep hard eyes watching.

The man was looking out at the evening.

"At the light that was fading," the Duke told Harwood afterward. "Regarding it contemplatively," he said later, "as if it were something important, to be gravely considered."

It had only been for a moment; the head turned.

"We must hurry," the Duke said. Taking hold of Harwood's arm by the elbow, he pressed forward.

The train crawled past shipyards, past the tight-packed roofs of the slums, following the river. The Duke sat up in his seat. It was his second night without sleep but he was no longer tired. "He did not see us," he said in a rapid, low voice, his eyes shining. "He was not looking for anyone. He would not have expected anyone." His own face beamed. "But he was seen."

The sun's rays had disappeared. The plain of the river had become a cavernous darkness. Harwood did not care to look at it.

"Why should you be the one?" he grumbled.

The conductor had come through, collecting the tickets. The Duke paid both fares.

"Compensation," he said cheerfully. "You must admit I was owed something. It was my decision which sent him to his death. I felt the pain of it. It comes down to that, I think. Payment for sorrow."

Harwood frowned. The dead man, sitting no more than a dozen rows ahead, did not look very dead. Yet from the back it was difficult to make judgments.

"I could walk up front," Harwood suggested, "to the lavatory."

"What would you see?" the Duke objected. "He was no one you knew."

"I could see if he looks like a man."

"He does," the Duke said flatly.

"I could see for myself."

"Isn't it enough that I told you?"

"You!" Harwood nearly shouted. "Why you?"

Beyond everything it was this which had troubled him. If the world had changed, if this was an instance of its changing, why had he been excluded?

He looked around miserably. "Why should it be you who noticed?" he asked.

But His Grace had already given his answer. "Perhaps it only happens in pieces," he added sympathetically.

"What?"

"Just a bit at a time," the Duke said. "Only changing things that he thought should be different."

"That who thought?"

The Duke looked at him doubtfully. "Wykeham," he said.

Harwood shook his head. It was the same argument they had had in the bank; he was still adamant.

"Not Wykeham. Not pieces either," he said.

He was remembering the woodcut that hung over his desk. The pattern, he recalled, once altered, changed incrementally from one tessellation to the next. Yet, looking back, he had never been able to tell just where the change in the pattern had started. A hundred times he had tried to find the place but always there were shadows, glimmerings, a place farther off for every place he looked.

"No," he said fiercely. For an instant he looked straight at the Duke.

"There are differences," he said. "But they had always to have been there. Or to seem so, afterward." In his excitement, he leaned forward.

A lock of his ginger hair had fallen into his eyes. He pushed it back with his fingers. He said, "What changes one thing, I'm afraid, Your Grace, changes everything."

"But it was William," the Duke persisted. "Or at least it was Joseph."

"What makes you think," Harwood asked, "that only he could be the cause of it?"

"Cupheag," the conductor called sharply, announcing the station.

"Metichanwon," he said later.

But when he should have shouted out Bristol, he did not.

The train slowed. The conductor came into the car and then left it. Three or four times the Duke noticed him in the passage between the car and the engine, speaking to someone up front. Each time he came back into the car he was frowning. The Duke wished the man would stay in one place. The movement along the aisle was annoying and he was trying to think.

"Your pardon," he said the next time the man passed him.

"There's been a delay," the conductor replied curtly.

"How long?"

The man shrugged.

It grew late. The Duke let his forehead rest on the window. The sound of the wheels came softly through the floor, a faint, even throbbing that made the sound almost tender. He glanced up. Houseman, to his relief, was still there.

For a moment he felt safe again.

He had listened to Harwood, had tried to think honestly what the younger man had meant. He knew that something had gone terribly wrong and equally that it had been put right again. A man was dead. Over and over he had tried to grapple with the shifting tides of that responsibility but he had felt himself being pulled under. Now Wykeham had changed it. "There is a place to stand again," he might have said. He had been beginning to drown.

"Christ Almighty!" exclaimed Harwood.

The Duke dragged himself up.

The passengers rumbled awake, their sleep-slackened faces jolted into alarm.

The river was burning. Across the water-meadows and the marshes on the outskirts of Bristol they saw the bright sheet of flame: a thousand tongues of light, not upon the water but within it, gleaming balefully. It grew bigger and brighter. But it was itself without height. Without heat. Without sound.

"Like a reflection," Harwood whispered.

He looked up. Even in the glare of the burning, his face grew pale.

"It's the city," he gasped.

"But how —?"

His Grace was staring.

The train crossed a small bridge. After a few hundred yards there was another. The sound of the wheels, rocking, echoed softly. Then the track, following the long curve of the bank, straightened. Suddenly the station was ahead of them. In the bright distance behind it the roofs of Bristol were engulfed in flame.

At the front of the car the door opened. The conductor walked through. He closed the door, locked it. The stricken faces of the passengers watched, unmoving.

"You must stay in your seats," he said evenly. "We will take only as many as we can. There is no need for panic. There are police on the platform. Everything has been arranged."

"What has happened?" someone cried.

"Fires," he said stiffly and went down the aisle and through the next door into the car behind.

The Duke did not watch him.

All around him was the confusion of the yard. Acres of track were sliding by him; odd little sheds and old carbarns flickered past. Usually untidy and blackened, they were now curiously enlivened. Touched with fire-gold and copper, they bloomed. The engine gave a small moan. The car bumped. Along the narrow platform, marshaled behind gates and high railings, crowds of people gathered by tens and by hundreds. The Duke did not feel their stares. His body did not seem to belong to him but to be floating above them, as the car passed, slowly, out of darkness, into light, again into darkness . . .

In the car the lamps were switched on once more.

He did not feel the blast of heated air as the outer doors

opened. All but unnoticed, Dr. Holmes, pushing his way through the men scrambling down the aisle, threw himself, exhausted, into the seat beside His Grace.

"I had fallen asleep," the Duke said afterward, as if that justified it.

But now he was strangely awake. His eyes ran down the rows of new passengers. More than a score had to stand, awkwardly, holding on to whatever they could find. He could not see Houseman. But he was there. The Duke was certain of that. The car was noisy with questions; he pushed his face next to Holmes's.

"Your wife?" he asked, almost shouting.

"I got her away this morning," Holmes answered. "With the children. Off to Cambridge." He was very nearly shouting himself. Yet some dread that had been in him relaxed a little. Still, his eyes did not soften. He said, "As far as anyone can tell, it is only this valley."

"It's only here, isn't it?" Harwood said. "Surely not in New Awanux." He had just remembered his wife and his daughter.

Holmes shook his head. "There were rumors this morning," he said. "When I came into the house, everyone was talking. We had time."

"We heard nothing."

"Then perhaps in the south there was nothing."

Harwood had to hunch forward to hear. "We were in New Awanux until evening," he cried. "No one said . . ."

Holmes's voice, raised above the voices nearest him, had at least the sound of honesty. "No one knew. There were only rumors at first. It was hours before anyone saw them and then they were so few. We just looked at them. Everyone went out into the streets. We all stood around on the steps of the houses, looking up."

His color was high, but it seemed less anger or resentment

than a kind of sad embarrassment, as if he had seen what should have been hidden. He turned, not meeting their stares.

"They fell so quietly," he said. "Here and there we saw one, on the ground, standing alone by the bridge that crosses to Redding, walking undisturbed in the conservatory garden. They were waiting as we were. But we did not know that they were waiting until there were more of them.

"All we dared do was watch. We did not speak to them. Yet I cannot help but wonder what I might have asked, what answers they might have given me.

"The odd part was they seemed to have nothing to do with us. Perhaps they were just watching. I counted seven on the lawn at Saint Stephen's before I went in to have my lunch. The house was empty, the bedroom empty. The shutters in my daughter's room were open. She had washed her hair, had been drying it in the sun before she left. I have tried to think if I shall ever see her.

"But I suppose I shall not," he said after a moment. "It would appear they are only men."

Harwood stared. "They?" he asked at long last.

"Indians," the Duke explained irritably.

Holmes looked away. "When there were too many to count," he said, "they began burning the churches."

4.

 "Flukes and flames!" the man cried, not yet seeing her. " 'The Pequod . . .' "

He leaned unsteadily against the counter and waved the book in the air.

" 'Freighted with savages and laden with fire!' " he shouted. " 'Burning a corpse and plunging into that blackness of darkness . . .' " The voice ended in a strangled yelp.

A moment later the book sailed by her head. Landing in the gutter outside the shop on Abbey Street, it joined dozens of volumes, their torn, stained pages fluttering in the breeze that prowled the late afternoon. The headmistress, thinking the man had simply been drunk, realized that he had been reading.

She stood in the doorway, clutching the envelope she had carried with her from the academy. It had taken her two whole days to trace the name.

"You are, I trust, finished throwing things," she said, fixing him with her fiercest, most reproving stare, the one she reserved for recalcitrant students and, more rarely, for their parents. "It is safe to enter."

He held on to the counter. By his elbow there was a mound of books. On the floor hundreds lay scattered. It looked as though there had been an explosion.

"Finished?" he asked severely. "Not till I'm rid of the lot of them."

"It is your business, I believe," she said calmly. "I am quite certain of that." She marched into the shop. "I had it investigated."

"No more it is," he announced, loudly. "I've stopped for good. Stopped forever." He picked up a book, spread the pages at random.

" 'Give not thyself up, then, to fire,' " he read, " 'lest it invert thee.' "

All at once his thin shoulders heaved; tears rolled down his cheeks.

"There, you see," he said helplessly. "It's all like that."

"Like what?"

"Like that. All opera and savages . . . howling infinities and poetry. Every bloody word of it."

He pressed the book between his small fingers.

"It was a book about finches," he said, trembling. "A very nice little book about the different shapes of their bills. But it isn't now. None of them are. They're all changed."

"I wouldn't know about that," she said.

"Almost no one knows," he said with terrible seriousness. His eyes were red. He looked ill. He stood up and staggered out into the room. "But I read them," he said savagely. "Hardly anyone did. Did you know that? But I did and I remember." He went to the shelves and began pulling books down. "Not these!" he cried, kicking them as they fell. "When I was at sea, sitting by myself with the engines, I was in the habit of reading: Darwin and Homer, Shakespeare and the Evangelists. I remember what was in them. Even now I haven't forgotten."

He put his head in his hands.

"You have a wife," she said.

He looked up. "I am not referring to that," he said.

"You have a wife," she repeated indomitably.

"No."

"And sisters," she said. "The oldest was an instructress at Bristol Academy. That was nearly fifty years ago. You were the youngest, the black sheep, if you will forgive me for saying so. I have had it all carefully researched. You drank, I am told. You were years at sea. When you came back, you brought a young woman." The headmistress was holding out the envelope upon which the name was written. "I have met her," she said.

Carl Brelling's face, as much of it as was visible between his grizzled beard and his sailor's cap, was red.

"Lies," he said. "Damn bloody lies."

He seemed so vehement that at first she hesitated, uncertain whether she ought to go on. She had devoted two days to calculating the new and wider scope for powers which, by the chance of a name on an envelope, had been opened to her. She would not let it pass. It now seemed that she had spent all her life preparing for just such an opportunity. Admittedly, it had sometimes not seemed much of a life: the headmistress of a second-rate private school, not even in New Awanux, but in a city of no particular importance. And little as it had been, she had had to struggle for it, without allies, by the sheer force of her will. The vagueness and obscurity of those years, the smug and yet indifferent faces of the trustees especially, stirred old bitternesses. But all the while something had been leading her. Forces she had not imagined or guessed had been tugging her into place. She had failed to notice. Then out of the blue Wykeham had come to the academy, bringing a woman. And suddenly the world that had so often seemed elusive and disappointing revealed itself to be, to have always been, her own.

"Your wife came to see me," the headmistress said, watching him closely, "in the company of a young man."

She could see his face more sharply now. She saw as well the poverty of the shop, knew he had never made much of a living at it, that now he would make none at all.

"Mr. Brelling," she said, "I am going to be of some help to you."

He was on his guard. "What kind?" he asked uncertainly.

"You are not a wealthy man," she said. They looked at one another. "I quite understand. For longer than I should like I have myself been lacking proper resources. There are many, however, who are not similarly troubled." For a moment she let him ponder that.

"Is there any good reason," she asked, "that either of us should continue . . . as we have been, when there is one young man for instance, who never had to give a thought to how he would manage?"

He seemed not to be listening.

His head was sunk on his chest, his eyes vacant. She was casting about for words to draw him to her, to fit him, a small, unhappy but very necessary piece, into the great cunning pattern she saw opening before her when he said: "She was only a child when I met her, no more than a girl with a head full of dreams."

Speech left him and he began to sway. He looked down at himself with contempt.

"I was old enough to know better," he said. "Yet, you know, in a way she warmed my heart. She wanted to marry a sailor." He shrugged his thin shoulders. "It seemed wrong to let her find out what dreams usually come to."

He shook his old head.

"Do you know," he said, "I was remembering her and I thought: suppose I had never gone to Bodø, never saw her striding down toward the sea, would I think of her? Would I still wonder if something were missing?"

He had gone beyond her, into his memory, but she knew she must not press him with questions. He was drunk and bad-tempered and, because he was feeling sorry for himself, likely to do anything. Yet she needed him. "There is a plan," she said carefully. "A definite pattern."

He lifted his eyebrows.

"The most insignificant parts," she said, "have a use and a purpose."

"What good is that?" he asked truculently.

"It helps," she said.

"How?"

"If you know a little, you can predict the rest."

He looked at her uncomprehendingly. "Why should that matter?"

The headmistress smiled.

"Though you had never met," she said evenly, "you would have missed her."

But again he did not seem to be paying attention.

He looked around at the shop, at its ruin. The air of the shop smelled of whisky. At last his eyes met her face.

"But she is gone," he said lamely.

"Then you must go and get her back."

"I couldn't . . ."

"That is why I have come," she said. "To take you." She turned on her heels.

He was not certain, even afterward, why he followed. But a moment later he was in the street, trotting behind her. He coughed and muttered but she would not hear. She was in a hurry, walking briskly. He trailed after unhappily.

Old as he was, it seemed to him that he had always been at the mercy of women. He had never intended it. Though they seemed always in a jumble, he had had dreams of his own; but then suddenly a woman would turn her eyes on him. He was not a big man, but he always felt himself getting smaller.

His fingers found the opening in his coat. Cleverly, he brought out the flask.

"It was not what I wanted," he grunted.

He put the flask to his lips. "It is not as it should be."

He could hear the gurgle of the whisky going down. His teeth chattered.

But it's the way it is, he thought bitterly, feeling himself in fact growing smaller. He had been sucking at the flask like an infant for a good half minute and was now very near the end. Soon, he knew, he would not be able to walk. Abruptly, he threw back his head. But suddenly, his attention distracted, he began to grin.

"Stand straight," she told him.

But he was leaning into her, his head lolling.

"Why's the sky red?" he asked, leering foolishly, as though asking a riddle. His hand, no bigger than a child's, was outstretched and pointing.

Her head turned.

From the High Street, looking out across the wide commons, she saw the great steeple of the old center church rising in a pillar of flame.

"Aye, we know something about that," he said darkly.

For the first time she seemed undecided. "What do you know?" she asked.

He cocked a bleary eye at the heavens.

"Savages," he said, disgusted. "Damn bloody savages and poetry."

5.

"What I cannot seem to discover," Harwood repeated in a temper, "is how you knew."

The Duke pulled at his chin. "Knew what?" he asked innocently.

Harwood blanched. His voice rose. "That they would be Indians," he said too loudly.

In the Royal Charles there were no more than a score of small tables, each packed closely with men. At the last and the smallest the Duke examined his glass. Harwood was watching him narrowly.

Half an hour before, they had followed Houseman onto the platform. They had seen him bobbling in front of them among the few dozen passengers who dared leave the train so near to Bristol. But when they had gone into the yard, he was gone, swallowed up by the darkness. No one had suggested they go straight off to Greenchurch. "We must have a plan," Harwood had said, and they had straggled along at a distance behind a pair of elegant young men who, having borne away with them nothing but their expensive suits and black fedoras, announced bitterly to the evening the fate of any Indians who, by mischance, might manifest themselves out of the air.

There had been workmen and laborers behind them, put off

in Devon because they had been short of the fare. Staring as Holmes had been staring, they had looked up at the closed doors of the houses, seeking some sign of welcome. But the long street remained silent. The gardens, full of old-fashioned flowers, peonies and sweet william, hollyhocks and roses, were as empty of dogs as of men. At the bottom of the green, a small boy, peeking from a second floor window, was gathered in quietly, the shades pulled quickly after him, the last porch lamps extinguished.

But the lights of the Royal Charles shone like a beacon. On the step by the broad, open door a man was singing noisily, with equal enthusiasm and disregard for the tune. In his hands he had held a portion of a quilt which, rid of its feathers, he was shredding for bandages. Seeing them, his solemn face broke slowly into a grin.

"New recruits," he observed and, smiling gravely, waved them on.

The Duke stared but Harwood moved past him.

With its low ceiling and one small window, the bar seemed half a cottage, half a shed. Harwood stepped down into the room. The other two followed, picking their way slowly among the chairs and the tables. By the time they had settled, the man on the step had gone back to his song. ". . . Nine on the hills," he was singing.

Holmes sat very quietly, his elbows on the table, his small hands cupping a match. Quantities of blue smoke filled the air about his head. Listening intently, he pulled on his pipe. "One met him face to face," the man sang,

> "one man alone
> bore himself bravely
> seated in his saddle . . ."

Holmes waited silently. The man at the door went on with his song. "When the stallion stood," he sang,

"there dropped from the mane
dews into the deep dales,
hails in the high wood,
whence Duinn his harvest . . ."

Holmes remained motionless. His eyes had faint lines at their sides.

"Perhaps I just drew it out of the air," His Grace was saying. His voice was cold. This wasn't what mattered. There were more important things to attend to. He looked across at Holmes, as though for confirmation, but Holmes only glowered.

"By Christ," the Duke added, "it was merely something I said."

"But you were right," Harwood told him.

"I didn't know it."

"You knew something," Harwood said tensely.

"He has a daughter," the Duke said. "I know that." He felt around in his coat, touching the letter but leaving it. Nothing showed in his face. "I have come out to find her."

All at once Holmes dropped his small hands to the table. "She may not be there," he said softly. Both men looked at him but again he lapsed into silence. In itself that was not surprising. For two days he had been the quiet one, the one who watched and who listened. Now, for several minutes some deeper quietness had seemed to move at the back of his eyes. For a long moment he looked about the room. "There is at least the possibility, Your Grace," he said quietly, "that she may not be anywhere."

The Duke lifted his head. "You disappoint me, doctor." He spoke as if it were a challenge. "I was sent for. I am here for the purpose of finding her."

Again there was silence.

"I never questioned that," Holmes said at last, his face and even his voice expressionless. "In a way we have all been sent for. That was never at issue. The question, from the start, I

think, is not what we are to do but what has got hold of us."
He stopped for a moment. "Before we even knew there was
anything," he said, "before we had even started to notice, what
already would not let us go." His little gray eyes stared without
blinking. "Each of us," he said carefully, "not just the two of you."

The Duke frowned stubbornly. He was about to speak.

"No," Holmes said, gathering his thoughts together, calmly.
"You knew him." He nodded toward Harwood. "You both
knew him. I did not."

He drew again on his pipe. "It cannot be Wykeham," he
said, stopping, pulling the fumes from the pipe deeply inside
him, "however remarkable he is. Rather, if you are both right,
if somehow he has been given the gift, or the curse perhaps, of
living forever, then really he is the very last thing it could be."
He stopped, puffing once more. "Indeed, he could only be the
enemy of what has taken hold, of what —"

The Duke turned on him. "It is not the dead man," he said
angrily.

Holmes paused. "Not the dead at all," he said. "But the
thing, Your Grace, whatever it is, that sees to the killing."

"I don't see —" Harwood began, interrupting.

"Or you never read," Holmes put in quickly. "It comes
down, I am almost certain now, to a sort of biblical question.
Though, of course, it's in Milton. Everything's in Milton."

Harwood's voice was like something tearing. "What is?" he
asked.

"Angels," Holmes said. "Devils, too, for that matter. I
haven't been able to decide which. They both can have wings.
But they are all, every one of them, men. You have only to
look."

"Look where?"

"In the Bible," Holmes said. "From Michael to Gabriel.
Lucifer to Beelzebub." He paused once more to consider His
Grace. "Or on the platform," he said simply, "or the train.
Even here, in this place."

The Duke was staring out at the room.

"Have you thought . . .?" began Harwood, but Holmes cut him short.

"I have tried not to," Holmes conceded. "Not even to remember." His clear, open gaze was without emotion. They had not, even then, begun to suspect what that had cost him. "I have a daughter," he said, "had a daughter . . . a wife."

He was looking at the backs and the faces of the men crowded under the rafters.

"Though by now," he said quietly, "like all the rest, I suppose, they are gone."

At the front of the room a man stepped silently over the threshold. For an instant, blocking the light, his huge shoulders threw a grotesque shadow over the floor.

They were aware, at first, only of red hair sweeping out like the halo of a furnace, a long red face as ferocious and unsympathetic as flame.

At the center of the room the tall old man halted. Wearily, he began removing his coat, freeing from the large shapeless garment first one arm, then the next. He unfolded the third and the fourth from where they were strapped to his chest. His mouth turning, as from some trivial discomfort, he withdrew the last pair from his back.

The arms were long, their flesh mottled with bruises and covered with fresh welts and scratches. Skillfully, with three of six great hands, winding with each the little ragged strips of the quilting, he began to bind his wounds.

"Someone fought you, then?" the barman asked.

"Some will," Charon Hunt said defensively. Stung by the implied criticism of his work, he turned away, looking instead at the room full of men. His own large face was plain, his grim frown dogged as an old hill farmer's.

"Yet they must come with me," he said with a harsh pride. "For how shall they cross," he asked no one in particular, "unless I carry them?"

· · ·

The world fell silent, the men behind him gone. But whether they found some hole to hide in was their own business. House-man was not curious about them. He had no great interest in his fellow men. His duty, as he saw it, was simply to find his own way. If now in the plain, shuttered houses along the dark street there were no signs of habitation, it did not trouble him. Though he was dead, he was not remorseful. He was surprised, however, that he was clothed in a good black suit and a white shirt with a firm, starched collar.

In the drawings of the damned, which he had carried out of childhood, the damned had been aggressively naked. The draw-ings had stayed in his mind and, although he had never been able to remember where he had found the book, he recalled ever afterward the massive torsos and ponderous legs of large, scornful men falling shamelessly into darkness.

He looked himself over carefully. I will need shoes, of course, he thought, only half wondering why that one item had been neglected.

Yet he could walk. The soles of his feet had somehow hard-ened and he went quickly over the pavement. His lungs, though they filled gently, scarcely needed the air: he might just as easily, he imagined, have been sucking in the enormous emp-tiness of the space between worlds. What little light there was left on the hill was the light of worlds, distant and receding. When he had entered under the interlocking boughs of the wood, the stars were not even a memory.

Thereafter, in spite of the darkness, he had gone swiftly for what may have been hours, except that it was not a matter of time. It was not, he supposed, exactly a matter of space either.

It was more like a jigsaw puzzle. The vague gray shape of the hill, the snaking contour of a wall, even the wood's feral darkness, while useful as points of reference, were only phan-toms. There was a deeper order, an arrangement in which hills, walls and woods, the clearness or mistiness of the evening were merely decorative. Underneath their momentary divisions, deeper and more permanent, there were lines. He had thought of them as lines at least, although he suspected they plumbed the depths and rose up, virtually without limit, through the heavens. They could not be seen, could not, either with hands or by the shiver of the flesh, be felt, but he had known when he crossed them. Having seen and experienced nothing, he had been forced nonetheless to acknowledge that he had passed from one sphere of reality to the next.

He had recognized it first on the train. He had awakened into the light, coming back to awareness on an old, damp seat, staring out at the smoky yellow light of the evening.

He had counted three worlds then: the one he had been born into and in which he had toiled unceasingly, year by year, at the bank for a reward that, when fate had granted it, death had taken; death itself, which although it was dark and empty, he was certain was also a place; and the world after, which was not empty and not, he was equally certain, either world he had left. For one thing, it was summer.

He had watched the huge evening sun falling past the vast roof of Water Street station. Feeling the light sweeping through him, he had smiled, a slight yet cunning smile filled with purpose, as if, by daring and perseverance, he had outwitted an ancient enemy.

He had crossed the fourth line at Bristol. From the train window he had stared straight ahead at the fires, smiling his brief triumphant smile at the glowing ruins of houses. He had licked his lips greedily, watching the bright bands of flame.

But under the eaves of the wood it was dark again. The village was long behind him. As he pushed his way in through heavy brakes and sharp brambles, there was nothing to be seen. The hill had vanished, even the grim old trees were invisible and, conscious only of darkness, he was left with a feeling of inescapable dread. At the back of his mind he could hear now and then a distant crow complaining somewhere in the branches. But the sound seemed to come from everywhere at once. Perhaps direction itself, he thought apprehensively, is immaterial. And yet he felt more and more certain he was advancing toward the fifth line. At all events, it did not matter which way he came at it, it was now Wykeham land.

His jaw had fallen open and he was drooling as he lumbered on blindly. Twigs cracked under him and he nearly slipped on the path.

He must burn, Houseman thought, angrily, imagining the purifying breath of flame that alone could free him, that would free them all, he hoped, from the damned white-faced English. But it was the rustle of the bare soles of his feet over straw that convinced him that he was outside the barn.

He stopped and, for a time, stood staring wildly into the darkness. At last, grown impatient, ignoring the one clear order Wykeham had given him, he gave a heave to the door so that the car, riding the double line of the track, could enter. He had, he knew, really no alternative: a door will not open by itself. His long clawed fingers clung for a moment to the latch.

The stench as of some old heavy animal in its lair was overpowering. He coughed and clamped his mouth shut.

The sound of men running, when it came to him, was slow and unnatural. The roar of the gun itself was deafening. Something crossed in the air. With a jolt he felt it enter him, felt the wall of his chest ripping open. And yet it was not until he had been lifted by what seemed too many hands onto the back of the ancient Ford pickup that he noticed the odd treacly smell of his blood. He lay groaning. Bitterly, with the shattered fragment of a wing, the young dead man covered his head.

Nora put her hand on his bed, passing her fingers caressingly over the sheets. In the warm summer darkness she felt more than saw that he was gone. She had expected that. He rose early. But he has been here, she thought, and so sooner or later, would be there again. Everything returned. In all her life she had not known it to be otherwise. But all the same she had wished for one last meeting. During the night she had dreamed of him; now with the sight of his bed she remembered her longing. "Ah, men!" she whispered but, knowing only too well her own inadequacies, she sighed. Kneeling down, she gazed without jealousy into the sleeping face of the girl. Jane was quite naked, her wide, ungirlish mouth open. Her bare arms were stretched lazily above her head.

"It is time," Nora said.

The girl's breathing went on quietly.

Without another word Nora began to undress. When she had taken off everything, she went to stand by the window. A small, hot breath drifted over the sill. Her nostrils twitched curiously. There was something uncertain in the air. But the yard below looked as it always did, the gray meadow quiet and still, the gardens harboring darkness. In the dawn the tops of the tallest elms seemed to sputter. Nora drew herself up. Around her the room was gradually brightening. But for a long moment she stood undecided, examining herself in front of the window.

Even now her body was slim and white. Her knees and the tips of her breasts were likewise pale. She lifted her arms. Only there was there darkness, prickly and damp, in two spots, and a third, in the crease where her belly ended.

Nora shook out her hair. Her head filled with memory, she tried to recall the bodies of the girls in the faraway village and found, surprisingly, that she was ignorant of what had lain under their shifts. She had not, although they had shared but a single room, seen even her own mother naked. Finally, she turned. The girl, the sheet drawn away from her, was, she had to acknowledge, the limit of her experience.

Watching her, a brief smile passed over Nora's lips.

Deliberately, her hand no longer trembling, she reached down, touching herself. In the crease between her legs the feathers were not as yet thick, just soft black quills.

Jane did not speak but Nora saw she was watching.

"I cut them," Nora said. "In the pocket of my apron I carry a pair of sharpened scissors." She gave a short laugh. "There is always the chance a man may wish to sleep with me. And being men they are easily frightened."

She managed a grin. "But always they grow again," she said.

Jane's fingers moved restlessly down her leg. "I don't think he noticed."

"Not in the dark," Nora said. "Never the first time when they are filled with impatience." She no longer looked at the girl. Where on earth had she ever learned such things? she wondered.

Her husband, of course, had been frightened. Yet his misfortunes he had brought on himself. He had not touched her. In the ignorant way of men who have learned what they know of honor out of books, he had never taken her to his bed until they had married. What is done is done, he had said afterward; but in the small bedroom over the shop his eyes were swollen with sleeplessness.

"Why did you never tell me?" he had asked her once, abandoning all caution.

"It has always been so," she had told him.

Jane dropped her feet to the floor.

"You go out and I'll dress," she said.

Nora's smile lingered. "What is the need?" she asked. "They are gone."

In the kitchen Lizzy and Olivia were already naked. Lizzy was packing away the last of the dishes. Olivia lowered her eyes rather than look at them. "Who will take care of the house?" she asked. "Who's going to make breakfast?"

"They will have to manage without," Nora said evenly.

They went onto the porch and down the back steps. But they did not start out. They were waiting. In the east the immense sky shone like a mirror. Even under the elms there was a blink of watery sunshine. But in the wood under the hill there was darkness. The wind that only brushed at their ankles seemed to blow harder there. The old, dark trees seemed to beckon. They tried not to look. Instead for a time they stood quietly, sunk in memories of the house and of the men they were leaving.

At last they heard the sound of Plum's heavy feet on the gravel. She came around the corner of the house, the crow on her shoulder. Its wings were spread, its weight gently balancing on the air, so the murderous claws would not tear her pink flesh.

"Well, it's begun," Plum said. Her large round face was haggard. In their black sockets her eyes had an expression Nora had never seen in them.

Jane lifted her head. She was the youngest and her face conveyed her confusion. "It's women and children first, isn't it?" she asked.

"The children have already gone," Lizzy told her.

"There was a boy," Nora said all at once, remembering. But it was much too late. Under the eaves of Black Wood the village women were gathering.

V.
October Wars

1.

The letters that morning, because the postman had punctured two of his fingers with the toasting fork, were smeared with blood. "Daughters of Belial!" the postman muttered, thrusting both fingers into his mouth. Standing in the middle of his kitchen he glared at the window and wondered why it was not yet light. He had half expected to see his old wife spreading strawberry nets in the garden; but the garden, like their bed, was empty. "And I was ever kind to her," he announced to the rooms from which she had gone empty-handed. The postman shook his gray head. Lifting his bag onto his shoulder, he stepped out onto the porch.

Above the long village street the stars were still shining.

In Black Wood John Chance rocked contentedly, taking no notice. In the summits of the trees a high wind was blowing. The old man never lifted his head. He was remembering the starry evening Okanuck had come out of the darkness to sit with him, remembering the woman who had arrived the next morning, slept in his cottage and gone. To his mind they both seemed to stand at a beginning. He remembered them because they had brought on a feeling of profound anticipation and because they had shared, with only a difference of hours, the moment of Wykeham's return. After fifty years something was about to happen.

He had no desire to join in their lives; he only wished to see for himself what they did. His own life, he had come to believe, had taught him almost nothing. Not that this mattered. It only meant that one life was never enough. What was needed, he suspected, was not a few decades but centuries, time to feel and smell the grain of existence and uncover its possibilities.

"Young Wykeham's home again," he repeated to himself, only slightly puzzled by the swirl of dry leaves that came tumbling from trees that had been old when Adam, barred by the angel, walked away from the wood.

Hearing the postman, the Reverend Mr. Longford rushed out onto the dark porch in his socks.

The postman stared at the minister's feet. "You in a hurry, Tim?" he asked.

"It's the shoes," Longford answered. His voice was strained, his eyes wandered. "Three pairs," he said thickly. His gaze turned abruptly to the host of small stars that by now should have faded. "Tried each one," he said softly. "But they all seem to have shrunk."

"You might have Plum stretch them."

Longford looked away.

"She's gone then, is she?" said the postman.

Longford did not answer.

To cover the moment's awkwardness the postman dug into his bag. When he had fished out the letter, he thrust it into Longford's fingers.

The minister looked down distrustfully.

"There is something wrong . . ." he began.

"Cut myself," said the postman.

Longford brought the letter closer to his face. "Where did you get this?" he asked.

"At the station."

"It's from here in the village."

The postman nodded. "Her Majesty's Mail," he said glumly. "Everything goes first to Bristol."

"But it's only down from the hill."

"Sent two days ago," the postman admitted.

"You are certain?"

"Mr. Wykeham gave it to me himself."

Longford screwed up his eyes. In the shadows and without the aid of his spectacles, it was difficult to read. In order to see at all he had brought the letter up so close he could smell the ink and the paper.

"October, I think," he said irritably.

The postman looked puzzled.

"The postmark," said Longford. Out on the lawn something fluttered. He looked up.

From the gray hills a sharp exhalation flowed down into the village. The dawn wind, ruffling the grass, filled the yard with the cool, unmistakable breath of autumn.

An hour later, on the grimy steps of Hunt's garage the postman was shivering.

". . . and the sun was late," he muttered, adding to his list of complaints.

Hunt took no interest. With two of his hands, he was sharpening a scythe. The leaves that came spinning through the air dropped noiselessly at his feet. The only sound was the monotonous grinding of stone on metal.

"The birds are gone," the postman went on sadly, remembering how in the hedges there had been sparrows. Each morning when he passed the cemetery there had been a crow on the gate. This morning the gate had been empty.

"It's the women who take them," Hunt said.

"I expect they fly south."

Hunt smiled. With a free hand he rubbed the blood on his trousers. "Believe me," he said, "it's the women."

He tore open his letter.

The postman waited. In his own hands he was shuffling a pair of letters, stamped UNDELIVERABLE, that had come back to the village. Dr. Oliver Holmes, the postman read, turning over one envelope then the next, Professor Harwood. Hunt tucked the letter away in his pocket. Like the others it was an invitation to Greenchurch.

"You plan to go up there?" the postman asked.

"It's not a matter of choice."

The postman stared vaguely into the street. At the far end of the green a team of horses was hauling a well-laden wagon toward the hill that climbed to the House. "Do you think there will be women?" he asked.

Hunt shrugged one of his shoulders.

"I was kind to her," said the postman. "I was sober."

"Perhaps you've a hard heart," Hunt told him.

The postman sighed. "I've thought of that," he said miserably. "Or maybe no heart at all." He looked down at the blood still oozing from his fingers. "Do you think they can tell?" he asked.

Hunt only frowned. He went back to the scythe, his powerful, broad hands moving rhythmically. With his great strength he could mow an acre of barley in less than an hour. Nonetheless he was impatient. He drew the stone roughly over the metal. Men, he thought thankfully, were much shorter work.

The wheels clattered on the pavement. On the high front seat, the butcher was singing. His bass voice rolled over the green. Undiminished, it echoed among the houses. It was fortunate perhaps that Longford had gone in for his breakfast. It was a foolish song, but, with his theological turn of mind, it would have hurt Longford deeply. Yet it was the song's simple foolishness which most pleased the caroler, the plain fact that the song had nothing to do with the boxes of oysters or the fine pickled salmon soaking in claret, nothing whatever to do

with the six wheels of Midland Stilton cheese, the rib roasts or
the four Banbury cakes wrapped in paper, all of which and a
great deal more he had carried, at Wykeham's request and
starting well before midnight, up the river road from Bristol.
The butcher threw back his head.

"Shoes," he roared cheerfully,

> "I got shoes,
> You got shoes,
> All God's chillun got shoes . . ."

Holmes lay slumped on the ground, sleeping off his whisky
in the alley behind the Royal Charles. The song drifted into
his mind and then out again. The sunlight was cool on his face
but did not wake him. Finally, hearing odd gulping sounds, he
stirred. Harwood was sitting up beside him. He had wrapped
himself in his greatcoat.

"How did you manage to sleep?" he asked bleakly.

"It seemed more sensible than staying awake," Holmes answered. For the first time the doctor looked about him. "It
must have been hours," he said, looking into the morning.

Harwood sniffled. "It was longer," he whispered. In his voice
was the same weariness that showed in his face.

Propped wide awake by the wall while the others had slept,
Harwood had watched the bright stars swing through the heavens. Hour by hour he had watched them, the warm summer
stars sliding westward, withdrawing, the fall stars climbing colder
and fainter up from the east. Alone in the darkness he had felt
the world turning. With an almost infinite slowness, his muscles beginning to stiffen, he had felt himself turning as well;
and it had come upon him with sudden sickening horror that
he would surely die.

"How cold the wind is," he said with a shudder. He was
shivering but his forehead was damp with sweat.

At the bottom of the alley the Duke slammed the door of the

privy. Grasping his trousers with one hand, he clambered across the alley. With the other he was holding a letter.

"We can go there," he cried out excitedly.

Holmes tried not to grimace. "Just walk up to the house," he said dryly, unable to stop himself, "and inquire whether he is a murderer?"

"If you like." There was a pleased look in the Duke's eyes. "The point is he expects us."

"We knew that," Holmes said. "You are to save the daughter."

"Yes, of course." His Grace was smiling. The daughter was a matter beyond question.

"You could have gone before," Holmes persisted. "Probably any time you wanted."

"Not until seven," the Duke said. He dropped the invitation into Holmes's lap.

"When did you get this?"

The Duke went on smiling. "On the morning he went away, I'm afraid." He put his hands into his pockets. "Yet I seem to have carried it about with me since."

Straining to look at the paper, Holmes was baffled. "But this is not until . . ."

"— till hell freezes," Harwood said hoarsely.

On the front step, in the clothes they had slept in, they waited for the public house to open. Out in the street the procession of wagons continued. One after another they thundered up the hill and, in under an hour, came rumbling back empty. Swinging wildly without their ballast, they disappeared around the edge of the green.

Holmes listened to the last hurried shouts of the drivers. "I wonder how many are invited?" he asked.

"An army," Harwood whispered. They both looked at him, but Harwood had slipped into silence.

Damn him, the Duke thought, annoyed with the man's bitterness. Certainly there were worse things than spending the night in an alley. The Duke himself had slept soundly. Slept at once, he remembered, falling away into a stillness so deep that, had he listened, the movement of the stars might have seemed audible. In fact, he had heard nothing. The intent dark eyes that in the deepest moment of his sleep had turned as though from other, pressing thoughts to gaze at him had watched him silently.

He was too old, too confident of his powers to be lured away by a memory that on his waking paled. He had not let his thoughts dwell on it. He wondered instead what Wykeham was doing and what would come of their meeting. But there is nothing so small that it is unimportant, even the flushed red cheeks of a woman, met and all but unremembered in the stillness of sleep.

The air now was cooler, sharper. The patch of blue sky visible between the trees was shining. The Duke stood over Harwood. Somewhere within him a longing he thought he had put away quickened.

"It is time we were about our business here," he said roughly. Without quite knowing why, when Harwood did not move at once, His Grace kicked him.

"Your manners seem to have got lost altogether," Morag said. His conscience pricked him a little to say it. A man with his wife just run off was bound to be short on charity. Doubtless, he must try to be a bit more understanding. But Longford was being insufferable.

Morag stared enviously at the racks of clothes hanging in the minister's closet. "It is only the loan of a dinner jacket," he said.

"You're not invited," Longford replied wearily. He had climbed up on the bed with his last pair of shoes and was attempting, without noticeable success, to enlarge them by making holes with a knife.

"I was his guardian," Morag reminded him. He looked once more at the closet. His own jackets had hung there until someone, packing away the things of the dead, had disposed of them. For all he knew it might have been Longford himself. Still, it seemed mean-spirited to mention it. "I am expected," Morag said civilly. "There have to be nine at the table." He looked shrewdly at Longford. "I can assure you I am one of them."

Longford worked on without speaking.

Morag rested his small, plump hand on the windowsill. In the yard the light was already failing.

"We are to be his generals," Morag said. "His commanders in the field."

The shoes were a hopeless mess and Longford abandoned them. "You are not coming," he repeated.

"Who's Wykeham to find on such short notice?" Morag asked. "Nine are expected." His splotched forehead wrinkled. "Eight just wouldn't do. It would be the ruin of everything."

"It would be a blessing," Longford retorted, wishing to have a few hours free of the old man's company.

"Do you think so?" Morag turned. "This particular world in ashes?"

Longford looked at him oddly. He had been feeling that he must put his foot down once and for all; only, it occurred to him suddenly, he had no idea what Morag was talking about.

"The world . . .?" he began.

"There wouldn't be," Morag answered. "In any event not this one. And not the world he intended." Morag shook his old head. "Though I suppose there would have to be something. But what's the good of a world if you're no longer in it? And you wouldn't be. You can be quite certain of that." He took out his handkerchief and blew his red nose.

"So it has to be nine," he continued. "Just as there were the time before. As there will be now, if I may have the loan of a dinner jacket."

A final spasm of annoyance came over Longford. "You can't talk to me!" he shouted. "You're . . . why, you're . . ."

Morag nodded. "Quite right, of course. Here in this room, if you'll pardon me saying so."

Longford's face flashed with despair.

"But then," Morag went on, "as far as I can determine, they were most always dead."

There was a long silence. Morag saw that Longford had understood nothing.

"We are less distractable," he explained. "That is why, I imagine, it is generally old dead men. We remember the shape of our lives. That's the real point. To have seen it before. To know enough not always to be expecting new faces, new anything. Though, of course, Wykeham would challenge that."

Longford made a movement of irritation.

"You said nine," Longford whispered. Because the rest had seemed gibberish, he had gone back to that.

There were nine towers in the village. He had discovered them, one after another in the hills, on his tramps during his first weeks in Devon. Uncertain of their meaning, he had suspected nevertheless that they were bound up with the river, with its changing, and had recorded their positions on his map.

Longford took a deep breath.

"Why are there nine?" he asked quickly.

"I told you."

"Tell me again."

Morag sighed. "Because there were before."

Longford stared at him uncomprehendingly.

"Before what?"

"Before this!" Morag said, raising his voice. "In the world before now. In the last world Wykeham fled, making this in its place. Though it made no difference. But he wouldn't learn. He never did learn and so can't learn now, that's what I think. Because he never ended, never had to stop, and so thinks somehow he can just keep on, world after world. And yet you and I will help him, though it won't change anything. We will make a world again."

The words poured forth in one breath.

Longford lowered his head, understanding none of them.

"But why nine?" he persisted.

"That never mattered."

"Give me a reason."

"They all come to the same."

"I don't care."

Morag looked out the window.

"Because he fell," Morag said quietly.

Longford stared at him.

"Him," Morag whispered, "the Almighty Power hurl'd head-long . . ."

Morag frowned. ". . . Nine times," he continued, his voice flat, reciting, "the space that measures day and night."

Across the green the postman had dragged a chair out onto his porch. The old minister's eyes remained fixed on him.

"Because it is three times the Trinity and holy."

The postman climbed onto the chair.

Morag grew still.

"Because for eight days," he said softly, "Hobbamocko labored. But when each hill was piled up, when the oakwoods were thick and the great, holy river ran between Greylock and the sea, then on the ninth day Hobbamocko rested."

Longford was about to protest.

"Because," Morag went on obdurately, "once at the beginning of another world there were nine great kings whose hearts . . ." Helplessly, he watched the old postman swing his stiff, arthritic legs into the air.

Morag closed his eyes tightly.

"Not that it mightn't have been thirteen . . . or seven" — his voice faltered — "not that it would have made any differ-

ence if it had been. But once . . . and so ever afterward . . ."
He trembled. "Oh dear," he said. "Poor man."

Longford had never once looked out the window. No longer
quite listening, he found himself staring at Morag's feet.

"About that jacket," he said. "I don't guess. I mean, if I
were to let you borrow one, you wouldn't . . ."

"It is just one more instance," Morag said, interrupting him,
"just a bit of something to cover one's nakedness."

A shadow had gathered in his face.

"It began with a cloak," Morag said. "Did you know that?
A wondrous cloak probably, beyond cost, stitched with silver
and embroidered with gold. Yet to Duinn it was nothing. It is
said at least that the grave Lord gave it lightly, seeing only that
the boy was cold. With his cares, it is perhaps not so unlikely.
But Wykeham, we must imagine, never forgot. And though on
one world after another he might have taken a stand, might at
last have stood and faced him, out of pity, remembering that
one kindness, he . . ."

His old eyes found Longford's and, though the other did not
want to look, held them.

"I wonder if Wykeham ever knew," Morag said, "how many
worlds would come to ruin because of that?"

2.

In the men's kitchen George Tennison worried the joint with too small a knife. Norfolk took up a cleaver.

"Here, let me do that," he cried impatiently and gave two quick whacks. The blood splattered. Fortunately they were both wearing aprons; only George Tennison felt more foolish. Flushed with embarrassment, he turned and began taking down the dessert plates, setting them aside for the end. Through the door he could hear the voices of the men finding their seats at the table. He gave a final stir to something in a pot, poked at it tentatively, hoping that, whatever it was, it was now cooked, and dumped the unknown contents into a serving dish. The steam rose in his face. The smell and the dampness made him dizzy; opening the door with his shoulder, he scowled. He was hungry as well as exhausted. It seemed unfair that in order to have his dinner he should have to make it.

"Give way," Norfolk said, pushing a cart at his heels.

They came into the room almost at the same moment. As if waiting, the other guests remained standing. In the light of the hearth their faces seemed darkened and out of date, like the faces in old photographs. Did people really look like that, George Tennison wondered, trying to remember the old men of his childhood, men in shirts without collars, their oiled hair oddly parted. If the truth were known, he felt rather old and out of place himself. He put the platter down beside Wykeham.

The young master smiled at him.

"Your seats, gentlemen," he said.

There was a scuffling of chairs, the clink of crystal as one of the heavier men bumped the table leg. Norfolk, the cart unloaded, was the last to find his seat. From the bottom of the table he grinned up at Wykeham.

Wykeham nodded. Behind him the tall windows reddened.

All through the day the village men had been gathering, coming on foot or on horseback and building fires on the lawn. In the middle of the afternoon Norfolk had opened the larder and just before dark he had rolled a half dozen barrels down the wide steps and then out under the trees. Seeing him, the men wandered up. "But when we start," Norfolk had warned them, "when the last comes up onto the porch, then you must be silent."

The men laughed. Already one of the barrels had been hauled onto a makeshift table. Licking his lips, the sexton removed a broach from his pocket. "And how shall we tell," he asked mildly, "when the last have come?"

"You might count," Norfolk suggested.

The old sexton smiled. He looked back at the house. "Quite right," he said. "It was never our business to meddle." He rolled the broach over in his fingers. "Only, if you'll pardon me asking, how are we to know, what with all that coming and going, who is worthy of being counted?"

"It is not a matter of being worthy," Norfolk answered.

"Of what, then?" The sexton's smile broadened. "Just as a matter of clarification, if you see what I mean."

The others had drawn nearer. Norfolk stared at them grimly. "You'll have to ask Mr. Wykeham himself," he said.

"Aye, there's the rub," the sexton mused slyly. "He's inside and we ain't."

"Six more," said Norfolk.

He turned quickly. But partway across the lawn Norfolk slowed to a walk. They were his mates. He tried to remember that. It ill suited a man, raised though he had been above them, to seem too eager to leave them forever behind.

"I wouldn't have taken Fred for one of them," muttered Izzy Franklin, who for forty of his sixty years had run the feedstore on the far side of the green. He put down his tankard. "Fred Norfolk," he said petulantly, "Lord of Creation."

"So much the worse for the world," said the sexton. He fingered his rifle. "Still, it takes all kinds, I should think."

The storekeeper gazed at the drive. "But what possible use could Fred be?" he asked.

The sexton shrugged. "Must be that a drunken man remembers something worth keeping."

By now the wind, which was always about somewhere, had begun to tickle his neck. He looked across the lawn. Dusk was falling over the gardens. Except for the fires, the hill itself was fading. Which of us, he thought, will still be here come morning? But it was not a question which submitted to an answer. He sat quietly, waiting. It was becoming so dark he could scarcely see the Ford pickup making the last turn of the drive; but the sound, echoing harshly against the barns, he heard plainly.

"That will be the first," he said.

The old engine sputtered. The ancient doors rattled. When Hunt switched off the ignition, the whole frame seemed to tremble. Hunt gave a slam to the hood.

"You be quiet as well," he said, looking across at the Indian bound in the back. But the words went unheeded. Arthur Houseman stared with narrowed eyes at the fires.

Borne up by the wind, the sparks were carried into the darkness. In the upper air they grew smaller and more distant. Yet they were not consumed. Houseman leaned into the corner of the truck and worked at the ropes.

Something had come into the world. Or something had left it. He did not concern himself with which.

It burns, he thought joyfully.

"And the wood fires blinking on a winter's night," Wykeham said, gazing one by one into their faces. "The Royal Charles with Fred Norfolk sprawled on the counter."

His shadow, amplified by the firelight, ascended the opposite wall. He alone had remained standing. His glossy black hair had been parted in the middle. Brushed behind his ears, it had given his head an unexpected dignity.

Like the head of a bishop, Longford would recall afterward.

The Duke's tired eyes rested on the large open features. Like a tyrant, he thought, casting about in his mind for an image. In spite of the years it had been the longest he had looked at him.

On the lawn the men of the village had turned silent. Wykeham had himself stopped a moment. He smiled.

"The church draped for Christmas," he continued, "and Morag up in his pulpit, his congregation asleep, all the bored, bundled children staring out at the snow." He rubbed his chin. "And pigeons," he said, almost gaily, "crowds of wild pigeons in South Wood with spring coming . . . But the river first. The river before everything."

"The land?" Longford asked uncomfortably.

"This valley," said Wykeham. "Since I plan to keep what I like."

"What you must," Morag told him.

Wykeham made a vague gesture. "I had never intended to start from nothing, Michael."

"Could not," Morag told him.

Hunt shifted the mass of his arms. He got up and walked to the sideboard. Finding a fresh decanter, he brought it back. One way or another this business had to be settled and he was obliged to play his part in it. But until this moment, eased by a sense of familiarity, by the firelight and darkness, he had held his contempt in check. It was the terrible paralyzing emptiness that must be safeguarded against. Nothing else mattered. But death came, he knew, always, reasserting the pattern. Everything that had happened or that was likely to happen returned to that single and compassionate end. Whatever he attempted, Wykeham could not alter that.

Hunt laughed but now there was relief in his laughter.

"It is late," he said. "What is coming is already on its way."

"Not yet," Wykeham answered.

"A little while, surely."

"Time enough," Wykeham said. "Until morning." He had smiled again, his odd, quiet smile.

"You were only the instrument," he said. "Long ago I had given up hating you."

Hunt frowned.

"There was a river before you were here."

"I have not denied it."

"You have taken credit . . ."

"For what pleases me," Wykeham said. "From the start I took whatever attracted me. What otherwise would have been forgotten. And now it is stamped with my thought." He drew himself up. It was his house and his table. Smoke rose from the hearth, curled from Holmes's pipe. "And not only the fields and the miles of walls," Wykeham went on confidentially. "Certain conventions, some of the institutions of men. Did you suspect that?"

Longford looked at him uncertainly.

"What, for example?" he asked.

"Ministers."

Longford stiffened.

"Married priests," Wykeham said, explaining. "The just living by faith." All at once Wykeham grinned. "In the latrine at Wittenberg, in the rotted old tower I squatted down beside the young friar. I whispered in his ear."

244

Hunt turned in his chair. "He never did," he said and laughed again. "He never did much of anything. Not that lasted."

Holmes stared in dismay.

The musculature was wrong. The bones were impossible.

"He murdered a man," Holmes said quietly.

"Cured him," Hunt said. "And, of course, made him worse."

"Stopped him," Wykeham added. "But then I had run out of choices. I had given him only a single rule. Had he kept it, the world, for the time that was left, would have become infinitely wider. He would have walked this valley freely . . . as in a garden. And there, to make him happy, I would have sent him a woman — a daughter of my own flesh."

The Duke looked up.

"I have not forgotten," Wykeham said. "From the first you were to come with me. Still, what I gave you, you have by default."

His hands, long and hardened by a work only Hunt knew, clutched the table. For an instant he turned to the windows. There was only candlelight and hearthlight to see by, only the red gilding of the lawn from the bonfires.

"It is out of ignorance," Wykeham said, "you would have me be merciful. But the law in itself is the supreme mercy."

The Duke's eyes searched his, uncomprehending, seeking a motive.

"Ignorance is forgivable, Your Grace," Morag warned him.

"Only ignorance," the Duke said.

Wykeham's jaw hardened. "We do not, perhaps, quite understand one another," he said.

"I understand a little."

"Not enough."

"A man is dead," said the Duke.

"What you question is justice." Wykeham paused. "There was a law, Martin."

"— And I broke it," the Duke said angrily. "I went myself to the station. Though I had sworn I would not, I watched . . ."

With a swift, sullen movement Wykeham turned away so that the Duke would not see his face. His Grace remained staring.

Somehow the sky seemed to darken. It was as if a wall had come to stand between the house and the lawn.

For a moment the Duke thought he heard a rustling out on the porch. He turned but saw only shadows. Yet there was something. It had almost a smell, as of twigs and branches, the deep renewing recesses of leaves.

Wykeham was watching the darkness.

"That was merely for the Will," he said slowly, carefully. "It was of no consequence. I have told you there was but one law."

"Then I do not know it," the Duke admitted.

Wykeham was silent.

The men looked at one another but Morag was staring at Longford. He said nothing, only stared at him, waiting for understanding to come.

All at once Longford lowered his head. His lips grew white. "Dear Lord," he said softly.

One last time Wykeham smiled at them. It had been first of laws but it was broken.

"There is a Tree," he said, "One of many planted in darkness, drawing strength from the ground. Of these I had given you freely. But the One you may not see, may not touch. . . ."

By then the hedge had reached the second story. Norfolk, who had been sent to make certain, edged down the stairs carrying a broken section of a branch. He had torn it off as it had coiled in through a bedroom window. The gray brown stem continued to grow in his hand. He set it down gingerly in the midst of the table.

The doors had already been tried. Like the windows they were impassable. With all his strength George Tennison had given a kick to the mass of thick stems spreading over the sill.

A tremor had run through the wood. As though with pain, the queer dark leaves seemed to hiss at him and he had drawn back, afraid. All about him there had come scrapings and creakings, the muffled slither of limbs reaching furtively into the shingles. When he looked out, he was no longer able to make out the end of the porch. Soon, he thought, the roofs and the chimneys will be covered. He had gone back to the table. They had all gone back, from the west wing and the attic, from the little-used and out-of-the-way rooms that, since his return, Wykeham himself had not often visited.

They found their chairs silently.

Harwood disentangled himself from the twigs, which some-how had caught hold in his pocket.

"There are roots in the basement," he said. "Already they have broken in through the walls." A trickle of blood ran down the side of his nose. He blotted it with a napkin. "Thick as a man," he said, looking around at the circle of faces.

"I don't suppose we have an ax?" Holmes asked. He was nursing a cut on his forehead. Burrowing his way out of the kitchen he had snagged his coat and scratched his face horribly.

"Not much use if we had," Morag answered.

The old dead man kept his eyes averted. Even the nearer hallways were choked with limbs. He had just been able to clear a path through. Nearly gasping, he slumped over his plate. He was too old for this. For the first time in a long while he felt resentment for the thinness of his legs and the immensity of his stomach. He had always feared the physical world a little. But once his size and his clumsiness had protected him. He saw no reason now for Wykeham to call on what, before, no one had thought to ask of him.

"You have made your point too well, William," he said sadly.

"What point?" Holmes wanted to know.

Hunt's teeth showed between his lips. "That we are safe," he said.

Harwood swore. "You mean that we are hopelessly trapped."

"That may be," allowed Hunt; yet his voice, which seemed flat, had anger lurking under it. "Still, what is out there won't get in. Or at least not at first. So there may well be time. That is it, is it not?" His eyes stopped at Wykeham. "As though a hedge . . ." he began, grinding his teeth.

"What is out there?" the Duke demanded.

Hunt did not bother to answer.

"Living men, I hope," Harwood said in his place. "But beyond them an army of the dead. And beyond them again —"

"Duinn," Hunt said coldly and felt Wykeham's stare.

He looked again into the unmarked face and, watching, thought how, because Duinn had willed it, he had carried him, a boy, his eyes grown large with fear, across the holy river into the lands of the dead. And let him come back. Because that too had been Duinn's will. Or his pride, Hunt thought, or that vanity called pride.

Wearily he reached out. He took a drink from his goblet, unhurried, enough to last him.

"You are lord of this world," he said. "Yet he will not let you stay in it." He raised a pair of his arms, impatiently. In his lap his fingers twisted. He said, "It was never life he gave you. Surely, you must know that. Even he has not that power. It was only death he kept from you."

For a breath's space there was silence. Wykeham lifted his head. He smiled into his eyes. "Forever," he whispered.

"For as long as you do not tire of it," Hunt reminded him. "No longer."

"I do not tire."

Hunt put down the goblet. It was blood they drank. There was no other truth. Though a man yearned only for pleasure or searched for understanding, to the end of his days he would learn nothing more. "All that live must tire," Hunt said.

Wykeham's deep eyes in which the memory of a million deaths were drowned looked him steadfastly in the face. "Whatever must come," he said, "I shall be here."

"Protected by a few miles of wall?"

"And these few hills and a wood. And this house looking over them."

"And a hedge?" said Hunt. He scowled. "Like some damn story for children?"

"It was always for children."

"Where are the women, then?" Hunt asked him.

3.

"In Black Wood," Chance said, the wind of memory blowing through him.

He was silent a moment. "Still, I did not die of it," he said in a voice that quivered unexpectedly. He looked away into the fretwork of branches.

In the breeze the trees parried, drifted apart, only to return, limb by limb, to where they had been.

"The trees were mostly blackthorn then," he went on more quietly. "The only barn still standing Alf Jenkins's. And him only lately put underground and myself no more than a lad and feeling, the moment we entered the loft, a sinister dread on his behalf." He looked again into the evening. The cold had withdrawn a little. Emboldened, he said: "She was not yet sixteen. Still, it seemed a great difference." He managed a trace of a smile. "Before I had even touched her, she took off her dress."

"And you have thought of her since?"

Chance lowered his head. "Chiefly about other matters," he said. "But I have thought of her." He reached for the bottle, as the other had done, so that at a distance it seemed that the two figures sitting in the starlight were respectfully toasting one another. Once more Chance brought the bottle to his lips.

The whisky was strong and smelled of rainstorms and oak. He smelled other things; they floated out of his memory, the smell of fire, of earth, the old puzzling smell of dying. He looked around. When he recalled the scent of her hair, his eyes filled with tears.

She had had wonderful hair, brazen and red as flame. When she had looked up from under it there had been something touching about her glance, and something shameless too. She had not minded what the village women said of her. If things had come differently to him, he thought, if she had not been older, in his youth when a few years, it seemed, had been everything . . .

"I was seventeen when she married," he murmured. "She was twenty."

"Her young man died."

The breeze stirred and a shadow crawled onto the porch.

"Soon after," Chance said. "He is buried at Greenchurch."

"Then, had you wished?"

Chance half closed his eyes. "I was roaming," he said, "down to Bristol. Later to the docks at New Awanux." He seemed to shake his old head. "It was ten years before I was home again."

The boy sat with his legs dangling in the grass. He was looking into the darkness. The spikes of his black hair fell over his collar. He took up the bottle.

Chance tried to speak casually:

"There's no hurry, I suppose?"

"There are many I won't even sit with," the boy said.

"When that business up at the house is done," Chance said obstinately. "I've earned something, damn you, sitting in this place, keeping company with them who no one else would listen to."

"Have you had supper?" the boy asked.

"Don't eat."

The boy nodded. Unsmiling, he set the bottle down next to him.

"I've a paper," Chance said. "Sixty — seventy years I've had it."

He had thought he would be frightened but he was more angry than frightened. He hadn't planned when it should be but that it should be now, before he saw whether Wykeham, with all his years, had made any difference, was senseless. It was cruel. Bitterly he dropped his eyes to the floor. He could see his legs, stuck out straight and stiff, and tried to pull them back. It worked its way into his consciousness very slowly that he could not.

"Fifty years," the boy said.

"No matter," Chance answered, brushing those years aside, although at the end they were all that was left to him. "Time enough," he said hoarsely. He started to draw a new breath. He could hear his chest begin to suck clumsily. It made him angrier.

"And nothing of him changed," he whispered. "While to me . . ."

The boy turned his head. The darkness had rubbed the expression out of his face. His eyes were now murky holes, his mouth a vague tear. Chance shut his sight fast against them. Do not feel, he thought.

After a little while he heard him get up.

"When I took her," Duinn said, "she was waiting alone at her window." His footsteps came nearer. "Waiting as she had night after night, hoping for another look at a red, naked man who, long after she had forgotten you, once waved at her from the midst of the air."

Presently Duinn put his hand on the weeping man's shoulder.

"Shall I tell you what I did?" Duinn asked.

The man did not answer.

"In fact, it is a little thing," Duinn said, almost diffidently. "Like killing a hare."

4.

It was late, too late, Willa Brelling was afraid, when she began her journey; but then, until the fires, she hadn't understood that it was within her power to go. It had not even been in her mind — a stone only watches, wood only waits — and with every nerve rigid, she had watched endlessly, waited endlessly, while the nights had piled up about her. In her innermost self she still felt the hands that long ago had pulled her down on the cot, still felt even now, in the darkness of classrooms and corridors, how he had covered her with himself. But she had no happiness out of the memory and though he had come again, he had gone. She could not follow. It was only because she was often at the windows that she had watched the fires.

For hours, becoming one substance with the glass, she had observed the Indians gathering. They had floated down from the sky, effortlessly, never touching the ground. All afternoon they had lingered in the air. The frost had turned the elms into torches of fire. It did not seem strange to her that the flesh of men should likewise burn. Like herself, the Indians seemed intent on no other business but waiting. It was not until evening that they came down onto the roof of the chapel. Dancing upon it and jeering at those within, they blew the sparks from their mouths onto the shingles. She saw the building begin to glow dully. From the main house a dozen figures rushed onto the lawn. When the chapel exploded, the odd-job man was still dragging up buckets of water. The fires that twisted on his back rose abruptly as he ran. Coming over the hill he looked like a shooting star. Her star. Rushing toward her.

The body dropped and lay still. She drew a part of herself into the front step and waited. Smoke escaped from the rags of its clothes but the life that had been there had gone. Yet something of its warmth remained. She did not mind that its chin was covered with bristles or that, in its agony, it had fouled itself. She was frightened, however, that someone might take it from her. She could hear the women drawing nearer and knew that she must conceal it from them.

All that was necessary, she thought, was to inhabit its legs. She could do such a thing. Every board and timber of the hall was filled with her. A body was much smaller.

She entered its feet through the soles, hastily, eager only to be done. But there was more room inside than she had imagined. She had a feeling of terrible vastness. In order to fill it, she was forced to draw herself down from the roofpeaks and out of the walls. Yet life can only be filled with life and, although she had pushed all she was into it, the sense of emptiness was appalling. Nonetheless she could make it stand. She could open its eyes.

She looked toward the road on the side of the hill. The road led toward the river and the trains. It led, she did not doubt, to Greenchurch and the house to which he always returned.

If she wished to, she felt, she could follow him.

She made the legs bend. They carried her down the hill. In her heart there was a sudden, overwhelming nostalgia for movement. Ignoring the sluggishness of its gait, she crossed the first poor square, passing into the narrow street beyond with an air of giddy anticipation.

The fires were not yet general. The few men stood about

idly, unnoticing, or sat in groups on the steps of the houses, talking in the lateness of the evening. But already the women were leaving. Each alone, with eyes shrewdly vacant, they strolled out onto the avenues. Yet they seemed without purpose and, if a man they knew caught sight of them, they smiled and went on without speaking. In the darkness their footsteps were soon gone beyond hearing. Unless one followed down the dim, shifting streets that led to the trains, one would never have guessed their numbers.

Bristol station slanted upward into the blackness. Out on the platform the women assembled. Their stares, which at first had been impersonal and questioning, warmed as they met the stares of others. Very little was said. They knew and, assured of the reasons, had no cause for concern. Some of the women had owls, others jays or wrens, in little wire cages or free on their shoulders. Unmindful of the soft twittering, the women looked across at the river. Their eyes had become clearer, the lines at the sides of their mouths more deeply satisfied.

"Go home, father," said the matron who was the first to see the old man climbing the stairs from the street. Her voice was kind but it was firm. "Get along home," she repeated.

Willa did not try to speak. It was the body of the man the woman was talking to. And the body was not interested. It was stiffening. Willa let it lean on the rail. The woman continued to speak to it.

"We — needn't — take — care — of — you," the woman said, spacing the words and giving them a certain triumph. "We needn't bathe you, though you need it. Needn't clean up after you. Not ever again. And there is no use in following." Pausing, she saw its face and mistaking what she saw there, said more gently but as earnestly: "You will just have to get by as best you can."

The body waited, unmoving.

To Willa, who was alone in it, the corpse seemed larger than it perhaps was, but it seemed even emptier as well. At last, robbed of any argument, the woman wandered away. Women hurried by, pushing past her. Willa watched the crowd of absorbed faces indifferently. The mouth of the corpse hung open. Its muscles and tendons were beginning to feel like iron. Soon, Willa thought, it will not move at all. But when the train pulled into the station, she dragged its halting feet over the platform, made its legs mount, heavily, one by one, the black metal steps into the car. With every step the corpse looked older and more vile. But, within, under the glare of the lanterns, the women recognized the dazed and temporary nature of its life. There was nothing to do, they decided, nothing worth the trouble of taking charge of, and so they did not protest. It only sat with its ropy hands hung between its knees, staring rudely at the many colored birds that shared the car, listening wearily to the unmerciful joy of their voices.

The young woman, her chin lowered and her hands in her lap, did not wake until the train started. It was the wrong place to sleep but her body was exhausted by the life stretching and pulling inside her and any respite had been welcome, forgetfulness most welcome of all. She twisted awake. Startled at finding the old man sitting next to her, she moaned.

"They have made you sit here," she said unhappily. "To punish me. Because I am already pregnant."

Its stench sickened her; still the woman did not move. She accepted the punishment as she had accepted the life growing in her, because she felt or wished to feel the presence of the man. The women, of course, had done this. She was certain of that. They had sent the old man, his head like a skull, to remind her of the mortality of earthly affection: the man, they as much as said, will become as this man.

She had known all the while they were leaving, going off to a much better world. Nonetheless when the man had come to her she had put that knowledge aside. Afterward, in the large rented room of the King's Hotel, although they had talked on for hours, they had never discussed the possibility of a child. When he had gone away, the man had gone away unknowing.

Carolyn let her head fall back on the seat.

In the darkness of the river she could see the darkness of his eyes. It was odd, she thought, to think of him that way, not eyes black as the darkness but the darkness as black as his eyes. But she knew it was fitting.

The women in the library had been kind. They had tried to be comforting; yet, she had seen the disdain in their faces. Poor nasty fat thing, they had said, without speaking a word. Poor thing, they had whispered, watching her waddle between the rows of books, lugging the life about with her like something in a sack.

"In the new world," Carolyn told the old man, "they will always be thin." She kept hold of her smile, partially out of bitterness but as well from embarrassment. It was much the same smile that had lingered in Wykeham's mind when on the night he was leaving he had written her his last letter. "How can I explain?" he had written, saying the words a second time, to himself.

"And when they bear," Carolyn went on softly, "the child becomes as the woman, the one repeating the other. Without pain." She looked at the old man carefully and said, "So they have explained it to me. But I will never know for certain. Not with a life already inside me. Because of it, when the time comes, I shall not be permitted to cross."

She settled farther back in the seat. The darkness had not changed but now in the blackness of the river she could make out a succession of shadows. Moment to moment, they seemed to resemble a tree, a galloping stallion, a ship. She folded her hands on her stomach.

"Sometimes I am afraid," she whispered, wanting none but the old man to hear. "Suppose," she said, "it is something fit only for circuses." She pressed her plain fingers into the lap of her dress. "Something for Barnum, with stubs of wings or too many legs."

She discovered the old man watching her. Its chest moved.

"It's done in darkness," it croaked.

"Loaded in darkness," it insisted, its breath a dry hiss.

Not understanding, Carolyn merely continued to stare.

The corpse set its teeth. "Life," it said sharply. The body felt heavy and terribly cold. It had been dead only a few hours. But in fifty years, Willa knew, she had not learned to be ready.

"You can't see," the corpse said, her voice in its voice, its cold breath touching her own dead heart with awe. "You can't ever see. You must simply wait."

An army, the stationmaster thought in his sleep, listening to the tramp of feet on the platform. He had been no more than a boy during the Great War; but the trains, coming down from the north, had passed through quite often. Now and again, because of delays on the line, the troop cars had stopped at the village. The men, spilling onto the street, had had time for a smoke or, if they were daring, just time enough to run the quarter mile across to the Royal Charles — though, of course, it had been the Royal Edward then.

The night breeze blew stiffly through the office window, stirring the stationmaster's memory. It was the same sound, he decided without waking. Though, in truth, it wasn't the rumble of boots he heard but the shared sense of purpose and hurry that was missing from the scramble of ordinary passengers. The sound was continuous and, for the space of several min-utes, deafening. Yet by the time he had struggled out of his sleep, it was gone. He stuck his head out into the cold night air.

Except for the very pregnant young woman leading an old man across to the stairs, the platform was empty. He watched them go down slowly into the street. He looked at his watch. It was not quite two-thirty. The train, he decided, was late.

"I am slowing you," the corpse said. It was not an apology.

Carolyn was silent. She did not say that her own careful slowness was as much a matter of her sickness and pain. Left alone she would never have been able to keep pace with the scurrying feet of the women.

Far ahead the last had already vanished under the trees. A ridge of cloud was creeping up from the south and it had become very dark. Had it not been for the birds screeching about the entrance to the path, she would have missed it entirely. Carolyn's eyes flickered up at the branches. She was frightened.

"There are Indians," she whispered.

"I have seen them."

"Perhaps you should not," she said pointedly. She kept looking over her shoulder.

It was the first time in her life she had stirred from New Awanux, the first time, apart from Wykeham, she had dared much of anything. But it had done no good. In the damp chill of the wood she saw nothing that had any meaning, only half-things that were constantly changing. She walked more painfully. For a moment even the lame old man was in danger of drawing ahead of her.

The air smelled different. They were among the stones. She could feel their vague huge shapes looming over her.

"It is strange to think," she said, "that it is all a mistake." She stopped and rubbed her hands on her dress. With the back of her wrist she pushed her hair away from her eyes.

"We will come to water soon," she said. "There he who will carry them across will be waiting."

Her hands which had been seeking something to hold, something to touch, fell helplessly.

"Someone has blundered," she said.

The old man looked blank.

"A Redd Man," she whispered. "Can't you see that? The fetcher, the stalker by streams."

She peered desperately into the eyes of the corpse.

"Red as the old cock salmon," she whispered, "red as blood."

Her hands, which at last found some purpose, now hid her face.

"A Redd Man," she cried out, a sob breaking through the mask of her fingers. "A Redd Man," she wailed. "Never Indians."

5.

 Deep into the evening a tender little breeze moved through the hedge. It stirred the tall curtains, shaking, ever so faintly, the cloak which hung by the hearth.

The Reverend Timothy Longford watched the rotted old fabric as though transfixed. The fire-light had touched its veins of gold with a bright rime of flame, its threads of fine silver with radiance. He tried to moisten his lips.

"Dear Christ," he whispered.

In his mind the flickering vision of God and His angels still lingered. He felt a mortifying guilt. For twenty years, as rich and as holy a mystery, the woman, forsaking all others, had clung to him. In sickness and in health, he said, not aloud, but his lips moved reciting the service. He looked again at the cloak. How could he have been so mistaken?

"Dear sweet Christ," he repeated. But it was the woman who was gone.

At the table the discussion went around him.

The Duke refolded the paper. Returning it to his pocket, he became aware of a swift flutter of pain. Still, it was no more than a gentle pressure on his chest, and he hunched his thick shoulders, ignoring it.

"You wrote me a letter from Egypt once," he said. "I was at the bank, William, when I opened it, in the chair I was to give to Houseman."

Wykeham was looking away.

"Thirteen years ago," the Duke reminded him. "It was about women. Their bowing and nodding, you wrote, reminded you of birds."

His Grace shook his head.

"I would have thought they would have been herons," he said. "Or whatever white birds there are in Egypt. They were blonde after all. They were English women."

He waited and then cleared his throat. "But they were like crows, you said. Their eyes soulless like the eyes of crows."

"Not crows," Hunt offered ruefully.

With two large hands Hunt hitched up his trousers; with another he took up his cup and looked over it. "But all the same," he said, "like a flight of birds turning." His old red face glowered. "One creature," he said, "thinking one thought and turning —"

"But where?" Longford asked desperately.

Holmes was not listening. He was watching Hunt's arms. Yet, until he struck the match and saw the bright flame twisting above the bowl of the pipe, he had not remembered the photograph.

At once his head tilted up.

"What if," he asked, surprised, "from the very beginning we have had it wrong?"

It was only then that Wykeham looked at him.

"What then?" he asked.

"Suppose there were two Creations."

Wykeham frowned.

"Or twenty," Holmes said.

"Or hundreds," Harwood added disagreeably. It was the first time in a long while he had spoken. "Like beads on a string," he said, his voice too loud because he thought they were ignoring him.

"Only here, I think," Holmes said quietly. He was concentrating. "Only sharing this place," he said softly. "Only using this place and, though struggling, never able to get free of it."

There were endless worlds.

In this one there was water.

Carl Brelling edged to within a few feet of it.

He had tried to move carefully, avoiding the mounds of dead sticks and the briars, but scrambling over the maze of bleak walls in the heart of the wood he had fallen. Although he had managed not to cry out, his elbows were bruised and his trousers in shreds. But because he was sober he began to feel the cold. He stood in the reedy grass at the water's edge, cursing the darkness and shivering.

It was like coming to the end of the world.

It was just that, he thought, the world's end. The shame was he was alone at it.

The woman who had marched into the shop and whom, half in a daze, he had followed, was gone. She had driven him, he thought, along the river. He remembered the car at least. He had got into the corner of the back seat and had paid no attention while she had gone on about Nora and the young man. It was not that he was uninterested; he could no longer make out the meaning of the simplest words.

What was love? he wondered.

What, damn them, were women?

He did not pretend these were original questions but, despairing of answers, he dug his small boots into the dirt of the bank. The night wind had come and chilled him. It had been hours, he thought. Perhaps longer.

For a long time he had looked out the car window.

At the beginning, on the plain, the fires had been everywhere. Like the swift streak of a line-squall fires exploded over the roofs of New Awanux. They erupted from chimneys and doorways, fell hissing out of the low sky. He sat and stared without speaking.

Bristol, when they came to it, was already in ruins. The flames formed a ring halfway across the horizon.

The woman peered out through the windscreen.

"It is still dark up ahead," she said gravely.

The houses of the village had come up on the left. All at once at the crown of the hill there were women. The street and the sidewalks had been filled with them. By hundreds, they tramped through the bare gardens and over the lawns.

The headmistress stopped the car at the top of the green and climbed out.

"Where are you going?" he asked, but she moved away with the others. When he opened the door of the car, no one stopped to look back.

His poor eyes squinted into the darkness.

On the side of the green there was a garage, its doors closed and its dark windows shuttered. The field beside it was wild and overgrown. Unmindful, the women poured into it. At a distance he watched them.

The path they made twisted; it wound among the rough stands of burdock and thistle. Conscious only that he had been left behind, Carl Brelling started after them. He went toward the far edge where the ground fell steeply. He ran. Inside his chest he was suffocating. Just once, out of the corner of his eye, he still saw them. But as the trees at the margin of the wood came up at him, he stopped, gasping, dragging the cold air back into his lungs and found only their clothing.

He closed his eyes tightly. But it was not the nakedness of the women he was imagining but the hallway in his mother's house, long ago in New Awanux. He had been the youngest, a boy in a house of women. His big, grown-up sister had left her stockings curled at the foot of the stairs, her skirts on the railing.

Trudging up to the landing, catching up one thing then another as she went, his mother had thrown each one back to him. The mound of his sister's clothing had grown in his arms.

"She has no sense of decency," his mother said. She stopped outside Willa's room and glared in.

"And this is the way you treat me," his mother said bitterly to the girl on the bed.

He had peered around his mother's waist.

"Like a servant," his mother said.

Frightened, he had pressed his face into the loose jumble of garments. But the smell of them, damp and faintly sour, rising like a guilty transmission, cut through him.

Willa's long bare legs dropped to the floor. She had not looked at him, perhaps had not even know he was there. But he fled.

At the head of the stairs where the light poured in through the window he tripped over a pair of worn pumps, which, after her slip, were the last things she had abandoned.

Carl Brelling had scarcely taken a half dozen steps when the sensation of water brought him back to himself.

The light began on the far bank. At first it seemed no more than a small ragged tear. But in a moment it was several yards wide. He stood and stared, praying that it would stop. Instead the light grew. Presently, in its brightness, he could see the many shapes of their arms, the endless variation of their breasts and their legs.

A thousand women were crossing the clearing, on their way up the great, fissured slope of a hill. Not a hill exactly. It kept rising, and a hill, he was certain, would not. He drew his hand to his brow, shielding his eyes from the light.

Far up, above the highest tops of the water oaks, he saw the first branches. They were distinguishable only because his eyes were still fixed on them. But as long as he looked they were everywhere — straining outward with immense sweeping arms. The wind stirred them and was itself stirred, was filled with fluttering leaves. He forced his head higher.

It was in that instant he saw her, saw only her.

"Nora!" he called.

The harsh slit of her mouth opened. It vomited flame.

Turning frantically, Carl Brelling bumped into a man.

He tried to run, but the man had got hold of him.

Ducking, scrambling on hands and knees, he tried to crawl. Suddenly there was another in his way. Reaching out when already he knew he should have stopped, he felt the prickly wool of her dress. The distended sack of her belly jutted over him.

The woman stared down at him in horror. He was not old and he was thrusting his small wet hands in her dress.

"Get away from me!" she screamed.

Whatever was there in truth was perhaps no great matter. The eyes Willa looked through saw the face clearly. She remembered his lies. She had taken her own life to be with him.

The corpse shivered. Its tongue went stiff in its mouth.

"You were not dead!" it cried. "You were never —"

It was not a man's voice, or a woman's. But it was old and terrible and made desperate by longing.

Carl Brelling turned his head.

The arms grasped him tightly and twisted. At that same moment something came loose in his memory. The name came to him without his seeking it. It did not matter whose name. There was a woman, and a man. There was water and darkness, a child about to be born and a man dying.

It did not matter whose death.

He could feel his breath squeezing out.

"Is that you?" he asked, whispering soundlessly, because now he had no breath at all.

The hands that held him dug into his neck.

"Please," he said meekly.

Their dark shapes, though scarcely bigger than himself, loomed over him. They were cradling his head and pulling it. He felt the vertebra crack, heard it splitting. He smelled the quick, sour exhalation of air rushing under him and, for one last moment, looked back on the red, pumping stalk of his neck.

It was fine. The breeze had dropped. Its cold breath was gone from her breasts and her legs. The branches stretched invitingly toward the pale windless dawn. Smiling, she hurried along them, mounting from starlight to shadow and back into light. About her the tree was thick with singing birds, with blackbirds and sparrows. Above her the crows shook out their splendid wings. The women, walking close beside her, were fair. The world would always be as it had been in her childhood, when the dreams had gone with the morning, and the man, who, like the God who had made her, was not even a memory. She would no longer dream of him. She would no longer grieve for what, now unremembered, was lost.

On the cold bank below something lifted its head.

She did not mean to look but it called to her.

Nora stiffened.

"Woman!" it cried.

There was something moving under the tree. She saw the tender crown of his forehead. His tousled hair made him appear younger than he was. Yet she knew him. Surely she had always known. His skin was pale; his eyes, watching her nakedness, much too innocent. Uncertain, she made herself laugh.

"Nora," he whispered, finding her name.

"He is not here," she called back.

The boy's small face darkened, as though he felt she was deceiving him.

She did not need to ask the reason why he had come, but she did ask.

"Why," she whispered, "should he be where I am?"

His eyes looked up.

"You followed him."

She laughed again, more bitterly. "With little hope," she said, "and no more chance than you of finding him." There was a touch of defiance in her voice but her mind raced, trying to think of a way to flee from him and yet terrified that he would hear her thoughts.

Indeed, her thoughts lay before him, as the thoughts of all living things came to him. Even then he would have wept for pity of her. He took no joy in the killing. In the gray twilight he had made, he gathered the dead. In the halls of blackened stone, he kept them. It was the Redd Man who did the slaughter. But Wyck had brought his fearful servant to the Great House, ringed by its walls and a wood, and set him there within a hedge beyond his reach. Thwarted, Duinn's face was weary but his jaw was set.

He lifted his head.

Then at last, in the shadow of his cheek, she saw the cheerless, grizzled color of his hair and the long hands partly hidden in his cloak; and where the cloak was parted, she saw the ax.

"There was a man," he said, "who would have loved you."

There was a silence.

"In the house," he said. His grimness softened, for a moment he looked a boy again.

"What do you need of me?" she asked.

"I would have you bring me where he is," he said.

Her perch in the tree was high above him. Still, she shrank back. She said: "Lord, I have come too far."

The sky was even higher than she was. But she wondered if even that were high enough. With stubborn terror her mind sought a place more distant.

It was almost morning. The setting moon had dropped within the maze of limbs; slipped in between the branches, a blade of its wan light, touching her fingers, made them visible. The feathers sprouted from her nails. Feathers grew without pause from her wrists and arms. With one wild push, she brought them up. In the first silver chill of morning their hard, bright edges caught the air.

"Lady," he murmured.

But in that vast place the light was empty. Even the tree that from the beginning in countless worlds had rooted at his will was gone; only the man was left.

An icy wind blew cold against the bank. Lodged between the stones, the white body of a crow, grim with frost, lay frozen stiff.

For a moment Duinn gazed at it. But if there had been pity in those eyes, when he turned them toward Greenchurch, it was gone.

In the final hour, in that gentle darkness which comes before dawn, there was a stillness. Wykeham watched the men before him. The table was cleared, the bottles emptied and returned to the shelf. Grumbling, the Duke examined his watch. Morag mopped his damp forehead. But nothing was said. In the hearth the last live coal glowed once faintly, then went out.

When the stillness was deepest, Longford's tired blue eyes filled with tears.

Wykeham laid a hand on his arm.

"It is the worst time," Wykeham said. "The hour when death seems most welcome."

The minister's face twisted. "It is not for myself," he said. "I would not care for myself, if I were certain. If I knew —"

"Then let him tell you," Hunt said.

Longford's head came up in astonishment.

"Tell me what?"

Wykeham looked at him. No muscle in his long face changed but he avoided the question.

"At dawn there will be a wind," he said.

Fred Norfolk groaned. He had kept out one last glass for himself and now he drank it. "By Christ," he said loudly, "there is always a wind. A queer wind, blowing up mischief." He put his glass back down on the table and stared at it. "But it wasn't a wind that I looked for," he complained. "It was a war, I thought." He waved his hand toward the window. "It was what they thought, those men on the lawn. Staying up all night, waiting just like we were waiting." He grunted. For a long moment he studied Wykeham in silence. "God damn it all," he said at last, bitterly, "a man can't fight wind."

"It will be a great wind," Hunt said, "with the dead riding it."

"Which dead?"

No one looked to see who had spoken, for each had had the same thought. Each sat very still, remembering, peering into nothingness and trying to think of a way to keep, for good or ill, what had been.

Amelia, Holmes whispered.

Nora!

Olivia!

Plum!

Wykeham had shut his eyes, but not against them. He could feel the fierceness of their longing. Before him, even with his lids clamped shut, he saw the lonely tangle of their separate lives; saw Longford in his bed, with Plum beside him; saw the little room of Harwood's study and the arching rosemary barberry that twisted beyond the kitchen door in Cambridge when Holmes was six. Fondly, through Morag's keen, unfaded eyes, he saw all the wonders of women and porter the old minister had left, too soon, behind. He saw the dusty yards and barns and the high sun over the hills where Norfolk had wandered. Reaching with long, scarred hands, he touched with Martin Callaghan's fingers, not his own, a son, a boy with jet-black hair who never was.

He moaned.

A branching labyrinth had opened before him. Beyond the ragged sounds of his own breath he heard the great surging hiss of their memories filling the channels, coursing through them, heaving the weight of their dreams to break and form again, like waves against a shore. Beneath that avalanche the long hill shook, the house shook on its old stone, and the earth and sky for an interminable instant tore.

It seemed only a moment. But in that moment he bound them, rejoining what they most remembered, gathering all that elsewhere had been quickly lost, the laughter and the vital nerve of longing, the snow-mired streets, the sure, swift hazards of sun and wind. All that had been his hope and theirs he took and forged, until, clear in its common shape, it moved before him. A world moved, a substance of shadows, a substance of rivers and mountains and unbroken light.

Wykeham threw back his head. His black eyes flashed open.

It was George Tennison who stood. Angrily, seeing no vision, the old workman pushed his way through the hedge. But now, when he touched them, the rough, gray limbs fell. He stood stock-still among the wreckage.

The lawn was empty; only the cold, useless stumps of the fires remained. It was not quite day. A bare light shone on his face.

Harwood had come out beside him. One by one, parting the hedge, the men followed. Wykeham stood nearby, his face watchful.

Harwood opened his mouth, but there was no sound.

The men looked at one another. They looked over the trampled grass and gardens but there was nothing to be seen. From the depths of the wood there came a cold silence.

The wind began with the dawn.

"Look there!" Norfolk shouted.

At the very edge of the wood the wind sprang. Out of the wrack of branches a turbulent black stream came tumbling. A thousand dark shapes filled the air. Some solitary, others in knots and wheels, pitching out of the shadows, they leapt and soared. There were none the same. Shooting out over the wide brown meadow, their black wings churned a booming thunder from the air. They rose. Then, all at once, almost cloud high, they turned and, swept on by the gale, came direct as an arrow toward the house. Shapes that had become dim specks grew breasts and arms. Eyes, where they had been only unheeding shadows, peered out from under strands of streaming hair and smiled again.

Norfolk rushed out on the lawn. Yet even as he ran it seemed to him that the sound of the wind had changed. That it beat against the earth with antic wildness. It tugged at his sleeves and tore the buttons from his shirt. He placed his hands on his hips and laughed. Morag had run out after him; Longford followed.

"Listen," Norfolk cried. "Listen!"

Morag craned his neck and simply gasped.

He did not know how Wykeham had managed it.

He himself, he hoped, had never wronged them. Yet, whatever rage was felt against the race of men, whatever insult had been kept and harbored, by whatever cause, no longer mattered.

The wind whisked through his fringe of hair. It would never be still, he knew, could never be held to one thing without turning. His eyes by now had a curious dreaming look.

All about him, over the wide bright lawn, the women were floating down.

Morag flung out his arms.

Plum loomed above him. The white of her breasts, the white of her neck and shoulders were suffused with a deepening blush, her cheeks the color of red petticoats. They watched each other's eyes. Conscious that they were drawing nearer, both chuckled. Each leaning forward, they swayed, almost touching, until one final gust blew them together and they fell in a quivering jumble on the grass. Plum squeaked. Morag giggled and nuzzled her ear.

Longford could not bear to look. There had been but one woman he had loved. He stumbled out into the middle of the lawn. "Plum," he wailed. "Oh, Plum!"

Hearing him, the stout, gray-haired woman, the bald head of the old gentleman supported like a baby in her lap, looked over her shoulder. As though it gave her exquisite pleasure just to look at him, she smiled.

All the while Norfolk was pulling little Welsh girls by their pigtails down from the wind. There were three already clinging to his knees, grinning merrily. But he was not able to pull them down quickly enough. He had been thinking of seven but had only got five when he caught sight of Lizzy bearing down on him. He gave a mild shrug. With one last backward wink and more courage than he had thought himself capable of, he accepted Lizzy bravely into his arms.

One after another the women were caught and brought down. The men who had spent the night on the lawn, hiding themselves, now got up quickly. The sexton, hoping to get the best pick, had climbed onto a barrel, where, waving his thick arms, he barked in a voice of thunder: "She is mine! She is mine!"

Nobody challenged him. There were only a few dozen men and the women, it seemed, were without number.

Holmes came down from the porch, staring around guiltily for his wife. He walked into the noisy yard, his hands held behind him. Leaves and thistledown were blown over the edge of the lawn. There for a moment he saw her, drifting toward the barn, the stationmaster trotting along under her. Her small, fishlike mouth parted happily. She waved to him but her thoughts were occupied. Holmes turned away. He scarcely saw the young woman in the air before him.

"Good sir," she called out to him, "why are you filled with sorrow?"

He did not want to look but courtesy made him answer.

"I do not know," he said. He thought of the woman who had shared his bed. "I had a wife," he said, "yet even then I grieved for something."

The young woman smiled. "I was a wife to someone," she answered, "but I have been blown about by the wind today and

I do not think, even if I found him, I would take him back."
For the first time he truly looked and saw the plain, brown, eager face. He was almost relieved she was not beautiful.

"What will come of this?" he asked.

"Like you," she said, "I do not know."

"That much is certain," he answered, but with a brief, grave smile he drew her down.

The gale had tipped a wagon on its side and sent a line of haystacks blundering toward the fence. Half of the new shingles George Tennison had hammered onto the roof had broken off and lay scattered across a hundred yards of lawn. "There will be work again," Olivia told him. George Tennison nodded.

"We can put it to rights," he said confidently. Slyly, pretending to survey the damage, he drew a hand around her waist.

Something, however, had to be done about the women who remained in the air. A few too many men, finding much delight in the women they had landed, had already begun to slip off with them, leaving their less fortunate sisters stranded and just beyond reach. The neglected women rolled about helplessly, bumping and generally getting in each other's way. "Bitches! Husband-stealers!" they cried out to the women on the ground. The village policeman, reinforced by a thin, dark-haired lad from over the line in West Redding, came back from the stables with a pair of painters' ladders and were kept busy for hours, untangling and drawing them down.

Martin Callaghan took his hands from his pockets. Two or three times he had been about to go down, but he had held back, not frightened, but watchful. On the hillside the bodies of men and women moved over one another in the grass. From the porch he could hear their soft voices. He stepped back. For no clear reason he trembled. Around by the sheds Harwood was speaking quietly to a young woman. He was touching her neck. In front of them a small blonde girl was playing. Even Hunt had not gone off alone. His face strangely resolute, he sat out under the elms, squeezing the pink nipple of a plump, white-faced woman between the blunt fingers of his huge, blood-red hands.

Martin Callaghan turned his head irritably. "Is this the world, then?" he asked in a low voice.

"Part of it," Wykeham told him.

"And the rest?"

But Wykeham was still watching the wood. Once it had been spring there, then summer. Now even the last warmth of autumn was leaving the air. As he watched, what he took for a flock of wild gulls came swirling over the lawn.

Wykeham shut his eyes and still saw them. The sky was turning white with their wings. They beat against the blank screen of his eyelids, falling, settling down on the earth.

When he looked again, they were standing in front of him.

Nora was first, before them all on the steps. But Willa was mounting behind her.

"I have come," she said simply.

"As I promised," Jane said.

"As you dreamed," said another, coming nearer. Synchronously, a spirit of laughter touching their brains, the multitude smiled on him.

VI.

Winterking

 He waited as a man waits in a cell. The gray, silent hills, drawn away from him, seemed to rise like the walls of a prison. This also will be a place of darkness, he thought, dismayed. He had a sense, again, of terrible emptiness, as if the valley itself, in spite of cities and towns, in spite of hedgerows and the hundred million boughs of the wood, was, in fact, the pitch-dark corridor of a hideous dungeon. Wykeham gave a second jerk to the reins. But as quickly as the impression came it passed.

It was a dream, he was certain. Like any dream it was a jumble of pieces, each seeming to make the others impossible.

For one thing the long, twisting drive seemed to wind toward the sea. A little breeze had sprung up, carrying the wet flavor of salt. To his ears it carried as well the hurrying sound of waves. Turning his back to it, he gave a kick to the ribs of the stallion so that the animal broke into a lumbering trot. When he made the last turn of the drive, he could see Martin Callaghan waiting. Watching the intent, dark face in the dusk, Wykeham forgot he was dreaming.

"Where in the name of God have you been, William?" Martin shouted.

Wykeham dropped down by the front door, giving the reins into the hands of the stableboy.

"How is she?" he asked.

Martin made no reply.

Together they mounted the steps. But inside he knew it was a dream again; he was in an unreal house that only existed when he entered it. Still, it pleased him immeasurably to see the house spring to life around him. Women, hearing his boots on the carpet, peered out of hallways, looking up tenderly as he passed. He could smell potatoes and ham from the kitchen and knew that Lizzy would have a huge dinner waiting when he came down.

The room was on the third story, at the end of a passage that ran along by the side of the house. A dim light showed under the door.

When he went in, Morag was reading the service. Holmes was drawing the sheet over the head. The head made one mound, the breasts two large others. Wykeham knelt down, pressed his hands along the sheet. He was surprised, full of wonder.

"What did you expect?" Morag asked him.

"I'm the father, you son of a bitch."

"It could not be helped," Morag told him. "There was a storm. She was caught in it."

In the silence that followed, they could hear the wash of the sea below the house. Wykeham tried to move away but could not.

"God help me," he whispered.

The dream Callaghan stood behind him, watching quietly.

"It is the way the world is now," he said, unconcerned. He might have stopped but did not.

He said: "Tell me just what it was you wanted."

"Nothing."

The dream Callaghan shrugged. "As you please," he said. But Wykeham cried out:

"Nothing more than I had."

A frown settled heavily on Martin Callaghan's face.

"Very well," he said patiently, "but when?"

That, of course, Wykeham realized, had been the first error. But, in a way, he had half expected it, for he was always remembering a little more than he intended. Nonetheless, there were worse fates than too many women. If that was all that had gone wrong, he would live with it. He looked directly at Nora's slender corpse, aware that outside the dream he had saved her, that when he woke she would be whole again.

Beyond the window the gulls went on crying. In the darkness he could hear the cold waves crashing on the beach. He knew the sound. It was the same beach which, world after world, he had walked with Duinn. Still, it is a dream, he thought, reassured.

Wykeham lifted his neck.

When he reached out his arm, it was morning. Beside him there was a warm patch in the bed where Jane had been. The sea was gone. By the gentle vagueness of the light he knew it was snowing.

The women were up early. When Jane came in from the hallway, the kitchen was glowing with warmth. The kettle steamed and puffs of drowsy smoke escaped from a crack in the chimney. As though by right, Nora and Lizzy had the best seats, with Olivia, on the edge of the bench, squeezed in next to them. Mrs. Harwood, however, had to watch from the corner, her hands resting protectively on her daughter's small shoulders. Between mouthfuls of jam, the child was trying to count all the women. But the room was crowded and in the confusion her eyes kept coming back to the Welsh girls. Entwined in each other's arms, they sat on the floor by the wall exchanging glances and whispering about Fred Norfolk. Braving the snow before daylight, he had already gone twice to the shed where they had set up their housekeeping, to look in, he said, and see how they were doing. Lizzy went to rinse her cup in the sink. She had a

word or two to say about Fred Norfolk and didn't care much
who else heard. But as she stretched herself up there was a
thump on the porch.

A few too many thumps, Nora thought, who had been expecting only Plum.

But when the door opened, it was Plum in fact, standing on
the threshold with half a hillside of snow on her shoulders.

"Found her," she said, panting, pulling in a bedraggled young
woman, an even greater shawl of snow covering her.

The young woman blinked. Her skin, what they saw of it,
was blue and she was shivering. By the way she held herself it
seemed she feared something inside her would break.

The women sat her in a chair. They rubbed her all over,
toweling her long legs and thin arms until the skin was red
again and her hair a nest of limp, black curls.

Plum dried herself.

"Like you," she told Nora when Nora brought her a cup.
Plum drank it down.

"By the edge of the drive," she said, "as you were."

"Not like that I wasn't," Nora laughed.

"Mama," the little girl said, "the lady —"

Mrs. Harwood ushered the child from the room.

"Let's try not to think of it," said Olivia.

But the young woman by the stove was already asleep and
the talk left her even before it had started.

There were to be a great many women. The change wouldn't
treat them all just the same. A few, perhaps, would remain
as they had been. Nonetheless, it was a new world and the
women had expected everything to be a bit strange and were
astonished when they remembered even the smallest things
exactly.

"This cup has a chip," Lizzy said, "here on the bottom. Now
how would he know that?"

"Perhaps Fred —" Olivia suggested.

"Don't talk to me of Fred," Lizzy snapped at her furiously.

But in a moment, on her own, she had launched into a long, bitter complaint against the Welsh in general and Welsh girls in particular.

"And what does Mr. Longford think of Mr. Morag?" said Nora, speaking to Plum before Lizzy had run out of curses.

"God have mercy!" Plum exclaimed loudly and grinned. "It's an odd life I'm in for." She edged her way through the crush toward the kettle. "Like a bag full of cats and myself in between."

Jane looked around nervously.

"Like my William," she said.

"You mean Joseph," said Willa, entering the conversation for the first time. "Only it's all of us in the bag with him." Willa sighed.

She was a tall, handsome woman of about fifty. Her short black hair was obviously dyed but that was the way she remembered herself, a woman whose white skin had begun to pucker under the eyes, that instead of the dazzling beauty a dozen years younger whom Wykeham had transported to seaside hotels on holidays. If she thought about it at all, she would have said that now she was simply more comfortable. But it was clear enough, Willa thought without wavering, what Joseph saw in the girl.

"You're the very image of myself," she told Jane. "Although I don't suppose it was only that he saw in you." Her tone was hushed. It troubled Jane more than if she had blubbered.

Jane said reproachfully:

"He can have who he wants."

"Lord knows," Willa said softly. "But, if we are any measure, child, what he wants is always the same."

Several new women had come in from the hall.

Jane looked around at them, staring. "He will marry me," she announced.

In the chair by the stove the very pregnant young woman started screaming.

* * *

He was on the stairs when His Grace noticed Nora. Strands of her long yellow hair, shaken loose by exertion, stuck to her neck. She was hurrying. In her arms were towels and blankets, which she was carrying up to the third story, to Wykeham's room. There were plenty of bedrooms but in most the men lingered. Wykeham, however, had quit his room just as the house began bustling. His bed, Nora had told them, was the biggest, and when it had become available, with three or four to help, they had brought the young woman and laid her down in it.

Nora moved toward the railing to let His Grace pass.

He held out a hand to stop her. "Have I seen you?" he asked, watching her curiously.

"Forgive me," she said. "There is a young woman."

His hand had not left her elbow.

Nora's eyes darted to the top of the landing. "You were on the porch," she said quickly, "when we came. You were standing with William."

He nodded but it was not what he meant. His eyes took in the curve of her neck, the flamboyant blush that began at her throat. Surprised by her vehemence, he smiled.

"Sir, I must," she said firmly.

He watched her expression change from impatience to anger.

"Go on, then," he said.

But at the top of the stairs she looked back.

"There is a doctor," she called to him. "Please, if you could find him —"

In the middle of the stairs Martin Callaghan turned.

Off the second floor landing were a half dozen rooms. In the first two, when he knocked, he found strangers. "Holmes," he cried at the third and, without pausing, walked in.

Holmes was sitting up in the bed. The woman was mostly dressed. She was putting on stockings. Looking His Grace over hastily, she grinned.

"You're up early, Your Grace," said Holmes.

"It's habit. I'm sorry."

Holmes began to search for his trousers.

"There's a patient," His Grace told him.

By now the young woman was sitting down at the mirror, combing her hair. Just for a moment, when he had got his trousers onto both legs and half buttoned his shirt, Holmes's eyes shifted back to her.

"Which of us, do you think, is responsible?" he asked Callaghan.

His Grace did not see what was meant.

"I'll be quick, my girl," Holmes said fondly, "if I can." He went into the hall.

"There were nine of us," Holmes continued, trying to be perfectly clear. "But which of us," he asked very seriously, "thought of her?"

The young woman weighed down the bed. Her mountainous belly, spread over the sheet, frightened Martin Callaghan unreasonably. He sat at the far end, in the corner, giving everyone room. He was not wanted but he had come in with the doctor. He had climbed the stairs after him, holding the railing. He had been compelled to go slowly so that Holmes, who was hurrying, had been forced to look back. His Grace waved him on.

There was a chair, thankfully. The Duke thrust his heavy shoulders against the wood. But it was not his eyes, he thought, but the snow falling that made the room dim. The wind, sweeping across the roofs, made whines and moans as real as the whispers of women. The woman he had met on the stairs was busily filling the lamp. He consoled himself by watching her back. Once she turned sideways to look at him and then swiftly, her pale blue eyes still angry, looked away.

"She seems very near," Plum said flatly.

"She's in labor already," Holmes said. But his eyes seemed

uncertain. He guessed that the woman was trying to estimate the extent of his knowledge and so mustered an air of confidence.

"An hour, perhaps," he said. But honesty got the best of him. "Perhaps longer."

The women were looking from one to another.

"I'll need a bowl of water," Holmes said. "To wash my hands. And a fire. Do you think we can get a fire? It's cold as death up here." He finished buttoning his shirt. "There were other rooms, I suppose," he said. "Something nearer the kitchen. So why in the first place —"

He broke off when he saw the young woman staring up at him.

Her eyes wide and amused, she lay very still, watching.

Nora, not realizing his confusion, answered simply.

"Because it's William's bed," she said. "So it's fitting. The baby will be William's certainly."

Plum was squinting at her.

Nora laughed.

"By the looks of us," Nora told her, "there'll soon be a great many babies. But here's this one already, though the world's not a day old." Nora ran her fingers into her dress.

"It's his," she said carefully. "Either something he wanted or, if he didn't, that came anyway." She laughed again. "It's the one thing he never could stop, things coming back to him."

While Nora spoke, it seemed that Holmes scarcely breathed. The young woman in the bed was smiling at him. She was lying in the middle of the mattress, her large dark eyes attentive and critical, yet smiling as well.

"You needn't worry," Carolyn told him.

His hands moved quickly, bringing the lamp nearer, holding it up next to her, to be certain she had spoken.

"You don't have to think about it," she repeated. "Needn't concern yourself." She settled back on the pillows. "It's already done. I have seen him."

He waited for her to continue.

Carolyn smiled at his slowness. "Out there," she said.

She tried to turn but some heaviness restrained her. She must have them move the bed, she thought, so she might look with no need of turning and could watch and study him when he came again to the window. It was such a relief to see how tall and strong he had already become. He must be very strong indeed to climb so high, with great hands to hold onto the roof and large shoulders to ward off the wind. But he would be hungry, she knew, his hard, clever mouth seeking her. Feverishly, thinking of his hunger, she drew her hands up under her breasts, pushing them, as his huge dark face would push, to start the flow of milk. He would be hungry and lonely and cold. Such a cold morning to come into the world, she thought. Once more she attempted to look at the window.

"Do you see him?" she asked.

Holmes could see the sharp points of her breasts just under the sheet, see them left and fall with the fierce, failing struggle of breath.

Nora bent down beside her. In the lamp's glare, watching both faces, Martin Callaghan found himself filled, first with irritation and then with what he recognized was jealousy. "My God," he said suddenly, realizing they were the same women he had seen on the platform following William out to the train.

"What is she saying?" Plum asked.

Holmes shook his head. Not even hearing, he reached forward, touching the vein of the neck.

Though he was tired and sick at heart, the Duke stood. He went to the bed and, prying the lamp from Holmes's fingers, carried it to the window ledge. Just for an instant, looking out, he saw the deep drifted snow on the roof. The shoeless prints came up to the window and stopped. He turned his back on them, not knowing yet what they meant. But of one thing he was certain.

"He has one more death," he said grimly.

Nora glared at him. She could feel her whole body shake with rage against him, against all men who, finding a death, admitted no more than a single loss, one cruel absence, when it was worlds that went.

"The child," she said desperately. "And the child that might have come from that child and from that."

She was looking hard at him, seeing the dark molding of his flesh against the vague, snow-filled window. Her face was scarlet. For one awful moment each understood that she had meant herself.

"Hush now," he said softly; then quietly, as a father might take a child and yet not that exactly, though it was no less kind, he extended his arms and drew her to himself.

Wykeham sat without moving, the ragged cloak draped over his shoulders. The chairs, as the men had left them, were turned about in disorder. The women scratched at the door but he sent them away. Jane had come, incautiously, calling him. But when he did not answer, she had slipped away again to the kitchen.

His Grace listened to her footsteps retreating. "Which one is she?" he asked bitterly.

Wykeham did not try to look up. "From the school," he said.

"As before?"

"Yes."

"It was a girl's voice."

Wykeham turned his eyes on him. They were young man's eyes and it hurt His Grace to look at them. Wykeham rested his hands on the table.

"We tried to walk to New Awanux once," he said. "I don't suppose I wrote you that? One evening I drove to the school. It was late and I stood under her window in darkness, throwing stones at the glass. When she came down, she was yawning and only half in her dress. It was too far, of course." He looked down at his hands, thoughtfully, as though measuring himself against an obstacle. "We only made Bristol." He paused. "Before it was light, I found a cab to take her back." He stopped once more. "I do not think, Martin, there was a time when I was happier."

His Grace waited until he was certain Wykeham was finished.

"It was a risk," the Duke said.

Wykeham shifted; his face did not change.

"There were always risks. But none to myself. You must remember that. There was never a moment when I could not as simply have walked away. One more Wykeham vanished. Lost overboard, presumed drowned. Even now I could go out that door and in an hour I would be on a train. There are ships in New Awanux. I made certain I remembered ships. One would be waiting."

The words slowly took hold. "This house?" His Grace said.

Wykeham almost smiled. "I have told you."

"This room?" His Grace persisted. He looked around uneasily beginning to understand all that had been done. "Chairs?"

"Even chairs."

His Grace shuddered. "And in your bed?" There were tears in his voice suddenly.

"No!" Wykeham shouted. "No, I never —"

Just at that moment Longford burst through the doors. He tore the cap from his head, flinging cold drops from it. He stomped his boots on the carpet. Morag came after him, pawing his nose with his wool-gloved hands. But the stench clung to him, was mired in his clothes and his skin. Even the tramp through the fields, stumbling against the storm's icy fury, had not rid him of it.

"Burned," Longford said.

Morag closed the doors tightly. He did not want the women to come in.

"It is the one thing that was not supposed to happen," he said. "It was painted. I had seen to it." He looked briefly at His Grace, who was glaring uncomprehendingly.

"Greenchurch," Morag whispered, his face wretched. "Green as oaks, as a hedge. Not an English church." His old desperate eyes fixed on Wykeham.

Wykeham turned to the window, watching the storm.

"But white," he said softly, "when snow covered it."

Martin Callaghan moaned. He threw himself into a chair. "One of us had to think of that," he said, grumbling.

Suddenly they were all very still.

Wykeham studied them. "You will each deny it. I deny it myself."

For a while longer no one spoke.

"All the same it wouldn't matter," he went on, "if that were everything. If it stopped. But it won't." He was still watching them, his eyes settling on each face for a moment, considering. "How many are missing?" he asked.

"Five," Morag said at once.

Wykeham rose from his chair. "Then we had better find them," he said.

George Tennison came from the cellar, from making both coffins. His fingers were stiff from the cold and he was covered with sawdust. Fearful of a new catastrophe, he edged back the doors. Holmes, who had just come himself, pulled a chair to the table. "Where is Harwood?" he asked, glancing swiftly about the room. In fact, Harwood was sitting alone by the window, keeping watch on the hill. His face was unshaven and his head hung morosely to one side. In front of him the heavy wind washed streaks of ice across the panes.

Snow was everywhere. One of the great elms had toppled under the weight. It lay sprawled across the yard, its limbs fattened and nested until the shape was nearly unrecognizable.

Harwood stared, spellbound.

He had not heard the tree fall but it had fallen, he was certain, sometime during the night. The snow, he imagined, had muffled the sound. Still, he should have felt something. A tree crashing. A young woman dead. Each hour of the night he had lain awake, listening to the woman beside him, the child at the end of the bed. Outside the endless snow was filling the darkness. The world was being purified, was being remade. He had only felt cold.

He still was. He was shivering when, tilting his head, he caught sight of the sleigh. It was only a speck at the bottom of the hill. But the speck grew and, when it made the next turn, there were four horses galloping into the yard, sending up waves of white snow. For a terrible moment Harwood had the impression that the horses were coming onto the porch. Then he had a glimpse of red hair. A flurry of arms, jacketless, immune to the cold, jerked at the reins. When the snow settled, it was Hunt who climbed down. He handed the reins to the stableboy. Fred Norfolk followed after him. It was not more than a minute later they were both in the house.

"Greenchurch is burned," Morag told them.

"An Indian," Longford said.

"Though I had it painted," Morag added.

"But we never thought of the snow," Longford said bleakly.

Hunt moved across the room, passing slowly among the chairs. They watched his heavy shoulders and thick arms from which the snow had already melted, and thought how little it must interest him whether there were fires or blizzards or the earth itself opened. His dark quiet eyes looked around the circle of faces.

"And one of us must have thought of it?" he asked dryly, not bothering to look at one any more than another, not caring.

"Someone had to," Martin Callaghan said.

"And you will find him?"

The Duke nodded.

"And when he is found?"

The Duke stopped. He had been answering, not thinking where the answers led.

"There are women here," he said angrily. "A world just beginning." He turned abruptly, staring at Wykeham. "Lives" — he began.

"Against one life?" Hunt asked. "Where is the worth in that? What is saved in the end? You all die."

His Grace stood mute.

Quite unexpectedly he found himself remembering the young woman he had held in his arms. It was unreasonable. He had held her only a moment. How odd and old-fashioned he must have seemed to her, patting her shoulders, running his stiff, old hands along the side of her neck. Yet, although he admitted as much, he couldn't bring himself to feel ashamed.

"It matters," he said. "Although I never thought to stop its coming, it matters when."

"No longer," Hunt said.

The Duke had raised his head, to debate with him, when the house shook.

Suddenly George Harwood, who had been staring without point or purpose, began to scream.

For a moment there was no other sound, only his high, choking sobs and the creaking floorboards as the men rushed to the window. Then the house shook again. The flames in the hearth shuddered and in a dozen rooms the pictures of horses and cities fell from the walls.

The men stood before the glass.

On the windward side of the hill, where the whirling snow poured into the cuts and breaks between the trees, the nine advanced. Their shapes were tall and black against the frozen wood. Their ancient faces, carved and pitted in the rock, were sad and still. But when they moved, the earth groaned under them. And they went on moving, their heavy footfalls, slow, unturning, across the cold white lawn.

Harwood braced himself against the chair.

"What do we do?" he asked.

"Ah, Jesus," Longford moaned. "Jesus." He had closed his eyes.

But Wykeham bore the sight a few seconds more. It was the end, he knew. The world would be broken now, its last foundations pulled apart and scattered. He had imagined such a day as this. But it had always been far off. There seemed so little cause for it to happen. And yet it was not without justice. He had lived years beyond counting and his wrongs were many. He felt their weight, each like a stone, upon him. But the worst were these: he had abused love and he had murdered. But he thought: "Those I have left were dying and I could not die. And by taking life there were lives I kept." Still, he had found no peace.

He would have died once long ago, died well or badly, but died in fact had not Duinn, without cause or reason, spared him. He did not wonder now where Duinn was. He was near. At the end, when the hills were gone and the sky rolled up, he would step out on the empty shore. Would he pity then the dead he made? When the last were not even memories, when there were no more lives to grieve and dream, would the silence, empty of windstorms and faces, set him making worlds again?

In his mind Wykeham tried to imagine other worlds. It was then he smiled. Himself, he had made them. There was a meadow running down to the bluffs above Ohonowauke which was his indisputably. There was a line of workmen's cottages, slant-roofed and always falling down, worn by the use of men whom, one generation to the next, he had set to scratch and toil on the land. And the house itself, with its hallways and kitchens, its rooms of horsehair beds and wooden chairs, its black scalding stoves and cool cupboards of white china. Each he had set and ordered. And in their places, deliberately, the pattern clear before its start, men and women, ministers and a minister's wife, the honorable Callaghan, Norfolk and Lizzy, Harwood with his silent wife and sullen child, his all too visible sorrow and his attacks of melancholia, Willa and Jane, both Tennisons, and Hunt who from the first of worlds had followed him. One by one he drew them forth to look at them and smiled, contented. They were his and, although at any moment he might have changed his mind, he did not wish them other than they were. Their lives still filled him. Why then did everything end in death?

He had grasped his cloak, his long, blunt fingers worrying the cloth. It was no longer Duinn he thought of but Jane. "Who has done this?" he thought, his mind wrestling with the fabric of all he had made, seeking the flaw in it that it might be mended or, willingly, if every weave proved false, to tear it whole, to cast to the last and final darkness all that by the force of his will, his love and longing he had shaped and fashioned, if only she were saved.

What thread was lost? What one thing unremembered?

His mind flew back to Harwood's study, to the train. He thought of the tree, its endless branches spreading high and wide across the earth, and of the rout of withered leaves that blew through Black Wood. He remembered the hill at the edge of Bristol; and Jane, her figure dark against the windows of the hall, walking briskly, not paying the least attention, even at the last instant when she stopped: "Sorry, I was watching —"

He looked up, to see the massive shoulders of the stone. For a moment he was unnaturally conscious of the sound of the wind.

"It should have been an old Ford truck," George Tennison said. Scowling, rubbing his trembling hands on the glass, he peered down at the sleigh and the horses. "There has been a mistake," he said.

No one was listening.

"I see him!" someone cried. The others, staring, could not be certain whether it was one more shadow or a man that moved below them.

It was His Grace who realized that it was Houseman. The face was changed, the gaze colder and more insolent. The jaw, which was left open, seemed incapable of laughter or crying or any other human attitude save hate and fear. But even dead, the Duke knew him. He looked more real than ever he had in life. His voice cried out more desperately, remembering all he had lost, the bitter darkness he had been given in its place. He unfolded his wings. He lifted up his huge square hands, the torches in them red with flame.

But it was Harwood who saw the woman, not dressed for cold weather, running from the house. Her bright yellow hair streamed from her head. She was running very fast. Caught by surprise, he wondered, as he had once before, not who she was but where she was going.

The wind howled. But Nora had no time for that. Too many things had happened all at once. Even as she ran she watched the vast cold shapes, their solemn figures moving roughly into the yard. She had seen them in the wood and knew there must be nine; and, although they had not begun in her memory, she had called them forth. What need he had of them she did not know. Perhaps, if she abandoned them, they would pass from his mind as well. Surely they were the ghosts of something that had happened long ago. Yet it had seemed a sort of unfaithfulness to let them fade. Well, he had seen them now and he could make of them what he wished. For herself, she could not think of what to do with them.

For one brief moment she had considered Indians. Might they not sweep down from the valley's rim, an ancient host, reclaiming with fire and thunder the world they too had lost? But the rock was here before they came and death, she knew, could never take again what already it had stripped and robbed. Still, it had its use.

She had made his bed a place of death. Once, without watching, at least without knowing that she watched, she had seen the other woman at the train. Alone in his bed, wondering how many women had loved him, how many he had loved, it was this face, not the dark-haired child's, that stirred her memory. In the darkness of that bed, in the gulf between what is and what may never be, she called to her. And the woman came.

She was not surprised when death came after. It was fate, Nora thought, still recklessly, still not certain it was so. Yet it pleased her to see the ease with which she had repositioned all their lives.

She was well across the yard, nearly under the ragged elms, when, for a moment, she found herself wondering about His Grace. His arms, she remembered, had been warm and gentle about her waist. His dark eyes, looking down, had filled her with anxious tenderness. She knew she was frightened by those eyes and with her fear there came a desperate urgency, a sense of the quickly passing years. She ran.

In the torchlight even the stones' huge shadows glittered red. The snow was red about his feet.

"You keep out of this!" Houseman cried.

But she never could. She only hoped she had not forgotten anything.

It was only a little distance from the porch to the patch of broken ground where Nora stood by herself, watching Martin Callaghan opening the door. He blinked, trying to adjust to the cold and the wind. She was amazed how frail he looked. He came down the porch steps slowly, casting glances back at the house and then toward the wood. She saw his face darken as he noticed the man and the girl. They had stopped just short of the trees. Wykeham had been leading a horse by its bridle. Now they were both standing still, looking back at the house. Then carefully, showing her the stirrup, he lifted the girl onto the stallion's wide back. When he had climbed up beside her, he gave a flick to the reins.

The Duke never saw the stableboy. It was Nora who watched

him standing alone in the open door of the barn, quietly folding the rag of a cloak.

Nora made no move at all.

The Duke stopped.

"I don't understand," he said resentfully, realizing suddenly he knew a great deal more than he thought.

The snow was still falling. Without answering, she took hold of his arm. He limped a little as they walked together toward the house. She saw the pain in his face and knew that he was dying. Not all at once, but by inches, as men always died. Still, there will be a few years more, she thought. Time enough, when the world was her own.

At the top of the hill, because the trees were bare, she caught sight of the river. The hill was not of sufficient height to see the whole pattern but the river's jagged line, black against the snow-mired banks, described, she was certain, a nearly perfect figure.

"N" for Nora, she thought, smiling, remembering as well the little curving lake in Black Wood. "C" for Callaghan, she thought and went on smiling. From a distance both figures would appear to join, a piece of common mischief, shining out against the coming darkness, as if someone on the dwindling continent had left a message for a god.

EGRESS

Bridgeport — Ridgefield
March 1982 — September 1984